FUSION

Jackie glanced at Xander before she spoke. "Well, Peter, our theory is that Number 407 is now . . . inside a human being. After seeing the video, we suspect that It is within the girl, Alexis."

I know what 'deafening silence' means now, Xander noted, and one look at Jackie told him that she was thinking the same thing.

Dr. Gaige leaned forward. "Jackie, do you truly believe that The Organization would choose to plant one of the world's most powerful scientific discoveries inside of a teenage girl?"

"Yes, I do."

FUSION

TJ Amberson

FUSION

by TJ Amberson
www.tjamberson.com

Copyright © 2011, 2016, 2017 by TJ Amberson
Cover design © 2017 by Book Creatives
All rights reserved

ISBN 978-0-9892999-5-4

While every reasonable effort was made to ensure a product of the highest quality, minor errors in the manuscript may remain. If you have any comments, please contact tjambersonnews@gmail.com.

For the one who let me dream

ONE

Standing at the front of the cold, dimly lit room, Xander silently analyzed the tense expressions of the committee members who were seated around the table before him. Though his own pulse was racing, Xander revealed no emotion as he continued to wait. Finally, he heard someone speak:

"Xander, what you have just told us would change everything. Are you sure about this?"

Keeping his expression steady, Xander looked toward the source of the raspy voice. Dr. Gaige was seated in his usual place at the far end of the table, partly hidden in the shadows and watching Xander with his penetrating stare.

"Yes, I am sure, Doctor Gaige," Xander answered him. "The Organization has discovered Number 407."

"Well, where is It?" a woman at the table demanded. "And how is The Organization guarding It?"

Xander shifted his attention to the woman slowly, giving himself time to think. Although everything was going as he had anticipated, Xander knew that he needed to remain extremely cautious.

"We don't have that information yet," was Xander's deliberate reply. "However, it won't be long before we have more details."

"We don't want more details." Dr. Gaige's tone was disturbingly calm. "We want Number 407."

Xander turned to Dr. Gaige once more. "Of course. I only meant that . . ."

Xander trailed off, his concentration disrupted when he saw what appeared to be a red glow in Dr. Gaige's eyes. Startled, Xander blinked and peered more closely at Dr. Gaige, but the unexplainable gleam of red—whatever it had really been—was gone. Clearing his throat, Xander quickly continued:

"We will find It, Doctor Gaige. Soon."

Dr. Gaige observed Xander for a protracted moment and then made a gesture with his hand, indicating that the meeting was adjourned. As the committee members filed from the room, Xander discreetly glanced down at a new message on his communicator. The latest report indicated that The Organization had Number 407 on the move again, Its destination unknown.

Xander slid the communicator into the pocket of his suit coat, his mind working fast. *I have to find Number 407 . . . before Doctor Gaige does.*

***

Okay, stay calm. Act casual. And try not to make a complete idiot of yourself.

Alexis Kendall nervously pried open her locker's rusty door and pretended to rummage through the mess inside. After letting a few seconds pass, Alexis peeked again down the school hallway. Her heart skipped a beat. Not far from where she

"Nope. Either you say something to him or I will," Molly cut her off with an expression that made it clear she was not going to relent.

Alexis winced. She had no way out. With her hands starting to tingle and her mouth getting dry, Alexis anxiously checked her reflection in the cracked mirror that hung inside their locker. Sighing, she hastily began smoothing the frizz out of her long brown hair.

"Remember to act casual," Molly instructed.

"Casual." Alexis fixed a smudge of mascara under one of her green eyes. "Should be easy, considering that I feel like I'm about to throw up all over the place."

"And take your first period textbook," Molly continued, ignoring the sarcasm. "It'll appear more natural if you pass him on your way to class."

"Good idea."

Alexis reached for her enormous chemistry textbook, which she kept wedged near the back of the locker's tiny, over-stuffed shelf. But when she pulled on the book, it did not budge.

"This . . . stupid book is . . . stuck in here . . . again," Alexis grunted while tugging on the book several more times.

Faking a laugh, Molly flipped her curly hair and lowered her voice. "Tanner is looking over here."

"He's what?" Alexis stopped abruptly, her arms still stretched contortedly into the locker.

Molly let her eyes drift over Alexis's shoulder. "Yeah, Tanner is definitely watching you right now. Staring, actually. Drake and their other friends are, too. So you might want to get that book out, like, ASAP."

In a surge of desperation, Alexis gripped the book even tighter and yanked as hard as she could. Suddenly, the textbook shifted and came flying off the shelf toward her. Alexis had one split-second of relief before realizing that she was stumbling backward.

Alexis heard her own shriek fill the hallway as she stumbled to the floor. The gigantic book landed beside her, followed by everything else that had been knocked off the shelf along with it. As crumpled papers, highlighters, and an empty water bottle rained down around her, Alexis lifted her eyes and spotted a lotion bottle teetering precariously on the shelf's edge.

No, no, no, Alexis silently begged. *Don't fall. Don't—*

The bottle defiantly tumbled off the shelf, hitting the ground and splattering Alexis's jeans with floral-scented goo.

An uncomfortable hush settled over the hallway.

"Lex!" Molly gasped. "Are you alright?"

Alexis scrambled to her feet and brushed a clinging sandwich baggie from her sleeve. "Yeah, I'm great," she quipped, her face scorching. "Why wouldn't I be? I made a complete fool of myself in front of the hottest guy in—"

"I think you dropped this," someone behind her said.

Alexis froze. She saw Molly's eyes widen. Groaning inwardly, Alexis slowly turned around. Tanner stood in front of her, holding the chemistry textbook in his hand. Behind him, Drake was observing the scene with a smirk of amusement.

Alexis swallowed hard, weighing her options. *I could run away. Or pretend to pass out. Or act like I don't see him standing two feet in front of me. Or—*

Tanner cleared his throat.

Or I may have to talk to him, Alexis conceded, the idea causing her heart to pound. After three years, she was finally going to speak to Tanner Ricks. It was her moment. With a spark of renewed determination, Alexis stood straight, wet her lips, and opened her mouth.

Not a sound came out.

"Gee, thanks, Tanner," Molly piped up, grabbing the book from his hands. "That's, uh, mine, actually."

Tanner glanced confusedly between the two girls. "You're welcome."

Alexis saw Molly eyeing her. If she did not say something fast, Molly would probably tell Tanner that the only reason Alexis had joined the cheer squad was to spy on him during preseason football practices. Then Molly might even reveal how Alexis had—

"Hey, Tan-ner!"

The unmistakable, shrill voice reached Alexis's ears, causing her to wince. *Seriously? Her? Right now? Please let it be anyone but her.*

But as Alexis looked past Tanner, the sight that met her eyes only confirmed that her situation was about to get worse. Crystal Lark was charging toward them. With a toss of her silky blond hair, Crystal reached Tanner's side and gave him a playful nudge. Then she settled her concentration upon Alexis.

"Hi, A-lex-is," Crystal spoke to her, like always, as if conversing with a three-year-old. Her blue eyes moved down to the mess on the floor, and a sly grin revealed her bright white teeth. "Gosh, I love your jeans, but did you spill something on them?"

Alexis's reply was barely audible. "Um, yes. That would be lotion."

"Lotion," Crystal repeated, letting an uncomfortable pause settle over the group. She finally turned again to Tanner and Drake. "Are you guys headed to class? Wanna get going?"

"Nothing I'd rather do," Drake replied with a pointed tip of his head in Alexis's direction.

Crystal's smile widened. Linking her arm through Tanner's, she led him away. Drake tagged along, saying something that caused Crystal to laugh loudly before the trio disappeared into the crowd.

"So, uh, that didn't go too badly," Molly dared to say after a pause.

Resignedly, Alexis crouched down and started tossing things back into the locker. "Yeah, not badly at all. All I did was mortify myself in front of Tanner and give Crystal something to blab to the entire school about."

"Don't worry about Crystal," Molly stated supportively, kneeling to help clean up. "She acts like she's better than everyone else because she's captain of the cheer team. But I think she's jealous that you're a better dancer." Molly resolutely shoved an old cell phone case into the locker, and then her face brightened. "By the way, didn't Drake look gorgeous?"

Alexis could only laugh. "I wasn't paying attention to Drake. Sorry."

"I wonder if he's got a date to homecoming yet?" Molly stared off into space before handing the textbook over to Alexis. "Anyway, I take it you're off to the wonderful world of Mister Haber's chemistry class?"

Alexis got up, nodding unenthusiastically.

"It can't be all horrible," Molly pointed out, stuffing paintbrushes into her bag. "At least you get to start each morning with a view of Mister Haber's extremely handsome T.A."

Alexis raised an eyebrow. "Huh?"

"I'm talking about Noah Weston," Molly emphasized. "You know, the sophomore? Isn't he Mister Haber's T.A. again this year?"

Alexis shrugged. "I guess I haven't really noticed him, either."

"Haven't noticed him?" Molly appeared incredulous. "Well, take a moment to notice him. Everyone else does. Noah may be a science nerd, but he's gorgeous. And buff. And kind of mysterious. In fact, I almost think that seeing him each day would be worth suffering through chem—"

The bell rang.

"Oops! Gotta go! I'll see you in algebra!" Molly rushed off.

With the hall growing empty, Alexis shut the locker door and sighed again. The second bell rang. Hiking her bag onto her shoulder, Alexis ran to the other end of the corridor, turned the corner, and sprinted to Mr. Haber's room. She halted outside, the aromas of chemicals and used Bunsen burners rapidly filling her nose. Peeking through the narrow window in the door, Alexis spied the other students already in their seats.

"Alright, let us start with a review from yesterday," she heard Mr. Haber saying to the class. "Who can tell me how many elements are in the periodic table?"

"One hundred eighteen," Laura Bellows promptly replied from the front row.

"Correct!" Mr. Haber announced, causing Laura to sit up proudly.

Eyeing her empty chair, Alexis put her hand on the door handle, ready to slip in as soon as Mr. Haber turned the other direction.

"Of the one hundred eighteen elements," Mr. Haber went on, "how many—"

"So is this class standing room only now?" someone behind Alexis inquired.

With a yelp of surprise, Alexis spun around. She found herself facing a tall young man who was observing her sternly with his gray eyes. Sandy blond hair poked out from under his old baseball hat, and he wore a jacket over a faded t-shirt. Alexis vaguely recognized him and realized that he had to be Noah Weston, Mr. Haber's T.A.

"Oh, um, hey," she mumbled.

Noah did not smile. "Are you going in? Or are you doing this class by hallway correspondence now?"

"I'm going in," Alexis told him in defeat. "Sorry I'm late."

"You're late?" Noah checked his watch and reached for the door. "I guess that means I'm late, too."

Alexis did a double take and looked at him more closely. Noah only opened the door and waited for her to enter, his expression unchanged. So Alexis moved past him and stepped inside, the disruption causing Mr. Haber to break off from what he was saying to the class and peer at her. As usual, Mr. Haber's round wire-framed glasses sat slightly lopsided on his narrow face, and his stringy black hair was pulled into a low ponytail.

"Good morning, Miss Kendall," Mr. Haber greeted her. "Is there a reason you are late?"

"Oh, um, I was—"

"There was a chemical spill in the hallway," Noah interjected, coming into the room. "Glycerin, petrolatum, and cetyl alcohol everywhere. Alexis helped clean it up."

Alexis jerked her head in Noah's direction, but he did not seem to notice. While her cheeks burned, Alexis glanced down at the splattered lotion on her jeans and then faced Mr. Haber again with a forced smile.

Mr. Haber tipped his head. "That was kind of you to assist with the clean up, Miss Kendall. Now please have a seat."

Without another word, Noah walked off. He headed to the back of the room and went through a doorway into a large supply closet, which he and Mr.

Haber also used as an office. Alexis watched after him before making her way to her chair.

"Regarding the periodic table of the elements," Mr. Haber resumed teaching, "there—"

"Some elements are fake, right?" Sam Warren blurted out while flicking a paperclip into Laura's mane of red hair.

"Yes, some are synthetic. Depending on whom you trust, between eighty-eight and ninety-four elements are naturally found on this earth. The rest are man-made." Mr. Haber motioned to what was written on the whiteboard behind him. "In today's experiment, you will be using elements and compounds to perform the replacement reactions we discussed yesterday. Noah is setting out what you need. Please begin your experiments, and let us know if you have any questions."

The room quickly swelled with the sounds of conversation and activity as everyone got up and went to their workstations. Alexis pulled herself to her feet, grabbed her bag, and trailed unexcitedly after the others, heading for the workstation she shared with Julia Chen.

"So, Alexis, what scent is the lotion?" Sam sniffed obnoxiously and motioned to her pant legs as she passed by him. "Let me guess: something like Wowie Maui or Cocoa Butter Bliss?"

Alexis both glared and grinned at him. "It's a good thing I like you, or I'd break your Petri dish."

"Yeah. Be quiet, Sam," Julia added with attempted exasperation.

Sam bowed in feigned reverence. "Julia, your wish is my command. I shall be quiet. For now."

Julia blushed, put her head down, and began the experiment. Coming up beside her, Alexis also turned her focus to the assignment, warily eyeing the test tubes and powders that were set out on the workstation.

"Remember, time is of the essence. You must complete both a single replacement reaction and a double replacement reaction," she heard Mr. Haber counsel as he strolled past.

Alexis distractedly scanned the experiment instructions, scooped up some bright yellow powder, and dumped it into a test tube, which was propped up in a small metal rack.

"K_2CrO_4 in," Alexis mumbled as she worked. "$Pb(NO_3)_2$ added. Now watching for a precipitate . . ."

"If you have done the experiment correctly, you should be seeing a reaction at this point," Mr. Haber announced.

Alexis bent down, peered into her test tube, and frowned. All she saw were chunks of powder floating in a hazy-colored liquid. She leaned closer to the test tube and studied it pleadingly.

Come on, just do your replacement reaction thingy, alright? I need something to go well this morning.

"Miss Kendall, that reaction does not appear to be happening correctly, now does it?"

Glancing behind her, Alexis saw Mr. Haber watching over her shoulder. With a glum shake of her head, she moved aside.

Mr. Haber lifted the test tube from the rack and held it up to the light. "Is there a chance that your measurements were not quite—"

"Ben?"

Mr. Haber looked toward the sound of his name. Alexis followed his gaze. Noah was approaching him with rapid, long strides.

"Sorry to interrupt, but I need to talk to you," Noah explained.

"Certainly," Mr. Haber told him pleasantly. "After I finish assisting Miss Kendall, I will be right with you."

Noah's eyes flew to Alexis and back to Mr. Haber. "Actually, I need to talk to you right now."

There was a strange pause. Alexis looked curiously at Mr. Haber. For only an instant, she saw his face stiffen.

"Of course," Mr. Haber responded with a catch in his voice.

Mr. Haber placed the test tube into Alexis's hand and walked off with Noah, a sense of urgency to his steps. Abandoned, Alexis could only watch as Mr. Haber and Noah moved across the classroom and entered the supply closet. Mr. Haber hastily pushed the door shut behind them.

TWO

Alexis checked the contents of her test tube. The liquid had taken on an odd shade of muddy brown, and the floating clumps of powder were growing larger. Glancing at the clock, Alexis confirmed that first period was nearly over. Meanwhile, her classmates were already finishing the assignment and putting their things away. Alexis anxiously looked toward the supply closet again.

I know Mister Haber is probably super busy, but I'll only ask him one quick question.

Test tube in hand, Alexis wove past the other workstations and strode to the supply closet. As she started opening the door, Mr. Haber came into view; he was facing Noah with his back to her. Alexis then began hearing pieces of their strained-sounding conversation:

". . . notification came only minutes ago," Noah was saying.

"The danger is immense." Mr. Haber spoke apprehensively. "We need to move immediately—"

Alexis opened the door all the way. Its hinges creaked, causing Mr. Haber to whip around. Alexis recoiled when she saw deep lines of concern on his face. Behind Mr. Haber, Noah slipped something into his pocket, his eyes staying on Alexis. There was a taut silence before Mr. Haber addressed her:

"Yes, Miss Kendall? May I help you?"

Alexis gulped. "Yes . . . I mean no . . . I mean, I will let you know if I need anything."

Without waiting for a reply, Alexis scampered out of the supply closet. Once she got to her workstation, she checked behind her. The door to the supply closet had been shut once more.

Yikes. What were they so worked up about? Mister Haber seemed—

"Alexis, do you need help?"

Alexis broke from her thoughts and found Julia watching her inquisitively.

"With your experiment," Julia continued, motioning to the test tube that Alexis still gripped in her hand. "I can talk you through it."

Alexis gave her an appreciative nod. "Thanks. That'd be . . ."

She trailed off when the overhead lights unexpectedly went dark. An instant later, the floor started shaking hard.

"Earthquake!" someone shouted.

With shrieks of alarm, students began diving under their workstations. The shaking of the ground increased, causing racks of test tubes to fall from the counters and shatter across the floor. Books tumbled off shelves, and a huge chart of the periodic table crashed down from the wall. Plaster crumbled from the ceiling. Even the windows vibrated, causing an eerie hum to fill the room.

But as quickly as it had started, the shaking of the ground ceased. The lights came on with their familiar, soft buzz. There was a moment of shocked quiet, and then everyone began talking excitedly.

Still crouched beneath the workstation, Julia cautiously removed her hands from her ears. "That was crazy! I've never been in an earthquake before!"

"Neither have I." Alexis stood up, unable to keep her eyes from drifting uneasily to the supply closet.

"Hey, are you alright?" Sam came toward them, his shoes crunching the broken glass that littered the floor.

"Yes." Julia let Sam help her to her feet. "Thanks."

Outside in the hallway, the bell rang.

Julia uncertainly slung her bag over her shoulder. "Do you think it's okay to go, even if Mister Haber hasn't said so?"

"Sure it is." Sam shrugged. "It's not like Haber cares. He hasn't even bothered to come back out here."

"What if something's wrong, though?" Julia bit her lip. "Could he have gotten hurt during the earthquake?"

"Haber didn't get hurt," Sam assured her. "Look around. This was not exactly a major earthquake—nothing but a few broken test tubes. Haber is probably staying in there to grade papers since he doesn't have class next period." Sam put on his goofy smile and raised his voice so that everyone could hear him. "We can't work under these conditions! I hereby declare that class is dismissed!"

There was a smattering of appreciative laughter around the room, and students began exiting into the hallway while continuing to chat animatedly about what had occurred.

Julia started trailing after Sam, but she paused. "Alexis, aren't you coming?"

Alexis was still by their workstation, staring at the closed door of the supply closet.

"Alexis?" Julia repeated.

Alexis blinked and shook her head. "Go ahead without me. I need to leave a note for Mister Haber about my experiment. Hopefully, he'll let me redo it before class tomorrow."

"Okay. I'll see you in the morning." Julia waved before she caught up with Sam and headed out the door.

Alexis bent down and fished around in her bag, stalling until everyone else had gone. Once the classroom was empty, she stood up again, eyeing the supply closet.

Mister Haber sounded totally freaked out. He said something about danger.

Alexis waited—but for what, she was not certain. The sounds in the hallway faded as the time approached for second period to begin. Meanwhile, the door to the supply closet remained closed. Nothing stirred. Finally, with a slight laugh, Alexis started gathering her things.

Sam was right. Whatever Mister Haber sounded so panicked about, it's definitely not worth being late to another class over.

Alexis turned to go when, out of the corner of her eye, she noticed a blinding flash of white light fill the crack underneath the closed door of the supply closet. An instant later, the light disappeared. Alexis halted and faced the door directly.

It's nothing, she soon told herself, despite the strangely apprehensive way she felt. *Mister Haber is doing some kind of an experiment in there. That's all.*

Alexis again stepped to leave when another burst of light—a vibrant orange—illuminated the space below the supply closet door. By the time Alexis threw up her arms to shield her eyes, the orange light had already vanished. Blinking spots from her vision, Alexis began lowering her arms only to be blinded by flashes of magenta and vivid purple that shone under the door.

Then Alexis felt her skin start to tingle.

"Mister Haber?" Alexis called out, increasingly unsettled. "Is . . . is everything okay?"

There was no response.

"Mister Haber?" Alexis took a step closer to the supply closet. "Noah? Are you guys alright?"

Again, she was met only by silence. Alexis checked the clock.

I need to get to second period. Besides, whatever experiment Mister Haber is doing in there, he isn't going to want . . . but what if Mister Haber and Noah really did get hurt in the earthquake or something?

With a wipe of her sweaty palms against her jeans, Alexis resumed moving forward. As she did so, the tingling of her skin intensified. Breathing quickly, Alexis pressed her ear against the door to the supply closet, but all she could hear was the thumping of her own heart. After another pause, Alexis reached out and pushed the door open.

She saw no one inside, and the only sound that reached her ears was the faint hum of the lights above. Guardedly, Alexis entered—the echo of her footsteps on the concrete floor disrupting the stillness—and peered around.

The supply closet was bigger than she had anticipated. Bookshelves lined the walls, all of them crammed full with papers, ancient-appearing textbooks, and dark containers labeled by faded sketches of chemical structures. To the immediate left of the doorway sat two desks; one was bare and the other covered in sticky notes and clutter. After she got her bearings, Alexis scanned the room again, confused.

There's no other way out of here. Where did Mister Haber go? And where's Noah?

A blast of turquoise from the far end of the room caught Alexis's attention. She noticed a small wooden table against the back wall, which had something sitting upon it.

Something that was glowing.

Curious, Alexis walked toward the table to get a better look. As she drew near, Alexis discovered that the object on the table was actually a large white cube. The sides of the cube appeared shiny and perfectly smooth, and the entire object was emitting a soft white light. Fascinated, Alexis stepped even closer.

Without warning, a beam of yellow shot out from the cube and went straight up in the air, momentarily filling the supply closet with its incredible glow. Alexis jumped in surprise, which caused her bag to slide down her arm and collide into the table. The table wobbled from the impact, and the cube fell over the edge.

Alexis dropped her bag and lunged forward, managing to catch the heavy cube before it struck the floor. Immediately, the cool surface of the cube glowed brighter at her touch and Alexis felt a quivering sensation in her palms. A shimmering line then appeared near the top of the cube on all sides, tracing out what Alexis realized were the edges of a lid. She caught her breath.

The cube is a container. There's something inside of this thing.

Unnerved, Alexis set the cube back on the table and snatched her hands away. As soon as she let the cube go, the outline of its lid disappeared and the quivering in her palms stopped. Alexis remained very still, staring at the cube's mesmerizing white glow.

I wonder if . . . no, I shouldn't mess with . . . but it won't hurt anything. This is only ninth grade chemistry, for crying out loud. I'll just take a quick peek while I'm waiting for Mister Haber to show up.

Wetting her lips, Alexis reached out and put one hand on the cube. As before, the whole cube brightened when she touched it, and Alexis experienced the same peculiar quivering sensation in her palm. Next, the edges of the cube's lid reappeared, glowing invitingly. Alexis adjusted her footing and then used her other hand to open the lid.

A wide beam of blinding white light blasted out from the cube. Alexis shrieked and turned her head to protect her eyes from the overwhelming brightness, waiting for it to die away. But instead of fading, the white light intensified, and soon everything seemed to be sparkling in its glow. The overhead lights began to flicker. The floor rumbled, making the contents of the bookcases rattle as if in warning. Alexis staggered, took her hands off the cube, and fearfully grabbed onto the edge of a shelf to keep from falling.

For one second longer, the beam of white grew even more vibrant, and then an explosion of every color imaginable surged forth from the cube and spread rapidly through the air. As the stunning spectrum of color continued filling the supply closet, Alexis was struck in the chest by an unseen force and knocked hard to the ground. A strange heaviness pressed down upon her, forcing Alexis to struggle to get to her knees. Then she raised her head and gasped. She was totally enveloped by an array of beautiful, swirling colors.

The cocoon of light surrounding her was so overpowering that Alexis again had to lift her arms to shade her eyes. Only then did she notice that her hands were shining a fierce, pure white. With an exclamation of shock and wonder, Alexis moved her heavy arms higher. As she did so, streams of color began flowing gracefully through the air to her palms, making her hands shine more brightly still.

But only moments later, the colors that were dancing in the air started to fizzle out, gradually disappearing into nothing. The cube's glow faded. The shaking of the ground stopped, and the weight lifted from Alexis's body. The overhead lights sputtered on.

Alexis exhaustedly collapsed to the floor. *Am I crazy? I must be going crazy.*

She examined her hands, which appeared as they always did, all the way down to the chipped polish on her nails. In a daze, Alexis sat up and pensively eyed the cube, which sat on the table dull and lifeless.

It was one of Mister Haber's experiments. That's all. A really, really weird experiment.

Alexis stood and brushed off her lotion-splattered jeans.

I need to get out of here.

Trembling, she picked up her bag and fled into the main room. After a last glance behind her, Alexis hurried across the broken glass that glistened on the floor, exited into the hallway, and rushed for the stairs to Mrs. Frank's English class.

Back in the supply closet, the cube gave off a final, faint flash of white light.

***

Xander read the latest report and dropped his communicator onto the desk in frustration. Somehow, the operatives had lost track of Number 407. Every trace of It had unexplainably disappeared. It was as if Number 407 did not exist anymore—at least, not in the same form.

THREE

Alexis yawned and tried opening her eyes, still somewhere between sleep and wakefulness. At first, visions of the white cube and swirling colors filled her hazy mind. But as her thoughts cleared, Alexis recalled the humiliation of falling down in front of Tanner and being mocked by Crystal the day before. Letting out a groan, Alexis pulled the bedspread over her head.

At least today can't be as bad as yesterday.

Pushing the blanket from her face, Alexis rolled onto her side. Through the open door that led into her bathroom, she caught her reflection in the mirror. She stared, blinked, and stared some more.

It looked like she was floating in the air.

Alexis instinctively reached for the mattress beneath her but felt nothing. After another bewildered check in the mirror, Alexis looked down. She saw her empty bed, several feet below, in its normal place on the floor. With her mind beginning to whirl in sleepy confusion, Alexis surveyed the rest of her room from her surreal bird's-eye view: wrinkled clothes scattered across the carpet, finished homework on the desk, and her cheerleading outfit hanging over her chair.

I'm still dreaming. That's all. This is a dream.

But when Alexis sat up, a whack of her head

against the ceiling seemed to confirm the unbelievable: she was hovering in the air.

Suddenly, her alarm clock went off, blasting music throughout the house and jolting Alexis into a panic. She began flailing her arms and legs in a desperate attempt to get down.

"Alexis, are you awake?" she heard her mother, Liz, call from the bottom of the stairs.

"I'm awake!" Alexis screeched, her heart beating so hard that it hurt.

Liz sounded as though she was coming up the stairs. "And are you out of bed?"

"Yep, I'm out of bed!" Alexis made a frantic attempt to grab the window curtains to pull herself to the floor. "I'm definitely out of bed!"

"Your music is still playing," her mother noted suspiciously from right outside the bedroom.

Stuck floating helplessly near the ceiling, Alexis saw the doorknob begin to turn. She shuddered and shut her eyes tight.

Mom will freak out when she sees me like this! She'll call 911! I need to get down! I need to get down right now!

The bedroom door was opened.

"Honey, are you going to turn that thing off?"

She's taking this more calmly than I expected.

Alexis opened her eyes. Her mother was standing in the doorway, holding her hands over her ears as if nothing was out of the ordinary. Alexis then realized that she felt carpet beneath her feet. Inhaling sharply, she peeked again at the mirror. Her reflection proved that she was standing on the floor near her bed.

I'm definitely going insane.

Shaking in spite of herself, Alexis reached over to her nightstand and slapped the top of her radio. The music shut off.

Her mother uncovered her ears, stepped over the piles of clothes, and placed a hand on Alexis's forehead. "Are you feeling okay, honey? You appear pale."

Alexis nodded stiffly. "Uh-huh."

"Alright, then you better get moving. Marcus and Molly will be here soon."

Her mother walked out and shut the door. Alexis stayed where she was, her thoughts churning. It was not long before her eyes tracked over to her chemistry textbook, which sat open on the desk.

The glowing white cube. Those colors. Is it possible that something happened yesterday and . . . no, don't be stupid. That was one of Mister Haber's crazy experiments. I'm totally fine. I was only dreaming.

Alexis noticed the time, slipped her cheerleading uniform over her tall, thin frame, and approached the bathroom mirror. Her hands were quivering so badly that it took four tries before she managed to put her hair up into a ponytail. As she finished getting ready, Alexis heard the familiar sounds of a car pulling into the driveway and two brisk honks of the horn. Alexis paused, examining her wide-eyed reflection.

Relax. I'm okay. Everything is alright.

The horn honked again. Alexis stuffed what she needed into her bag, bolted down the stairs, and hurried outside. Sprinting to the end of the driveway, she hopped into the back of the waiting car and slammed the door.

From the front passenger seat, Molly turned and faced her. "Hi, Lex!"

"H-hi," Alexis sputtered.

"What's wrong, Lex? No, wait, let me guess: the monumental stress of cheerleading is getting to you?" kidded Marcus, Molly's older brother, as he maneuvered the car out of the driveway.

"Shut up, Marcus," Molly snapped. But she, too, began studying Alexis closely. "Are you okay?"

Alexis plastered on a smile. "I'm great. My morning was totally normal. It was fantastic, in fact. A really fantastic, normal morning."

Marcus checked Alexis through the rearview mirror. "Whoa. Seriously, why so jittery?" His teasing grin broadened. "Is it because Molly roped you into cheerleading and the first football game is tonight? Or do you have a new crush this week?"

"Shut up, Marcus, or I'll tell Mom that you got home late the other night," Molly warned.

Marcus chuckled. "Fine. Go ahead and tell Mom, but good luck finding yourself another ride to school every morning."

While the siblings argued, Alexis stared out the window, her mind a whirlpool of jumbled thoughts:

Don't worry about this morning—it was a dream. Ugh, I cannot believe that I humiliated myself in front of

Tanner yesterday. What was in that white cube? Did I remember my lunch? Crystal has probably told the whole school about what happened in the hallway. Do I know all the moves for the new routine? Marcus needs to slow down because —

"Marcus! Watch out!"

Alexis had screamed before she realized it. With a startled shout, Marcus slammed his foot on the brake. The car tires screeched, and the smell of burning rubber filled the air. Alexis was thrust forward and then thrown back as her seatbelt locked. She heard Molly let out a terrified cry. Jerking her head up, Alexis saw a semi-truck run a red light and roar past only a few feet in front of them.

"Oh, Lex," was all Molly could utter as their car finally came to a stop in the middle of the intersection.

Marcus was gripping the steering wheel, visibly shaken. "Lex, if you hadn't said anything, we would have been . . ." he trailed off and leaned forward, checking down the street from where the semi-truck had come. "I don't know how you even spotted that truck coming."

The three of them fell into a stunned quiet as Marcus resumed driving down the road. With goosebumps forming on her arms, Alexis peered out the window at the dark skid marks they had left behind.

I never saw that truck coming, but I knew it was going to hit us. I somehow knew.

The rest of the ride went by in a fog. Only when Marcus and Molly started getting out of the car did Alexis even notice that they had arrived at school.

Grabbing her bag, Alexis slid out after the others. Marcus gave her a curious look before heading off to his class. Once the girls were alone, Molly faced Alexis squarely, her expression serious.

"Lex, I have to ask you something."

Alexis's stomach sank. *How am I going to explain this to Molly without her thinking I'm completely psycho?*

Molly continued eyeing her. "What do you think about an extra cheer practice tonight before the football game?"

"What?"

"An extra cheer practice," Molly repeated. "Look, I really appreciate that you're doing the cheer squad with me this year. I know it's not your favorite thing, even though you are really good at it."

"Oh, um, thanks. No problem." Alexis rubbed her aching forehead.

Molly went on, "Obviously, I despise Crystal as much as you do, and I have no desire to hang out with her any more than absolutely necessary. But she sent me a text about having an extra cheer practice before the game tonight, and I told her we'd be there. She claims other cheerleaders need to learn the new routine better, but I think she's the one who doesn't know it."

Alexis managed something like a smile. "No worries. I'd be glad to rehearse."

"Cool. Thanks." Molly smiled in return. "I'd better run to class. Sorry you have to go hang out with test tubes. I'll be sure to give Tanner Ricks a wave for you if I pass him in the halls."

"And if I see Drake, I'll be sure say that you're in love with him," Alexis weakly joked in return.

Molly giggled as she headed for the outdoor stairs to the second floor. "Don't you dare! Unless you arrange for Drake to ask me to homecoming, then you can say whatever you want. Anyway, I'll see you later."

Alexis waved and remained by the car, gazing blankly about while trying to make sense of what had occurred. But she could not. Nothing made sense. Nothing seemed real.

I'm tired, that's all. Extremely tired. Hallucination-inducing tired. Imagine-myself-floating tired. Clairvoyant tired.

The bell rang. Hoisting her bag onto her shoulder, Alexis passed through the school's main doors and robotically maneuvered the noisy, crowded hallways until she found herself standing outside of Mr. Haber's classroom. She hesitated—the disquieting thoughts of that morning and the day before passing again through her mind—before reaching out and opening the door.

Everything in Mr. Haber's room appeared as it always did. The mess from the earthquake had been cleaned up. Students were busy chatting with each other, using their cell phones, and rushing to complete homework. Laura Bellows sat in the front row, conspicuously studying for the next week's assignment. A few seats away, Sam was teasing Julia while shoving his pencil into an outlet. Taking in the scene, Alexis sensed herself relax. She headed to her desk.

". . . it's like no one else felt the earthquake," a classmate was saying.

"I know! People thought I was crazy when I told them about it at lunch!" another replied. "Were we the only class that noticed it? So weird!"

Doing her best to ignore the discussions around her, Alexis bent down and pulled her homework from her bag. When the final bell rang, Alexis lifted her eyes in surprise. Mr. Haber was not there. He had never been late before.

"Looks like there's no class today!" Sam called out, causing a few students to cheer.

Alexis continued scanning the room. She was unexplainably uneasy, like her instincts were telling her that something was wrong. Then a cold, pricking sensation started creeping over the back of her neck, causing Alexis to shiver and hunch forward uncomfortably in her chair.

The other students were growing restless when the door to the supply closet was opened. Everyone hushed and turned toward the sound. Mr. Haber stepped out and strode to the front of the class. Alexis observed him, unable to ignore that his ponytail appeared uncharacteristically disheveled and there was darkness under his eyes.

At the same time, the main classroom door creaked and Noah came in from the hall. Seeming oblivious to the way everyone watched him, Noah's intense gray eyes were focused on nothing as he headed straight for a chair at the back of the room. As he passed by Alexis, she noted that he had in tiny earbuds. The sight nearly made her laugh aloud.

Even Mister Haber's own T.A. finds this class so boring that he has to listen to music to get through it.

"Good morning," Mr. Haber greeted everyone, sounding tired. "I do apologize for being late. Let us begin by reviewing the homework assignment from yesterday. Does anyone have questions?"

Laura raised her hand. "Will you show us how to do problem number sixteen?"

"Certainly, Miss Bellows. This question requires you to use a unit of measurement called moles, which is based on how many atoms are in twelve grams of the element carbon-12." Mr. Haber faced the whiteboard and continued speaking. "This constant is named Avogadro's number. Does anyone know what it is?"

"6.0221415×10^{23}."

Without turning around, Mr. Haber nodded. "That is correct, Miss Bellows. However, we usually round—"

"Laura didn't give the answer," someone interrupted. "Alexis did."

The room went quiet. Students shifted in their seats to view Alexis, not bothering to hide their expressions of surprise.

Mr. Haber looked over his shoulder and found Alexis in the crowd. "Very impressive, Miss Kendall. Yes, you are correct. Although, as I was saying, we usually round to 6.02×10^{23} for simplicity."

"Right. Okay. Thanks." Alexis sank low in her chair, cringing under the stares of the others and growing unnerved. *I don't know what I just said! I don't* have any idea what that Avo-whatever number means! I've never even heard of it!

Mr. Haber gestured toward the workstations. "And thank you, Noah, for pointing out who gave the correct answer."

Noah? Alexis tipped her head. He was actually paying attention?

Pretending to reach for something in her bag, Alexis glimpsed behind her. As if he had anticipated what she would do, Noah met her gaze. Alexis blushed and quickly faced forward again.

Mr. Haber seemed struck by an idea. "Miss Kendall, since you have a grasp of this, please come up and assist me with the next problem."

Alexis nearly choked. "Oh, gee, thanks, but I don't really—"

"Come up! Come up!" Mr. Haber insisted, his enthusiasm returning. "You obviously have a good understanding of these principles! Come!"

Alexis groaned. She was stuck.

With everyone still gawking at her, Alexis dragged herself to the front of the class. As soon as she reached Mr. Haber's side, he promptly handed her the whiteboard pen.

"Alright, Miss Kendall, this is a tough question, but I think you can get it started for us. Please use Avogadro's number to calculate how many atoms are in twenty-two grams of copper."

"2.09×10^{23} atoms," Alexis heard herself say.

Mr. Haber's eyes grew big, further magnified by his glasses. "You are right."

"Hey, genius!" Sam called out. "Slow down for the rest of us!"

Alexis, more shocked than anyone, peered out over the room. Most of her classmates were observing her with astonishment, Laura was glaring haughtily from the front row, and Julia proudly flashed a thumbs-up sign. Then Alexis spotted Noah. He was leaning back in his chair and studying her intensely with his gray eyes. Alexis swallowed hard.

"Miss Kendall, you did that in your head?" she heard Mr. Haber ask incredulously.

Alexis faced her teacher again. "I guess so."

"Well, how about we attempt an even harder problem." Mr. Haber eagerly checked his notes. "This was going to be my extra credit question for today: how many atoms of chlorine are in sixteen-point-five grams of ferric chloride? Obviously, this is a very difficult problem, requiring conversion tables to—"

"1.838×10^{23} atoms," Alexis answered before she could stop herself.

Mr. Haber stared at her.

"Is she right?" Sam demanded.

"She is right," Mr. Haber replied.

Students began murmuring.

"You planned this before class!" Laura insisted hotly.

Mr. Haber shook his head. "No, we did not."

More whispers filtered around the room.

Alexis was starting to feel faint. "May I sit down now, Mister Haber?"

"Yes. Of course." Mr. Haber sounded mystified. "Thank you, Miss Kendall. Excellent job."

Alexis kept her head low and charged to her desk. But as she took her seat, she sensed that someone was still watching her. Lifting her eyes, Alexis saw Noah observe her for another long moment before he turned away.

***

"Xander, have you reviewed my latest report?"

Leaning away from his computer, Xander picked up his communicator and spoke into it. "Yes, Jackie, and I agreed with your conclusions. Number 407 has got to be there. I sent an operative to the site this morning, who confirmed your findings. I now have another operative with a response squad on the way there."

"Good. Something very big is going on." Jackie sounded almost breathless. "The amount of activity going on in that area is unlike anything I've ever seen before. I'm still in the lab, but I'll get over to your office as soon as I can."

Jackie is as passionate about the science as always, Xander thought with a smile. But as he glanced at the computer screen, his smile faded. *Too bad things aren't as innocent as a PhD program anymore.*

"You know, Xander, The Organization used some incredibly clever cover. We were lucky that we found It again," Jackie remarked.

There was a pause before Xander replied:

"Yes. We were very lucky."

FOUR

"If the bathroom on the first floor wasn't always closed for repairs, this one wouldn't be so crowded all the time," Molly complained, shoving her way toward the mirror. "Can you believe algebra today? I thought Miss Carlton was going to talk forever."

Alexis only laughed as she reached the bathroom mirror and began fixing her ponytail. Algebra or not, she was in a great mood. It had been over two hours since Mr. Haber's class, and not a single freaky thing had happened to her. Everything was finally back to normal.

Molly finished smoothing her cheer skirt and examined her reflection with satisfaction. "Okay, I'm ready to go. I hope Drake is in the cafeteria today—I put on extra lip gloss for the occasion."

Alexis grinned at her friend, and the two girls slipped out of the bathroom and headed downstairs to the first floor. Crossing the courtyard behind the gym, they entered the cafeteria but lingered in the doorway so Molly could pretend to check her phone while discreetly inspecting the scene.

"Over there," Molly soon whispered with the slightest movement of her head.

Alexis peeked over at where Molly had indicated. Drake and several other guys from the

football team were seated around a table in the middle
of the cafeteria. Alexis shrank back when she saw
Tanner among them.

"No way. We aren't going anywhere near
Tanner. You know what an idiot I made of myself
yesterday."

"You didn't make an idiot of yourself. You . . ."
Molly twisted her mouth, clearly trying to think of the
right words to say.

"Looked like a klutz?" Alexis suggested dryly.

"No, you—"

"Hi, Tan-ner!" a voice rang out.

Alexis and Molly groaned in unison. From
their vantage point, they watched Crystal Lark waltz
across the cafeteria and take a place beside Tanner
with an exaggerated flip of her cheer skirt. A flock of
Crystal's friends followed and sat around Drake, who
clearly did not seem to mind.

Molly made a weird growling noise. "Sorry,
Lex, but this is war."

Before Alexis could protest, Molly grabbed her
by the wrist and began marching directly for the table.
When Crystal noticed the two girls approaching, she
set down her pink energy drink and flashed a broad
smile.

"Hi, A-lex-is! Hi, Mol-ly!"

"Hey, Crystal! How are you?" Molly replied
with equally artificial warmth, slipping herself
between the other girls so she was right next to Drake.

Left standing, Alexis saw that the only
remaining vacant chair was directly across from
Crystal. Giving Molly her you-so-owe-me-for-this

eyebrow raise, Alexis slid past the rest of the group and dropped into the empty seat.

"Hi, everybody," Alexis said in monotone.

Crystal gave her a contemptuous once-over before shifting to face the other way. One of Crystal's friends scrutinized Alexis and then whispered something to Drake, causing him to stifle laughter. With an inward sigh, Alexis put her head down and made herself busy getting her lunch from her bag. But then she heard someone say:

"Hey, Alexis, how's it going?"

Alexis recognized the voice and froze in surprise. Then she raised her head. Seated across the table, Tanner was looking at her.

"You'll be cheering at the game tonight, right?" Tanner continued, his expression kind and his tone sincere.

Alexis blinked, glanced around, and then ventured a slight nod. "Yes, um, I'll be there. Um, what about you, Tanner? Will you, um, be at the game?"

Immediately, Crystal and her friends started snickering and exchanging looks.

Alexis sensed her cheeks burn with embarrassment. *I just asked the team's quarterback if he's gonna be at the football game. The player who's so good that he's a starter as a ninth grader. Could I have said anything more stupid?*

But Tanner did not seem to think her remark strange nor notice how Crystal was nudging him. Keeping his attention on Alexis, he replied simply,

"Yep, I'll be at the game. So I'll try to give you something to cheer about."

The way he spoke made Alexis's stomach do a flip. After a beat, she dared to break into a smile. Tanner smiled back at her.

Abruptly, Crystal stopped laughing. Glancing between Tanner and Alexis, she spoke loudly enough for everyone to hear. "A-lex-is, did you get the message that we're having cheer practice before the game? I thought you could use it, since you're not exactly light on your feet, if you know what I mean."

The table came to a complete hush.

Alexis dragged her eyes from Tanner to Crystal, who smirked at her victoriously. Too stunned and mortified to muster a response, Alexis could do nothing as Crystal leaned close to Tanner and whispered in his ear. Alexis blinked hard, sensing tears that she was not certain she could hide.

I wish . . . I wish Tanner would realize that Crystal is nothing but a clumsy, lying fake with a stupid bottle of pink water!

"Hey, watch it!" Tanner suddenly yelled.

Tanner leapt up, frantically trying to wipe away a pink liquid that was soaking into his shirt and letterman's jacket. Next to his seat, Crystal's tipped-over drink was still spilling onto the table and floor.

"Tanner, I'm so sorry!" Crystal exclaimed, scrambling to pick up her bottle.

Tanner sighed. "It's okay. I know you didn't mean to—"

"Seriously, I'm so sorry! I don't know what happened!" Crystal went on, distraught.

"You knocked your drink over, that's what happened," Drake snapped, handing Tanner a wad of napkins.

"But I didn't! I swear!" Crystal insisted. "I never touched it!"

Drake rolled his eyes. "Right. Your drink magically tipped over on its own."

Tanner dried his hands and picked up his bag. "I guess I'd better go clean up. See you all later."

Tanner and Drake walked away. Crystal watched them go, visibly crestfallen, while the other football players eyed her with disapproval. As Crystal's friends gathered consolingly around her, Molly took the chance to grab Alexis by the arm and tug her toward the cafeteria exit.

"That was incredible!" Molly laughed as they burst outdoors. "I can't believe Crystal pretended that she hadn't knocked over her drink!" Molly's exuberance died away when she saw the blank expression on Alexis's face. "Uh, Lex? Hello? Crystal humiliated herself in front of Tanner, and he was talking to you in there. You should be celebrating right now."

Alexis met Molly's quizzical stare in silence. Her throat was tight and her pulse was climbing. No one, Alexis realized, had seen what really happened. No one else understood that the drink had tipped over on its own, as if pushed by an invisible hand.

I made that drink fall over just by thinking about it.

When the staggering idea struck her fully, Alexis's mind went into overdrive, replaying the memories of floating in her bedroom, shouting at

Marcus to stop the car, and giving answers to chemistry questions that she had no idea how to solve. As the unexplainable events kept swirling relentlessly in her head, Alexis knew that she could not deny the astounding truth any longer: somehow, she had developed strange and unpredictable . . . powers. Even more terrifying, Alexis knew that she had witnessed her mystifying powers do something bad to someone else—something she never truly intended—because of one fleeting, emotional thought that had flown through her mind.

What other awful things might I accidentally do to people? What if I cause something really serious to happen? What if I hurt my friends or family with these powers that I don't know how to control?

Fear rose fast within her, and Alexis knew it was time to seek help. But to whom could she go? She was sure that Molly would never believe something so incredible. And if she tried explaining things to her parents, she would probably wind up in a psychiatrist's office. Alexis concluded that there was only one person who might take her seriously: Mr. Haber.

Molly tapped Alexis on the shoulder. "What's wrong?"

"Nothing," Alexis lied. "I need to go speak with Mister Haber. That's all."

Molly's jaw dropped. "You want to go chat about chemistry rather than how Crystal embarrassed herself and Tanner was flirting with you?"

Alexis was already stepping away. "We'll talk soon, I promise. But I have to go. Sorry."

Alexis spun around and rushed across the courtyard toward the classrooms. As she hurried through the corridors, she became consumed by the same foreboding feeling that had filled her during first period. And when the back of her neck started prickling, Alexis broke into a full-on run. She was panting by the time she reached Mr. Haber's room, yanked open the door, and charged in.

"Mister Haber! I need to—"

"Miss Kendall? May I help you?"

She halted. Mr. Haber was in the middle of speaking to a class of seniors. While Alexis racked her brain for a sane-sounding way to explain her intrusion, Noah stepped out from the supply closet with his arms full of experiment equipment. Noah did a double take when he saw Alexis, appearing as caught off guard as she was. But after a glance at Mr. Haber, Noah proceeded to start setting up the equipment like nothing was wrong.

Alexis watched him, confused. *Noah's a T.A. for this period, too? Doesn't he have other classes?*

"What can I do for you, Miss Kendall?" Mr. Haber prompted again.

Alexis jumped and faced him. "I need to talk with you. In private, please."

Out of the corner of her eye, Alexis saw Noah stop what he was doing.

"Certainly," Mr. Haber replied. "As soon as class is over, I would be happy to meet with you. You are welcome to wait in here, if you would like."

"But I . . ." Alexis broke off, very aware that a bunch of upperclassmen were listening. She cleared her throat and tried appearing casual. "Yeah. Okay. Sure."

Mr. Haber resumed speaking to the class. Alexis migrated self-consciously over near the large windows on the side of the room to wait. Noah observed her, went into the supply closet, and came out carrying a chair, which he set down by where he was working. He gave Alexis another glance. She scurried across the room and gratefully took the seat.

"Thanks," Alexis whispered.

"You're welcome," he mumbled, not bothering to look at her again.

Okay, so apparently Noah's not one for conversation, Alexis noted with a roll of her eyes, turning away from him.

Try as she might to focus on Mister Haber, though, Alexis could not relax. She was unable to ignore the sense of foreboding that coursed through her body and the questions burning her mind.

How can I explain to Mister Haber what happened? Will he even believe me? Does he have a way to fix—

The soft clanking of glass brought Alexis to awareness. Noah continued working beside her. Trying to distract herself, Alexis began watching what he was doing. With steady motions, Noah measured brightly colored powders and poured them into a row of small beakers. While observing him, Alexis could not help but notice Noah's strong features and intense gray eyes.

Molly was right, Alexis finally acknowledged. *Noah might be a science nerd, but he's definitely . . .*

Blushing, Alexis faced forward and tried to concentrate on the front of the room.

***

Xander studied the newest satellite images on his computer monitor and then spoke into his communicator. "Victor, how long until you and the response squad are in position?"

"Three minutes," came the operative's reply.

"Copy," Xander said. "I will await your video and audio feeds. Over."

Deep in thought, Xander set the communicator down on his office desk. The events that were about to play out were critical. With every move he made as Head of Intelligence already scrutinized by the committee members, who were openly skeptical of him because he was only thirty-three, Xander had to remain one step ahead of the others while executing his assigned duties perfectly. And he knew that Dr. Gaige continued to watch him closely—at times, suspiciously. In such a precarious position, Xander was astutely aware that if he slipped up even once, his years of sacrifice would be for nothing and the results potentially catastrophic.

With such sobering thoughts weighing upon his mind, Xander contemplated the huge risk he was taking. He was sending one of his best operatives to a public location—a high school, of all places—and in only a few minutes, Xander would know if his gamble paid off.

FIVE

Alexis shifted in her chair. She remained extremely uneasy, even though nothing seemed amiss: Mr. Haber was still teaching the class of seniors, and Noah had gone into the supply closet to continue working.

Be patient, Alexis told herself with another agitated view of the clock. *Everything's fine.*

Despite how she tried, however, Alexis could not shake the gnawing feeling that something was very wrong. As she checked the clock again, a movement out of the corner of her eye caused her to whip around and face the windows. But she saw nothing outside except a thick hedge of plants right next to the windows, and the school's parking lot and soccer fields beyond.

With a jittery sigh, Alexis faced forward and surveyed the room for what she guessed was her millionth time. Mr. Haber was writing on the whiteboard, his back to the class. Students were whispering, texting on their cell phones, and taking notes. Nothing appeared out of the ordinary, yet Alexis remained convinced that something ominous was afoot. She warily peered outside again. The sky was clear, the autumn sun shone brightly, and a breeze had begun rustling the plants by the windows.

Rubbing her hands on her cheer skirt, Alexis made herself turn away.

Calm down. There's nothing—

A terrible, icy sensation suddenly washed over Alexis, causing her gasp aloud. As the haunting coldness spread fast through her body, Alexis shuddered. Somehow, she knew that something really was out there.

Slowly, Alexis faced the windows once more. Her heart slammed in her chest when she spotted two small, glowing red objects deep within the thick hedge outside—objects, she realized with horror, that were someone's eyes. Alexis then began to make out the silhouette of a man hiding in the bushes—a man with red eyes who was watching the room.

Alexis could barely breathe. *I have to tell Mister Haber.*

Shaking so badly that she needed to grip the chair for balance, Alexis stood up. As she did so, the shadowed stranger turned his head, putting his red eyes directly on hers. Frozen with fear, Alexis could do nothing as the lurking stranger raised his arm and pointed something at her.

Just then, Noah came out of the supply closet carrying a box of supplies. Alexis attempted to scream a warning, but her throat was too dry and tight to utter a sound. She made one desperate, staggering step toward Noah before her legs gave out and she began to fall.

"Alexis!"

There was a crash as Noah dropped the box and dove to catch Alexis before she hit the ground. At the same moment, a beam of red light came shooting through the window toward them. With her remaining strength, Alexis pushed Noah out of the way of the red light and then instinctively pointed her arms at the stranger outside. A blinding white light blasted from her hands toward the windows, the force throwing Alexis to the floor.

The classroom burst into commotion.

"There was an explosion at the experiment table!" one student cried.

"That girl passed out!" shouted another.

"Alexis?" she heard someone asking tensely. "Can you hear me? Alexis?"

Alexis moaned. As her vision came into focus, she saw Noah crouched over her. His jaw was clenched, and he was breathing fast.

"I can hear you," she told him weakly. Her head swam, and her hands were hot and aching painfully.

"Students, there is no need to panic," Mr. Haber was explaining over the chaos. "There was a minor chemical reaction at one of the workstations. Please exit into the hallway calmly and quickly, and we will take care of Miss Kendall."

As students started hurrying from the room, Noah leaned down close to Alexis. He spoke in her ear in a hushed, tense tone. "We have to move. Now."

Alexis detected the urgency in his voice and tried sitting up. But she collapsed weakly, her strength gone. Without hesitating, Noah slung one of Alexis's arms over his shoulders, lifted her off the ground, and carried her into the supply closet.

"I'm okay. Really," Alexis managed to say, sensing her strength beginning to return.

Noah helped her into the chair at Mr. Haber's cluttered desk. He got down in front of her and searched her face. "Are you sure that you're alright? You aren't hurt?"

"I'm not hurt. I'm . . . I'm fine."

Alexis had to look away so Noah would not see the frightened tears in her eyes. She was still trembling as she rubbed her throbbing hands together. There were several seconds of silence before she heard Noah speak again:

"So do you often deflect light attacks and save the lives of high school T.A.'s?"

Alexis took a sharp breath in and met Noah's gaze.

Noah's gray eyes remained locked on hers. "Is this what you need to talk to Mister Haber about?"

"Yes," Alexis nearly whispered. "This is what I need to talk to Mister Haber about."

Their conversation was interrupted when something started beeping. Noah reached into his pocket and pulled out a black device, which looked to Alexis like a strange cell phone. Noah pushed a button on the device, causing the beeping to cease, and then appeared to read a message upon it.

The door to the supply closet was opened, and Mr. Haber hurried in. "Miss Kendall, are you alright? Someone said that you passed out."

Noah got to his feet and held up his device. "Ben, we have a Priority One."

Mr. Haber halted. He let his eyes track meaningfully from Noah to Alexis and back to Noah. "Since Miss Kendall is here, perhaps we can excuse ourselves to chat about—"

"Ben," Noah interrupted, "Alexis is the Priority One."

Mr. Haber's expression changed. He took the device from Noah's hand and read the message that was on it for what felt to Alexis like a very long time. Eventually, Mr. Haber peered at her over the top of his glasses.

"Miss Kendall, I think this is a good time for you to explain why you came to see me."

Alexis was overcome with relief. She had no idea what the message on Noah's weird device said, but it did not matter. She was going to tell Mr. Haber what happened, he would fix her, and then everything would go back to normal. She would never have to think about powers or glowing red eyes again. Taking a deep breath, Alexis started speaking fast:

"Yesterday after the earthquake, I wanted to make sure that you were alright. So I came in here and—"

"You came in here? How did you get in?" Mr. Haber interrupted with obvious concern.

Alexis motioned apologetically to the supply closet door. "It was unlocked."

"Unlocked?" Mr. Haber faced Noah. "How could we have been so careless?"

Noah yanked off his baseball hat and ran a hand through his hair. "We were in a hurry, Ben. We had no warning."

Mr. Haber knelt in front of Alexis. "What happened when you came in here?"

Alexis looked to the back of the supply closet. The wood table remained, but the white cube was gone.

"I saw a cube sitting on that table," she explained, pointing. "The cube was glowing, and colors were shooting out of it. I thought it was one of your experiments. I wanted to see what it was, so I opened the cube. I know I shouldn't have, and I'm really sorry that—"

"You opened the cube," Mr. Haber repeated, going pale.

"Yes. And everything got heavy, and all sorts of colors flew into my hands!" Alexis heard her voice rising. "Now I'm doing hard calculations in my head, I made Crystal's drink tip over without touching it, I knew a semi-truck was going to hit us, and I woke up floating in my bedroom!" She broke off only for a moment and then frantically continued, "And I knew something was wrong even before I saw the man with red eyes hiding in the bushes outside!"

There was a terrible pause.

"There was a man outside," Mr. Haber finally echoed.

Alexis shivered. "He shot a red light at me."

"He shot a red light?" Mr. Haber got to his feet. "He shot at you, Miss Kendall?"

"Uh-huh. The light almost hit Noah." Alexis quivered at the memory. "I fired a white light back at the man. I don't know how. The light came from my hands . . . I think."

Mr. Haber gawked at her.

"It's true," Noah said to Mr. Haber, his voice low. "She saved me from the operative's light attack and somehow defended herself."

Mr. Haber handed Noah's device back to him. "I see."

Noah furiously shook his head. "I was in the supply closet until she was attacked, Ben. I never saw the operative. He was only feet away, and I didn't know it."

Mr. Haber faced him squarely. "You are not to blame for this. I am the one who should have detected that an operative, and the squad that was undoubtedly with him, got so close. What happened was my fault and my fault alone."

Noah said nothing more and began pacing with agitated steps. As Alexis watched the exchange, her worry and confusion grew even deeper. It was obvious that something was extremely wrong— something significant, which involved more than her. But did she really want to know? Alexis could not say for sure anymore. Almost reluctantly, she peered back at Mr. Haber and waited.

Mr. Haber observed Alexis, deliberating, before he spoke again. "Miss Kendall, I am about to explain something to you that can never be mentioned to anyone else."

Noah stopped in his tracks. "Wait, what are you doing? We can't involve Alexis in this."

"We do not have a choice." Mr. Haber gestured toward the table where the white cube had been.

"But it's not fair." Noah's words were strained. "It's not fair to her."

A look of pity crossed Mr. Haber's face. "I understand how you feel. However, based on what happened, we must. You know that."

Noah flinched and glanced at Alexis. She returned his glance with an uneasy, inquiring look, but Noah only turned away. As a lump formed in her throat, Alexis addressed her teacher:

"Okay. If . . . if it's the only way. I won't tell anyone anything, Mister Haber. I promise."

Mr. Haber made no response. He stepped over to the door and swiftly locked it. Then he walked over to a row of bookcases that lined the opposite wall. "This will make more sense in a moment, Miss Kendall," he finally said over his shoulder.

Alexis watched as Mr. Haber reached into his shirt pocket and pulled out a device that looked similar to the one Noah had used. Mr. Haber pushed a button on his device and, to Alexis's astonishment, a bookcase slowly started dropping down into the floor, revealing the entrance of a dark passageway behind it.

Alexis's mouth fell open. "Are you kidding me? A secret passage? What's in there? Or do I not want to know?"

But Mr. Haber did not answer. Putting his device away, he scurried into the passage and disappeared. Left behind in the strained silence, Alexis peeked at Noah. He was staring straight ahead, his strong arms folded across his chest. Alexis got the message that Noah was in no mood to talk, and she remained still. Tense minutes passed before there was noise again in the passageway. Mr. Haber reappeared from the darkness, carrying a square metal box.

"Ben, what are you doing?" Noah exclaimed, dropping his arms to his sides. "Why aren't you wearing protective—"

"There is no need. There is no activity in here at all," Mr. Haber replied breathlessly.

"What are you talking about?" Noah's eyes were big.

I've been wondering the same thing, Alexis thought dryly.

Mr. Haber set the box on his desk. "I am not surprised, actually. Given what Miss Kendall just told us, I suspect that if we had done another check on this after locking It up yesterday, there would have been no activity detected at that time, either."

"That makes no sense," Noah countered. "We checked It immediately after It arrived. Activity levels were off the chart."

"Yes." Mr. Haber looked up. "But that was before Miss Kendall got her hand on It. No pun intended."

Noah drew his brow together, and his eyes began moving restlessly between Alexis and the box on Mr. Haber's desk.

Alexis could remain quiet no longer. "Hey, I know you guys are all up to speed on everything, but how about explaining to me what's going on?"

"We shall, Miss Kendall," Mr. Haber replied kindly. "We shall explain things right now."

Mr. Haber proceeded to lift the lid off the metal box, reach inside, and pull out something Alexis recognized: the white cube.

Alexis jumped to her feet and backed up. "Keep that thing away from me."

"Do not worry. It is harmless. It is most definitely harmless now," Mr. Haber assured her with a hint of regret. He held the cube out to Noah. "Scan it. You will see."

Noah's focus drifted briefly to Alexis before he took out his device and pointed it at the cube. Nothing happened.

"You see? No activity at all," Mr. Haber uttered, sounding astonished.

"Activity?" Alexis was growing testy. "What activity?"

"There is no activity." Noah sullenly put his device down. "Not in the cube, at least. That's the problem."

Mr. Haber set the cube in the metal box and pulled his own device from his pocket. "Miss Kendall, please remain right where you are. I need to confirm something before I explain. I promise that you have nothing to worry about."

Mr. Haber raised his arm and pointed his device in her direction. Alexis winced but did not move. Almost instantly, the device in Mr. Haber's hand lit up and began making a shrill sound.

"Incredible," Mr. Haber whispered. He put his arm down, and the sound ceased.

Alexis had finally had enough. "Can you guys stop being so cryptic and tell me what's going on?

Actually, I don't even want to know. Just fix me, okay? I'm done with this!"

Mr. Haber's expression softened. He gestured to his empty chair. "Forgive me. So much has happened, and we are still sorting things out. But I shall tell you as much as I can."

Alexis dropped into the chair and crossed her arms impatiently.

Mr. Haber seemed to collect his thoughts prior to speaking. "Miss Kendall, scientific discoveries are being made every day. Miraculous discoveries. Powerful discoveries. Unfortunately, there are some who would use such discoveries for evil purposes and—"

"Mister Haber," Alexis cut in, "is this an acceptance speech for a Nobel prize or something that has to do with me?"

"It has something to do with you," she heard Noah interject.

Surprised, Alexis looked over at him. Noah was watching her with striking intensity, his gray eyes filled with both worry and fierce resolve. Alexis had to catch her breath before she turned back to Mr. Haber and motioned for him to go on.

With a tip of his head, Mr. Haber resumed his dialogue. "Centuries ago, a few devoted scientists recognized the danger of their discoveries potentially falling into the wrong hands. Those scientists created a secret group, simply called The Organization, vowing to defend their discoveries from those who would use them for evil. Since that time, The Organization has remained dedicated to guarding the world's most important scientific truths from all who might use them for the wrong purposes. Miss Kendall, I am part of The Organization. Noah is my trainee."

Alexis started laughing. "You want me to believe that there's an ancient, secret club of science nerds out there?"

"Something like that," Mr. Haber replied.

Alexis's laughing immediately ceased. "You're not kidding, are you?"

Mr. Haber shook his head.

Alexis took a moment to let the idea sink in. "You mean, this whole high school chemistry teacher thing is a cover?"

Mr. Haber smiled. "Who would suspect me of anything?"

He definitely has a point there, Alexis silently agreed, observing him.

Mr. Haber spoke again. "Now I shall try to explain how this all pertains to you, Miss Kendall. Yesterday, under the most emergent of circumstances, Noah and I received something profoundly important to hide and protect. Something many would consider one of the most powerful discoveries in history: a new element."

Alexis's ears perked up. "You mean, like an element on the periodic table?"

"Exactly." Mr. Haber seemed pleased.

"You said there were only one hundred eighteen elements, and that a bunch of them were man-made," Alexis recalled.

"Again, you are correct. At least, mostly correct. As far as the world-at-large is concerned, there are only one hundred eighteen elements, many of which do not even occur in nature."

Alexis eyed him skeptically. "So let me guess: even though all of the scientists across the entire world have never found or made more than one hundred eighteen elements, you're going to tell me that The Organization somehow discovered another naturally occurring element and managed to keep It a secret."

"Precisely." Mr. Haber apparently thought it made perfect sense. "Yesterday, we received the element that has 407 protons. The possibilities of what It can do—and the truths about the Universe we may learn from It—are almost unfathomable." His face clouded over. "Unfortunately, soon after It was discovered, those who would use It for evil got on Its trail. So instead of studying and learning from the element, The Organization was forced to hide It. That is why It came to me."

Alexis motioned to the metal box. "So the element is kept inside the cube?"

"The element *was* kept inside the cube," Mr. Haber clarified.

"Well, if It is so important and so secret, why'd you leave It sitting out on the table yesterday?" Alexis demanded.

"I can make no excuse for what happened yesterday," Mr. Haber acknowledged guiltily. "All I will say is that Noah and I had extremely short notice before It arrived, leaving us with almost no time to prepare. In our hurry, I forgot to lock the door into this supply closet. While Noah and I were making preparations to store the element safely, you must have come in and found It."

"Storing It safely? So the element is unsafe?" Alexis leaned away from the box.

Mr. Haber drummed his fingers on the desk. "We cannot say for sure, since no one ever came into direct contact with It—that is, until you did. And as you seemed to demonstrate, encountering the element without protection would affect someone. Somehow."

"Like causing someone to become a floating, calculation-solving weirdo?" Alexis quipped. "So shouldn't you lock up the element before It affects someone else, too?"

Noah cleared his throat.

"That is a good question, and the most interesting part of all." Mr. Haber seemed to be speaking carefully. "You see, when Noah scanned the cube just now, he confirmed that there is no trace of the element in it any longer. However, when I scanned you—"

"Scanned me? That's what you were doing with your device? Scanning for the element?" Alexis felt the color drain from her face as a horrible thought struck her. "And your device made a noise when you pointed it at me because . . ."

"Because when you came into contact with the element yesterday, It somehow transferred into you," Mr. Haber finished. "The element is part of you right now. It is miraculous."

Alexis went numb. "What?"

"I do not fully understand what occurred," Mr. Haber continued, "but one day I—"

"Don't understand? One day?" Alexis heard her voice shake. "Mister Haber, you don't have any idea how to fix this—to fix me—do you?"

"No. I do not think anyone does. At least, not yet."

Alexis stood so fast that she knocked her chair over. "You're telling me that you're one of the world's most super secret scientists, but you can't fix me? You're saying that I'm stuck like this forever?"

Mr. Haber put out a hand. "I am saying that this has never happened before. But The Organization will figure things out. That is why I need you to come to Headquarters with me."

Alexis refused to believe what she was hearing. "Headquarters? You want me to go with you to science nerd headquarters? Why? So I can become your next experiment? Your new show-and-tell?"

Mr. Haber tried again. "I know this is extremely unexpected and difficult, but you must come. The element that requires protection is now inside of you. We must decide what to do and ensure that you are safe."

Alexis could not think. Everything was spinning. She staggered as she retreated. "No. Absolutely not. I'm not going anywhere."

Noah stepped close and braced her by the arm. "Alexis, the truth is that you're not safe. The man you saw was an operative who works for Doctor Gaige. Doctor Gaige is the most ruthless seeker of everything The Organization tries to protect. After seeing how you saved me and defended yourself, that operative now knows of the powers you possess. He will tell Doctor Gaige, and Doctor Gaige will come after you."

"Yes, Miss Kendall, it is vitally important that you come with us to Headquarters," Mr. Haber implored.

Alexis blinked and shook her arm loose from Noah's hold, trying to clear her mind. But her thoughts and emotions were vacillating too fast.

They're not making sense, Alexis told herself. *None of this makes any sense.*

She took another stunned step back as confusion, disbelief, and anger swirled chaotically inside of her. With a defiant shake of her head, she moved for the door.

"No. I'm not going. I'm not going to become your science project, okay? I have a family, I have friends, I have a game to cheer at tonight, and unlike you guys, I have a life!"

Tears spilling down her cheeks, Alexis pulled open the door and bolted out of the supply closet without looking back.

S I X

"I have a visual on the classroom."

Victor's words were barely audible on the badly distorted video recording. The grainy footage, which had been captured by the tiny video camera Victor had worn, showed how he had approached the high school classroom alone despite orders to wait for his squad to get into position.

Hiding himself in a thick hedge of plants outside the classroom windows, Victor had observed while a teacher wrote on the whiteboard and students took notes. From his vantage point, Victor had also been able to see a girl in a cheerleading uniform who was seated near the back of the room. The girl looked out the windows and then checked the clock. Soon, the girl faced the windows again and looked directly at where Victor was hiding. She stood up, holding onto the chair for support, with a terrified expression on her face.

"Victor, we're detecting interference." Xander's voice had come over Victor's communicator. "Are you alright?"

Victor's reply could barely be heard on the recording. "There's activity beyond measurable levels! Request permission to deter assailant!"

"I did not copy, Victor," Xander had said tensely. "Did you say that there is an assailant?"

"Affirmative! It's a girl who somehow—"

Static on the video cut out the rest of Victor's words.

"Do not attack, Victor. Those are kids in there," Xander barked. "Proceed with evacuation immediately."

"But she has seen me! She must be prevented from—"

"Victor, I order you not to attack. Evacuate now," Xander repeated.

As the video showed, the girl swayed and began to fall. At the same time, a young man entered the classroom through a doorway in the back. He could be heard to call the girl's name—Alexis—as he rushed to catch her. By then, Victor had raised his weapon and shot at the girl. The girl pushed the young man out of the way and held up her hands. Everything went white. Victor screamed.

The video ended.

None of the committee members spoke as Xander turned the video off, raised the lights in the room, and faced the group.

"That is all we have," Xander told them.

"Was Victor reprimanded for disobeying your orders?" Dr. Gaige inquired.

Xander still showed no emotion. "No. After evacuation, Victor was taken to the infirmary, where he remains. The light attack generated by Alexis caused him significant wounds."

"I assume that you take full responsibility for Victor's injuries?" demanded an overweight man at the table. "He is one of our best operatives."

"As Head of Intelligence, I take responsibility for everything that happens during an operation, Gerard." Xander's breathing was deep and measured. "However, Victor's injuries were his own doing. He approached the school without permission and chose a foolish place to hide. He did not evacuate when instructed to do so. He launched a light attack against orders, which led to the retaliatory injuries he received. Had Victor followed the plan, none of this would have happened."

"Ridiculous," Gerard muttered, blotting the perspiration on his forehead with his tie.

Dr. Gaige motioned to a woman across the table. "Jackie, tell us what you've made of this development."

Jackie waited until Xander took his seat, and then she stood up and nodded curtly to the group. Her aura of confidence more than made up for her small stature. She pulled a remote from the pocket of her white lab coat and pushed a button. The room lights dimmed once more, and a slide appeared on the projection screen that read, 'DATA ANALYSIS.' Clearing her throat, Jackie began:

"As you know, about three weeks ago, our operatives started noting increased activity of The Organization's agents in Switzerland. This, of course, strongly suggested that The Organization had come across a new discovery."

Jackie clicked to a new slide, which was filled with complicated calculations. "In the region where agents were most active, we found subtle alterations in electron quiver and gravitational forces. Xander proceeded to direct further investigation into the agents' actions while I headed up the scientific tests, calculations, and confirmatory studies. Ultimately, the combined data of our efforts led us to conclude that The Organization had found the element with 407 protons. Again, Xander mentioned this to you previously."

Jackie stopped only to push aside a strand of auburn hair that had fallen loose from her bun. Then she went on:

"The Organization quickly realized that we had learned about their discovery. They managed to keep the new element, Number 407, one step ahead of us by transferring It across Europe and overseas. Only when similar changes in electron activity were detected in the U.S. did we get on Its trail again."

The next slide showed a map of the United States with several cities highlighted.

"Working with Xander, we continued tracking The Organization's movements, which eventually led us to an area surprisingly close to our base here. Yesterday morning, we were closing in on Number 407's exact location when something extremely unusual occurred: all signs of Number 407 vanished. One minute our analysis indicated that It existed, and then It was gone."

"Number 407 deteriorated?" asked a woman with black hair.

"More likely they slipped It out from under your noses," Gerard grumbled.

"Neither, actually." Jackie went to the subsequent slide. "The Organization's activity remained high in the same area, suggesting Number 407 was still located nearby although we couldn't detect It anymore."

"That's a reckless assumption, don't you think, Xander?" sneered a woman with a nasally voice.

Xander set his steel-gray eyes on the woman. "Reckless? Perhaps, Leslie. But the assumption also proved to be correct."

Xander gestured for Jackie to continue. With a tip of her head, Jackie clicked to a slide showing diagrams of unrecognizable chemical structures. Unable to keep from smiling when she saw everyone's puzzled expressions, Jackie started to explain:

"Early this morning, we began measuring all sorts of bizarre chemical activity and new bends to gravitational forces in the same area where Number 407 had last been detected. Soon, this activity became so strong and so unusual that we couldn't fully analyze it anymore. Shockingly, it appeared that this activity was being unleashed in a completely uncontrolled manner."

"Perhaps it was a distraction? A decoy?" an older man suggested.

"We entertained that possibility, Jacob, but multiple calculations confirmed that what we were detecting was real. Number 407 was still there, but It had been significantly altered," Jackie told him. "As the morning progressed, we did our best to track this peculiar activity, which ultimately settled at a high school, of all places. As best as we could conclude, that was where The Organization had chosen to hide Number 407."

"A high school?" Leslie scoffed. "You can't be serious."

Xander stood up. "Potentially the perfect cover. Hiding It in plain sight was clever. Changing Number 407's form so we were unable to analyze or track It was frankly brilliant. Fortunately for us, the level of activity that Number 407 emitted in Its new form was something we could detect, otherwise we may never have found It again."

A man with thick glasses raised his hand. "So how does that tie in to what happened to Victor? Who was the girl? Was she involved with The Organization or not?"

Jackie glanced at Xander before she spoke. "Well, Peter, our theory is that Number 407 is now . . . inside a human being. After seeing the video, we suspect that It is within the girl, Alexis."

I know what 'deafening silence' means now, Xander noted, and one look at Jackie told him that she was thinking the same thing.

Dr. Gaige leaned forward. "Jackie, do you truly believe that The Organization would choose to plant one of the world's most powerful scientific discoveries inside of a teenage girl?"

"Yes, I do." Jackie had to hold up her hands to quiet everyone before she could go on. "Do I understand why The Organization would do such a thing? No. Do I think it wise? Not at all. I'm simply reporting the facts and what I conclude from those facts. Everything supports the theory that Number 407 was altered and made more powerful. And we all saw the video of that girl defending herself against a light attack. I can only conclude that she carries Number 407 within her."

"This is crazy!" Gerard proclaimed angrily.

Jackie faced him, unwavering. "Why? The powers of Number 407 are now magnitudes stronger after transferring into the girl. Perhaps The Organization chose to sacrifice secrecy and security for that increased power."

Dr. Gaige shook his head.

"You agree that Jackie has run wild with her theory, Doctor Gaige?" Leslie gloated.

Dr. Gaige swiveled in his chair. "No. Jackie is correct to conclude that Number 407 transferred into the girl. The video proves that. However, her assumption about why It was transferred cannot be accurate. The Organization would never give up the security of something so precious, even for magnitudes of increased power." His tone took on a hint of resentment. "Perhaps The Organization always intended to hide Number 407 at the high school, but something unexpected must have happened to involve the girl."

Peter gaped. "You think Number 407 transferred into the girl by accident?"

"Yes! That has to be it!" Jackie exclaimed, her eyes big. "The girl's powers are so strong—so uncontrolled and easy for us to detect—The Organization never would have done that on purpose!" Jackie dropped into a chair and looked with astonishment at Xander.

Jacob raised a hand. "What will we do about the girl? If she has Number 407 inside of her, are we going to go after her?"

"I shall, of course, defer to Xander on this," Dr. Gaige said with a wicked smile.

Xander absorbed every ounce of Dr. Gaige's meaning. It was a challenge, meant to test him. But Xander kept his affect unassuming.

"We will get Alexis," Xander told them. "In fact, I already have a plan in place."

SEVEN

Step forward, one-two. Arms up, three-four.

Although she knew the cheer routine by heart, Alexis made herself concentrate on every move. She wanted to keep her mind busy. She needed to stop thinking about Mr. Haber and Noah, light attacks, and frightening powers.

"Great job, ladies!" Crystal clapped once the music finished. Putting her hands on her hips, she looked over the group, pausing with undisguised disdain when her eyes fell upon Alexis. "Most of you, at least, will give a great performance tonight. So let's get out to the football field!"

While the rest of the cheerleaders enthusiastically began chatting and gathering their things, Alexis remained quiet as she distractedly scooped up her pom-poms. Molly observed her, leaned in, and whispered:

"Don't let Crystal get to you, okay? She's jealous. Not only are you a better dancer, but Tanner flirted with you at lunch today. She can't stand it."

"What?" Alexis looked at her friend. She nodded appreciatively. "Oh, um, thanks."

With Crystal in the lead, the cheerleaders filed through the back door of the gym, stepping out into the crisp fall evening. Lost in thought, Alexis dropped to last in line as Crystal hurried the group across the school grounds. Soon, the football stadium came into their view, its lights shining with impressive brightness against the night sky. Scurrying through the stadium gates, the cheerleaders wove their way to their designated place on the sideline.

Once she got into position next to Molly, Alexis paused to take in what was happening around her. Since she grew up in the football-crazy city, Alexis thought she knew what to expect at the first high school game of the season. But Alexis quickly realized that nothing could have prepared her for the scene before her. Pre-game anticipation seemed to electrify the air as the marching band played, scents of hot dogs and popcorn floated past, and crowds excitedly filled the bleachers. Local news crews were setting up by the end zones while groundskeepers worked meticulously to prepare the field.

Am I really about to cheer in front of all of these people tonight? Alexis wondered, struck by a jolt of nerves. *I must be nuts! How did I let Molly talk me into trying out for the cheer squad, anyway?*

Her thoughts were interrupted when the crowd broke into boisterous applause. Alexis spun around and saw the football players running onto the field. The other cheerleaders started clapping and waving their pom-poms, and Alexis hastily did the same. The band played a new song as the pregame activities got underway.

"I see Drake!" Molly squealed to Alexis over the music, pointing toward the center of the field where the team captains were meeting for the coin toss. "We have to stay after the game so I can talk to him, okay? Plus, that'll give you another chance to see Tanner."

Alexis was about to reply when Crystal let out a shrill laugh. Peering past Molly, Alexis saw Crystal surrounded by her friends and making an obvious show of using glitter paint to write Tanner's uniform number on her cheek.

"I don't think I'm the one Tanner will be looking for after the game," Alexis noted wryly.

Molly scowled in Crystal's direction. "Stupid glitter."

The referee blew his whistle, and the team captains came jogging to the sideline with Tanner and Drake in the lead. As Crystal adoringly shrieked Tanner's name, Alexis sighed and turned away.

"Lex!" Molly nudged her. "I think Tanner's trying to get your attention!"

Alexis checked the sideline again, and her eyebrows shot up in surprise. Tanner was watching her.

"Do something, Lex!" Molly whispered. "Wave!"

Alexis awkwardly lifted a pom-pom and shook it in the air. Tanner grinned and winked at her before turning to listen to what the coach was saying.

"Oh my gosh!" Molly did a little jig of excitement. "Tanner is into you! He. Is. Into. You."

Alexis kept staring at the field in astonishment, her worries and fears evaporating. What happened earlier in the day became nothing but a vague, strange memory. And she barely noticed the way that Crystal glared daggers her way. All Alexis could think about was how Tanner had winked at her—right at her.

Bursting with new enthusiasm, Alexis cheered louder than anyone when the referee's whistle sounded and the players headed onto the field for kickoff. Still cheering, Alexis turned to the crowd and moved her pom-poms high above her head. But then she stopped. Someone was watching her from the stands.

What is he doing here?

Noah Weston was barely visible amid the crowd. High up in the bleachers, Noah stood with his hands in his pockets, his baseball hat pulled low, and his jacket zipped up so the collar covered part of his face. It also looked like he had in tiny earbuds. Alexis dropped her arms, her elation disappearing as fast as it had come on, the sight of Noah a bitter reminder of every terrible thing she had so desperately wanted to forget. Because of Noah, her night had officially been ruined.

If Noah came here thinking that he can convince me to be their little science experiment, he can forget it.

In a huff, Alexis turned her back to Noah and the rest of the crowd. She managed a half-hearted cheer as the kickoff commenced. Soon, the referee blew his whistle again, indicating another break in the action.

"Alright, ladies, that's our cue!" Crystal declared with syrupy sweetness. "Time to perform our first routine!"

While the other cheerleaders jogged onto the field, Alexis looked over her shoulder to glare at Noah again for good measure. But when her eyes met his, something about Noah's expression made Alexis pause. He stood stiffly, as if on high alert, watching her with his brow furrowed and his jaw tight.

"And now, ladies and gentlemen!" the announcer's voice boomed out from the speakers. "Let's hear it for our very own Meadowville High cheerleaders!"

The crowd began applauding. Alexis pulled her eyes from Noah and rushed to catch up with the others. Shivering, she moved into formation on the fifty yard line and struck her pose, waiting for the music to begin. A hush settled over the audience. Alexis nearly cried out when her body grew cold and the back of her neck started to prickle.

No. Not again. Not here.

Her heart rate accelerating, Alexis looked again at the stands. She saw Noah shoving his way through the packed bleachers, trying to get to the field. The urgency in Noah's movements was all it took: Alexis knew she was in danger.

The music began playing. The crowd clapped, and cameras flashed. Alexis attempted to perform the moves she knew so well, but panic left her mind jumbled and her body stiff. While doing a spin, Alexis desperately checked the bleachers once more. Noah was gone.

A deafening screech of feedback blared over the speakers. The music cut off. The cheerleaders slowly stopped dancing, glancing at each other in confusion. People in the audience murmured.

Alexis spun around in a panic. Her body was growing even colder when a loud crash echoed through the night air. Then every light in and around the stadium shut off, leaving the entire area in thick, eerie darkness.

"What happened?" Crystal could be heard to ask through the blackness, sounding annoyed.

"Lex?" Molly called out with a nervous giggle. "Where are you?"

Alexis sensed someone come up behind her.

"I'm right here, Molly," Alexis said, turning around. "I . . ."

Two glowing red eyes were staring at her through the darkness.

For one moment, Alexis was too petrified to move. Then her body pulsed, and she lunged to get away. But a man's cold hand swiftly clamped over her mouth, and his strong arm wrapped around her waist. As the man began dragging Alexis from the field, she flailed against the arms that held her tight, managing to free her face enough to scream:

"Noah!"

A cloth was stuffed into her mouth, preventing Alexis from yelling again. Something sharp jabbed her left arm. As her eyes watered from the sting, she felt a hot sensation spread through her muscles, and then her whole body became limp. The man easily slung Alexis over his shoulder and kept moving through the blackness. Her arms and legs paralyzed, Alexis could do nothing as the sounds from the stadium faded.

Soon, Alexis heard a soft crackling noise that sounded as though it came from something like a walkie-talkie. Then she heard her abductor speak:

"Xander, do you copy?"

There was more crackling before a voice replied:

"I copy."

"Objective completed," the abductor reported. "No complications."

Alexis heard the person named Xander speak again:

"Is she alright?"

"I repeat: no complications," the abductor answered without emotion.

"Very good," Xander stated. "The evacuation team will be there in six minutes. Over."

More crackling indicated that the communication concluded.

A tear rolled down Alexis's cheek, which she did not even have the strength to wipe away. Unable to move or speak, Alexis could do nothing as her abductor continued carrying her through the darkness. Her only solace was that the man apparently in charge—the person named Xander—had sounded as though he did not want her harmed . . . at least, not yet. With the warnings of Mr. Haber and Noah haunting her, Alexis wondered if she would ever see her family again. Or if she would even survive.

Suddenly, a flash of royal blue light illuminated the night. Alexis heard her abductor let out a horrific scream before he lurched and dropped to his knees. There was another burst of royal blue. The man cried again and fell forward. Alexis tumbled onto the dirt.

"Alexis, go!" a recognizable voice yelled.

Alexis desperately tried to move, but her body would not obey. Next to her, Alexis heard the abductor groan and shift slightly like he was coming to.

"Alexis!" The same person ran to her side.

The cloth was yanked out of Alexis's mouth. She gasped for air as she was lifted into a sitting position.

"Alexis, it's Noah," she heard him declare through the darkness. "What happened? What did he do to you?"

Alexis still could not speak. She felt Noah raise her arm and then let it go. As Alexis's arm flopped down uncontrolled, Noah drew in a breath.

"He injected you with a paralytic. It will wear off soon, but we've got to get out of here now because I only stunned this guy. He won't be down for—"

A flash of blinding red came from where the abductor lay. To Alexis's horror, she heard Noah groan and crumple to the earth. Without Noah's support, Alexis's body started tipping. She reflexively stuck out her arm and found that she was able to brace herself. Her strength was returning.

Weak but able to move, Alexis began crawling to get to Noah, but the abductor reached out and grabbed Alexis by the ankle, yanking her leg out from underneath her. Collapsed onto her stomach, Alexis kicked as hard as she could. She felt her shoe strike a face. The abductor howled and let her go.

Alexis staggered to her feet but was only able to move a few steps before her unsteady legs gave out again. Fighting to make her muscles respond, Alexis pushed herself back up and whipped around. All she could see were the abductor's red eyes. He sprang for her. Alexis screamed. Another flash of royal blue light flew through the night, striking the kidnapper.

"Get down!" she heard Noah shout.

Alexis dropped to the dirt as the abductor fired a streak of red at where she had stood. Hunched low and breathing fast, Alexis sensed her hands getting warm. A sudden recollection of what had happened during the attack in Mr. Haber's room caused Alexis to point both of her arms at where the abductor remained concealed by darkness. A blast of stunning white shot from her hands, the force thrusting Alexis onto her back. She heard the abductor bawl with terrible pain.

"Alexis, run! Get out of here" Noah sounded as though he was sprinting past her. "Go while I . . ."

Noah broke off when a beam of yellow light flew in from their left, cutting through the blackness. Alexis sat up just in time to see the yellow streak slam into the abductor straight-on. She heard him hit the ground. Then there was silence.

An instant later, the veil of darkness melted away. Alexis could once again see the moon overhead and the stadium lights in the distance. As her eyes adjusted fully, Alexis realized that Noah was crouched in front of her, facing a man who was motionless on the grass. Noah was holding his black device, which he kept aimed at the man for a long time before he finally put it into his jacket pocket. Alexis lowered her eyes to the abductor, who did not stir.

Is he . . . dead?

She felt a swell of nausea and looked away, and she spotted a trail of flattened grass extending all the way back to the football stadium. Staring at the path her abductor had carried her, Alexis felt the color leave her face. Her skin got clammy. Noah started speaking to her, but his words were muffled by the rushing sound that was growing in her ears. Through dimming vision, Alexis thought she saw Mr. Haber running toward them from the left. Then Alexis swayed. Noah reached out to support her, which caused the front of his jacket to open wide. Alexis saw a large patch of blood on his t-shirt.

"Noah, you're hurt," she mumbled.

Then everything went black.

***

"What do you see out there?" Xander demanded.

"We have a man down, and there is evidence of a light battle covering an approximate fifty-foot area."

Xander's jaw clenched. "A man down?"

"That is correct."

Xander leaned forward, watching the live video feed as it came through on his office computer.

The video was tinted a ghostly green due to the night vision equipment that the evacuation team was using to scour the area for information. Xander could see several patches of singed grass, undoubtedly from light attacks, and scattered drops of blood. Far in the distance was the high school football stadium, from which faint cheering and applause could be heard. Finally, when Xander saw Yuri's body on the ground, he turned away. Though the team would continue searching for clues, Xander had all the information he needed. There was no other way an operative could have been stopped.

Someone at that school is a Protector for The Organization. Someone is there who can get me to Alexis.

EIGHT

"What were you thinking by trying to fight an operative alone? You should have sent an alert! I would have been there sooner!"

Alexis heard Mr. Haber's voice and opened her eyes. Dim lights were above her, and there were people moving to her right. As her vision cleared, she realized that she was lying on a cot in the supply closet.

"I did send an alert, but no one responded," was Noah's reply. "Alexis was in trouble, so I had to move on my own."

There was a sharp break in the conversation.

"They must have figured out a way to block transmissions around the stadium." Mr. Haber sounded deeply troubled. "This was an extremely well-planned operation."

"I'm glad you got there when you did. I don't know how much longer I could have held that operative off. With the dark shield down, I was afraid of hitting Alexis and so all I could utilize were stun attacks."

Alexis sat up. "Mister Haber?"

Mr. Haber spun around and hurried toward her. "How are you feeling? Are you alright?"

"I'm okay," Alexis insisted. "But Noah isn't. He's hurt. There was blood on his shirt."

"What?" Mr. Haber faced Noah again. "You are injured?"

"I'm fine," Noah said dismissively, averting his gaze.

But Mr. Haber walked over to Noah and pulled his jacket farther open, revealing the large blood stain on Noah's t-shirt.

"Why did you not tell me?" Mr. Haber demanded, clearly alarmed. He pressed a button on his device and began speaking into it like a phone. "Ralph, we need you in here again. Noah sustained a wound from a light attack. Yes, Miss Kendall is . . ."

Still talking, Mr. Haber lowered his voice and moved to the opposite side of the supply closet to continue the conversation. Alexis looked back at Noah, catching his grimace of pain as he dropped wearily onto a chair and focused on the floor.

"Noah, I'm sorry," she nearly whispered. "I didn't understand . . . I mean, I was such a jerk and . . . you saved . . . you got hurt and could have been . . ."

Noah lifted his head, setting his gray eyes on hers. "Don't apologize. I was only doing my job. You saved me once, and I saved you. Now we're even."

Alexis studied his face and did not reply.

The door to the supply closet was opened.

"Well, it appears she's feeling better," someone remarked.

Alexis checked behind her, and her mouth fell open. *The school janitor is in on this?*

To her shock, Alexis was staring at the elderly man she frequently saw on campus wiping cafeteria tables, collecting garbage, or sweeping the gym. He was dressed in his dark blue jumpsuit, complete with his first name stitched over the front pocket. His bushy white eyebrows rose with amusement when he observed the way that Alexis gawked at him.

"Don't worry, young lady," he said with a chuckle, coming to her and checking the pulse in her wrist. "I'm—what do you call it?—legit."

"Miss Kendall, as you were not lucid enough earlier, allow me now to make the official introduction," Mr. Haber offered. "This is Doctor Ralph Fox. He has been a member of The Organization for over forty years. He serves as a physician for us, and he was one of my mentors when I became involved."

"So what are you guys gonna tell me next? That the school bus drivers are ninjas?" Alexis asked only half-jokingly, looking between them.

Chuckling again, Ralph shuffled to Noah's side. "Alright, young man, I hear you have an injury that you failed to mention when I was in here helping Alexis earlier?"

"It's nothing," Noah insisted, though he winced as Ralph helped him remove his jacket.

Ralph's expression changed when he observed Noah's bloodied shirt. "Why don't you lie down? I'll decide if it's nothing."

When Alexis heard Ralph's tone, she got up fast and moved aside. Noah sighed sullenly before he walked to the cot and lay down upon it. Ralph followed. Pulling a pair of trauma sheers from his jumpsuit pocket, Ralph swiftly cut away Noah's t-shirt to fully expose the injury underneath. Alexis had to keep herself from crying out when she saw the deep, still-bleeding wound in his chest.

Noah raised his head to view his injury. His face went pale, and he dropped his head down on the cot. "That doesn't look right," he mumbled.

"But we will make it right." Ralph noticed Alexis still staring. "Young lady, would you like to assist me?"

Alexis shrank back. "What?"

"If you're feeling up to it, I could use your help," Ralph explained. "It would be optimal to do the initial wound care here as quickly as possible, and the more assistance I have the better. Then I'll take Noah to Headquarters for further treatment."

Alexis peeked again at Noah, who kept staring at the ceiling in silence. Although he was trying not to show it, she could tell that Noah was in immense pain. As she witnessed him suffer, Alexis's impulse to shy away from his injury was replaced by a powerful drive to heal it. Putting her eyes on Ralph, Alexis nodded earnestly.

"Yes, I'll help. Whatever I can do."

In response, Ralph went over to one of the bookshelves and pulled down a large container. He returned to the cot with the container and proceeded to pull from it an assortment of medical supplies. Mr. Haber brought over the wood table from the back of the supply closet. Soon, Ralph had the table covered with a sterile drape and his medical instruments placed upon it.

"Alexis, I'm going to have you do the initial wound cleaning while Ben assists me with preparing to place sutures," Ralph informed her.

Moving with measured though hurried motions, Ralph opened a bottle of saline, which he poured onto a stack of gauze pads. Taking one of the gauze pads, he started blotting away the blood from Noah's injury.

"I would like you to take over cleaning the tissue like I'm doing now," Ralph instructed her.

"Right. Okay." Alexis ungracefully donned the pair of gloves that Mr. Haber set out for her. "I can do that."

Ralph turned away and began drawing up medication in a syringe. Alexis picked up a new gauze pad and carefully started wiping Noah's wound the way Ralph had demonstrated. It was a while before he dared to look again at Noah's face. Flinching with agony, he kept his eyes focused on the ceiling and still said nothing.

Again, Alexis was struck by emotion unlike any she had experienced before. Noah had saved her life and been seriously injured doing so. Both overpowering gratitude and heart-wrenching guilt made Alexis long to say something to Noah—to apologize and thank him for what he had done—yet she knew her words would be woefully inadequate. So instead, Alexis lowered her head and continued her task in quiet, miserable to seem ungrateful but too afraid to speak. Keeping at her task, Alexis felt her hands get hot—though whether from the warmth in the room or her own nerves she could not say.

"Alright, Noah." Ralph faced him with a syringe in hand. "I'm going to anesthetize the area so you'll be more comfortable."

Noah cleared his throat. "Yeah. Okay. Sure."

Alexis moved aside, anxiously observing as Ralph bent forward and leaned over the wound to begin. She saw Ralph pause, and he seemed to pause for a very long time. Eventually, the elderly man's inquisitive eyes drifted to Alexis and then back to Noah.

"Now this is interesting," Ralph remarked.

"Interesting?" Noah lifted his head. "I don't like being interesting. Not when I'm a patient."

Ralph motioned oddly to Alexis. "Tell me what you make of this."

Alexis did a double take. "Me?"

"Yes, you," Ralph replied.

Puzzled, Alexis slid in to recheck Noah's wound. She blinked, wondering if her eyes were playing tricks on her. Noah's injury had nearly disappeared; all that remained were a few shallow abrasions.

"It's all . . . better," Alexis stuttered.

"Better?" Noah dared to look at his chest. "It's not as bad as you thought?"

"It's not bad anymore," Ralph remarked with astonishment. "I believe my young assistant has some sort of healing touch. Absolutely remarkable."

Mr. Haber peered over Ralph's shoulder. He exchanged an incredulous glance with Ralph, and then they both looked at Alexis with strange expressions.

Alexis rubbed her still-warm hands on her cheer skirt. "I don't know what you're thinking, exactly, but I definitely didn't make Noah's injury magically go away."

"I think you did," Ralph gently corrected her, further examining Noah's wound. "All I need to do is place a dressing. Noah, you are going to be fine. Simply incredible."

A ringing sound interrupted the quiet.

Mr. Haber pulled his device from his pocket and read a new message. "Miss Kendall, it is time for you to return to the football field."

"What?" Alexis exclaimed.

"What?" Noah echoed, sitting up despite Ralph's attempt to keep him still.

Mr. Haber put his device away. "I will be close by. You will be protected."

"Mister Haber, I can't go out there. I can't even go home," Alexis protested. "What if some red-eyed whack-job stalks me or goes after my family and friends? What if someone tries to kidnap me while I'm asleep? Earlier today, you wanted me to go to Headquarters, right? I'm ready to go now. I can't let . . . I don't want . . ." she broke off, her mind consumed by the terrifying memory of the abductor's glowing red eyes coming at her in the darkness.

"Miss Kendall, we have a very sophisticated surveillance plan in place, and our best Protectors are stationed to guard you and your loved ones. You will be safe," Mr. Haber told her. "Tomorrow, I promise that you will go to Headquarters. But tonight, you have to go out there. You cannot just disappear. I will explain more at another time, but for now I am asking you to simply trust me."

Alexis shuddered. "You really want me to go out there and pretend everything is normal?"

"Yes," Mr. Haber said frankly. "I know it is a lot to ask."

Alexis peered at Noah. "Is that what you do? Pretend every day that things are normal?"

Noah did not quite look at her. "Something like that."

"Come, Miss Kendall. We must go." Mr. Haber had already headed for the door.

Alexis hesitated and cast another longing glance around the supply closet. When her eyes met Noah's, she stopped for a drawn-out moment, her heart full. Then she forced herself to trail Mr. Haber out the door.

"You're a brave girl, and a gifted healer," she heard Ralph call after her. "You should consider a career in medicine."

Alexis rushed to catch up with Mr. Haber, who had walked across the darkened classroom and out into the empty school hallway. Together, they continued in silence until another set of footsteps was heard approaching from behind them.

"Noah, you should rest," Mr. Haber stated even before turning around.

Noah came to a stop in front of Mr. Haber and put in his earbuds. He had his jacket buttoned up to the top. "Ralph said I was okay."

Mr. Haber gave Noah a look but pushed the door open. The three of them stepped outside and headed along a path toward the football stadium. When they arrived, they found lights shining brightly, the marching band playing the school's fight song, crowds mingling, and newscasters reporting the results of the game.

Observing the carefree, celebratory scene around her, Alexis felt profoundly distant. Although everything appeared just as before, nothing was as Alexis had understood it to be only hours earlier. The world had become a completely different place—a frightening, complex, dangerous place.

"Miss Kendall, we will not be far away," she heard Mr. Haber say.

"What? Wait!" Alexis spun toward him. "I don't . . ."

She did not finish. Mr. Haber and Noah had already disappeared into the crowd.

"Lex, there you are! Lex!"

Alexis saw Molly calling to her from the middle of the football field, where she was talking with others from the cheer team. Alexis forced a smile and jogged toward them.

"Wasn't that the craziest thing ever?" Tessa Raines asked Alexis when she reached them. "It was, like, complete chaos down here! It was so dark! No one's phones were working, either! Did you hear the cops say that the whole area around the stadium also lost power?"

Alexis shivered. "No, I didn't hear that."

"Yeah. The cops also told the news reporters that no one knows why the blackout happened," Tessa continued, almost breathless. She put her hands on her hips. "Thankfully, the lights finally came back on so the game could resume!"

"Thankfully," was all Alexis could say.

"So what happened to you, anyway, Lex?" Katrina Norman inquired curiously. "When the lights came on, you were gone. Where'd you disappear to?"

Alexis kicked the turf with her shoe. "Oh, um, I got lost."

"You got lost?" Molly was clearly unconvinced. "What do you mean? One minute you were right beside me in the middle of the field, and the next minute it was like you had vanished."

"No, um, I didn't say I got lost." Alexis faked another smile. "I said that I got locked . . . in the second floor bathroom. The first floor bathroom was closed, of course, and so I had to go upstairs. But I got locked inside, and it took forever for the janitor to come and let me out."

Molly was now blatantly gawking at her. "You managed to walk in the pitch black all the way from the football field to the second floor bathroom? And you got locked inside?"

Alexis shrugged. "Weirder things have happened, right?"

The other girls laughed in agreement. To Alexis's relief, Molly laughed along with them. With her friends distracted, Alexis started scrutinizing everything that was happening around her.

Did that guy look over here? Who is that woman talking to on her cell phone? Why is that car driving past so slowly? Where is—

"Hi, Alexis!"

Alexis spun around. Julia was coming toward her.

"I watched you cheer during the first part of the game. You did a great job . . ." Julia paused when Sam Warren strolled past and gave her a playful nudge. Cheeks pink, she then resumed addressing Alexis. "I've got to go, but I'll see you in chemistry tomorrow, okay?"

"Um, yeah. See you," Alexis replied. *That is, as long as I haven't been attacked, kidnapped, or made into a science experiment by then.*

Alexis turned to rejoin the other girls but saw Drake making his way to Molly's side. So Alexis wandered over to the bleachers and sat down to wait for her friend, grateful for the chance to be alone. Gradually, the crowds thinned out and the stadium quieted down. As cool breeze brushed over her face, Alexis closed her eyes and dropped her head in her hands.

"Alexis Kendall, I was hoping to see you."

Alexis snapped her head up and felt her stomach jolt. Tanner Ricks was coming toward her.

Smiling, Tanner sat down on the bleachers and motioned playfully toward Molly and Drake. "Looks like you're waiting, too, huh?"

"Looks like it." Alexis laughed lightly. "Oh, um, nice game, by the way."

"Thanks. I didn't see you after the blackout, so I thought I had missed my chance to talk to you." Tanner looked at her directly. "Glad I caught you."

Alexis sensed her cheeks getting warm. "I'm glad you caught me, too."

They met each other's gaze and then both glanced away. There was a pause.

"Hey," Tanner eventually said, "the football team is having a bonfire party up in the canyon on Saturday. It'd be awesome if you came. Molly, too."

"Wow! Really?" Alexis exclaimed, not hiding her excitement.

Tanner's grin widened, which made Alexis blush even more. She hastily cleared her throat, attempting to sound nonchalant as she added:

"I mean, that sounds pretty cool. I think Molly and I might be able to go."

"Great. So how about . . ."

Tanner's words were drowned out by a loud clanging noise as some stadium lights shut off. Alexis jumped and peered skittishly into the shadows.

". . . if that sounds okay to you," she heard Tanner finish.

Alexis put her attention back on him. "Sorry, what did you say?"

"You'll find me when you get up to the bonfire?" Tanner repeated.

Alexis's stomach did another somersault. "Yes, I'll find you."

"Hey, Lex?" Molly called out.

Alexis and Tanner both looked toward the field. Molly was headed toward the bleachers with Drake strolling beside her.

"Marcus called," Molly continued grumpily, gesturing to her cell phone. "He says we have to go now. Sorry."

Tanner got to his feet and put his helmet under his arm. "Glad I got to talk to you, Alexis. I'll see you soon."

Tanner jogged to Drake's side, and the two young men headed for the stadium exit. As soon as they were out of earshot, Molly practically sprinted the rest of the way to Alexis's side.

"Did Tanner tell you about the bonfire party on Saturday?" she screeched. "Are you freaking out right now? Can you even believe it?"

Before Alexis could answer, a soft swishing noise caused her to peer over Molly's shoulder. Ralph Fox was coming around a corner, hunched over a large broom, which he was using to sweep the trash that littered the ground. He stopped to pick up a gum wrapper that Molly had dropped, and then he continued on his way. Alexis watched him go, until another motion beyond the bleachers caught her eye. Nearly hidden in the shadows, Noah gave Alexis a slight nod before he stepped out of view.

<u>NINE</u>

"Victor remains in the infirmary, Yuri was killed, and we still don't have Number 407! I hate to be the one to say it, but Xander has proven unqualified to lead this operation!" Gerard finished his rant by using his tie to emphatically blot the sweat from his brow.

Jackie sat up sharply. "Victor's injuries were his own doing, as we clearly determined at our prior meeting. As for what happened to Yuri at the football game tonight, that was . . ."

"That was my fault, you want to say," Dr. Gaige finished for her.

Jackie averted her eyes and did not respond.

"Jackie is correct, of course." Dr. Gaige looked around the table. "The decision to send Yuri to the high school football game to take the girl was mine. I asked Xander to oversee my plan."

Gerard hunched down in his chair and muttered something under his breath.

"I obviously don't mean to question your judgment, Doctor Gaige," Peter ventured, "but I am curious to know why you didn't allow Xander to execute the plan that he proposed to get the girl."

"I believed Yuri would be capable of doing the job," Dr. Gaige replied simply.

From his seat, Xander observed the exchange without revealing his unease. *Doctor Gaige is hiding something.*

Jacob spoke up. "So in light of the botched kidnapping at the football stadium tonight, now what is our plan for getting the girl?"

Dr. Gaige gestured for Xander to answer. Maintaining his unemotional demeanor, Xander stood and pointed at a map that was projected onto the screen behind him.

"As you can see, not far from the school's football stadium, there were marks of several stun attacks and the skillfully shot light attack that killed Yuri. Therefore, we must assume that a Protector is stationed at the high school and watching over Alexis. Now, after the failed abduction at the football game, we must also assume that The Organization will increase security around Alexis because they know we're on her trail."

"They'll be watching her like hawks," Leslie griped. "We'll have to engage in a full battle with their agents in order to get the girl."

"There will be no battle," Xander countered immediately. "Alexis and other innocent civilians were already put at far too much risk tonight. That will not happen again."

Leslie exchanged a look with Gerard, who shook his head with obvious disdain.

Jackie swiftly cleared her throat. "Xander makes an excellent point. If the girl is hurt in a battle, we run the risk of losing Number 407's powers altogether."

"Which is why we must completely change strategies," Xander went on with deliberate restraint. "We have lost our opportunity to easily take Alexis by force. So our best plan now is to recruit a new operative who can befriend Alexis and convince her to join us willingly. With Alexis viewing us as allies, not enemies, she will likely disclose a large amount of valuable information. Not only might we understand even more about Number 407 this way, we may learn about The Organization and their agents, other discoveries they have made, and perhaps even where their Headquarters is located."

"Not to mention, our testing of Number 407 will be easier and more productive if the girl is cooperative," Jackie added.

Gerard leapt to his feet. "This is absurd! Doctor Gaige, surely you can't be on board with this. Why are we worried about playing nice with a fifteen-year-old girl? It would take no effort to force her to do everything we want."

Xander's steel-gray eyes flashed. "Gerard, this is not your call to make."

The two men glowered across the table at each other until Dr. Gaige lifted his hand. Xander sat down. With another disgusted shake of his head, Gerard also took a seat.

Dr. Gaige leaned back in his chair. "While there may be disagreements about Xander's recommendations, we cannot argue with his results. We have repeatedly seen that things go well when Xander's plans are followed. We have also seen that things conclude poorly when someone—including myself—deviates from his suggestions. I therefore defer to him."

"Unbelievable," Gerard hissed.

Jacob smiled. "Xander, I admit that I am quite curious to know how you expect to find a new operative who can befriend a high school cheerleader."

***

Please don't be floating in the air. Please. I can't deal with that today.

With her eyes still shut tight, Alexis used her hand to tap around where she had been sleeping. She felt her mattress beneath her and breathed out in relief. Her respite was short, however, as the horrid memories of the day before rushed into her mind. Cringing, Alexis smashed her pillow over her face as if to block out the frightening recollections as well as the morning sunlight.

Alexis's head was throbbing, and she was exhausted. Fearful of another attempted kidnapping, Alexis had spent most of the night crouched on her bed, listening for intruders while gripping a pair of scissors in case she needed a weapon. Only the exhilarating thought of seeing Tanner at the upcoming bonfire party had made the hours of nerve-wracking silence slightly less miserable. It was not until the early morning when Alexis's fatigue won out over her fear. She last remembered checking the clock around four-thirty, and she realized that she must have drifted off to sleep after that.

With a weary sigh, Alexis rolled over to check the time. "You have got to be kidding me," she mumbled.

Her alarm clock, nightstand, and everything else in the room except for her bed were hovering a few feet above the carpet. Alexis pulled herself into a sitting position, almost too worn out to care. She slid off of her bed, snatched her clothes out of the air, and began getting ready for school. It was not long before Alexis heard the sound of a car pulling into the driveway.

"Lex? Molly's here!" called Alexis's younger sister, Nina.

Alexis scanned her room again. *What am I going to do? I can't leave with everything floating like this!*

"Lex?" Nina started opening the bedroom door.

Alexis leapt forward and stuck her foot out, preventing the door from opening any farther. "Hey, Nina, what's up?" she asked, positioning herself to block her sister's view of the room.

Nina peered up quizzically at her. "Mom told me to tell you that Molly is here."

"Thanks." Alexis swiftly shut the door in Nina's face.

There was a honk of a horn outside.

Alexis flinched. *I need my stuff to get down! Now! Right now!*

Desperate for a plan, Alexis turned around. Everything was back on the floor where it belonged.

Marcus honked the horn again.

Alexis sighed. *This is getting really old really fast.*

***

"I thought you handled yourself well in the committee meeting, Xander."

Xander swiveled his chair around and watched Jackie enter his office. She took a seat across from his desk, her face lit up with interest as she continued:

"Do you really think the plan for using a new operative will work?"

You can take the girl out of the science lab, but you can't the science out of the girl, Xander thought, observing her. He shrugged. "You tell me. You're the one who was once a teenage girl, not me."

Jackie laughed. "I'm not sure that I'm the best comparison. I was a teenage girl who spent her free time doing college-level science courses, not a teenage girl who cheered at football games or bothered to go on dates."

Some things never change, Xander noted.

Jackie's laugh trailed off. "But if anyone can pull this off, it's you."

"We'll see." Xander's eyes drifted to the file on the prospective recruit. "Maybe everyone will end up wishing Gerard was still in charge."

Jackie straightened her lab coat. "Absolutely not. Gerard was removed as Head of Intelligence for a reason. You're the man for the job. You have the right instincts for this."

Xander winced, having to take a moment before he responded. "Thank you."

***

"Be sure to read over chapter ten before Monday. Have a great weekend."

As the bell rang and students began packing up to leave, Mr. Haber stepped away from his podium and strode toward the supply closet. He passed Alexis as if she was not there. While her classmates started heading out the door, Alexis stayed in her chair, becoming confused.

Mister Haber said we were going to Headquarters today, so how come he's acting like I don't exist? And where's Noah, anyway? Did they change plans and not bother to—

"Alexis?" Julia asked. "Are you going to homecoming?"

Alexis faced her. "I don't think so. What about you?"

"I doubt anyone will ask me." Julia peeked at Sam as he walked out. She grabbed her bag and stood up. "Anyway, aren't you leaving for second period?"

"I have to ask Mister Haber a few questions."

Julia's eyes got big. "You? You're the one who got your experiment done in ten minutes today! If you have questions for Mister Haber, we're all in trouble!"

Alexis let out a poignant laugh. "Believe me: I definitely have questions for Mister Haber."

"You could have fooled me." Julia moved for the exit. "Good luck. See you later."

Julia left along with the others, and Alexis was soon alone. Surveying the empty classroom, Alexis sensed herself calm down.

Mister Haber had to wait until everyone else was gone, that's all.

Alexis remained seated. Minutes passed. When she heard the bell for second period, Alexis finally got up and went to the supply closet door.

"Mister Haber?" she asked, knocking softly.

There was no reply. Alexis knocked louder, but there was still nothing but silence. She reached for the handle and found that the door was locked.

What is this, some stupid joke? Mister Haber promised that we'd go to Headquarters today! How else are they going to figure out how to fix me?

Tired and angry, Alexis snatched up her things and stormed into the hall. Her bad mood was only made worse as she became surrounded by people who were laughing, chatting with friends, and talking on their cell phones.

They all get to be normal while I'm stuck with light attacks and kidnappings! It's not fair!

Glaring at no one in particular, Alexis pushed through the hall and started stomping up the crowded staircase for the second floor.

Mister Haber lied! He said we would get things sorted out at Headquarters. He—

"Alexis."

Someone had grabbed her firmly by the arm. Alexis looked up and saw Noah standing on the stair above her. She felt a powerful sensation in her chest as she stared up at him.

He saved my life last night.

"Mister Haber wants to review your last assignment," Noah stated, his voice without emotion but his eyes sharp and focused. "Can you come by his classroom during third period?"

Alexis caught her breath and nodded.

Noah's hand stayed on her arm. "Good. I'll tell—"

"Well, good morning, Alexis Kendall," someone else said.

Over Noah's shoulder, Alexis saw Tanner coming down the staircase. Noah followed Alexis's gaze, released her arm, and continued past her.

"Noah, wait," Alexis called out, turning after him. "I will . . ."

But Noah was already gone.

"Hey, Alexis, long time no see."

Head spinning, Alexis whipped back around. "Oh, um, hey, Tanner. How are you?"

"Doing alright, other than I'm late for class," Tanner replied with a laugh. "I'd better run, but I'll see you at lunch?"

"Yeah. Sounds good."

Tanner gave Alexis a wave and hurried off. She remained where she was, trying to sort out her thoughts. The bell rang again. Wistful, Alexis slung her bag onto her shoulder and continued up the stairs toward Mrs. Frank's room. But English class was about the last thing on her mind.

***

"We have successfully recruited a new operative," Xander reported, looking around the table. "Things are falling into place as anticipated."

"Very good." Dr. Gaige seemed pleased. "No doubt the thrill of working undercover made our cause an easy sell."

"It always does," Leslie interjected amusedly.

Gerard huffed and crossed his arms. "Well, Xander, I hope that this little game you call a strategy will actually produce some meaningful results."

Xander managed something almost like a smile. "The new operative can easily get close to Alexis. So as long as everyone carries out the plan, we will all get what we want."

***

The bell indicating the conclusion of second period had not even finished ringing before Alexis bolted out of Mrs. Frank's classroom and sprinted for the stairs. It was finally time to go to Headquarters. Someone would figure out how to help her. Soon, she would not have to think about weird powers, red eyes, or Noah Weston anymore. Life would make sense again.

Alexis reached the first floor and continued darting through the hallways. When she arrived at Mr. Haber's room, Alexis tore open the door and burst inside. She came to an abrupt stop. A group of students sat around one of the workstations.

"Are you here for the meeting?" asked a student in a Star Trek t-shirt.

"Meeting?" Alexis parroted. "You're here for the meeting, too?"

"Yeah. The science club meeting."

"Oh! No, I'm not here for the science club meeting." Alexis relaxed. "I'm here to see Mister Haber. Um, there's an assignment that I need to review with him."

A girl pushed her glasses up the bridge of her nose. "You need help with homework? We can probably assist."

Alexis grinned slightly. "Thanks, but I think these particular problems are best for Mister Haber himself to—"

The classroom door was opened, and Mr. Haber stepped in from the hall. An expression of surprise came across his face when he saw Alexis.

"Hello, Miss Kendall. I trust that you are doing well?"

"Yes," Alexis replied slowly, watching Mr. Haber walk to his podium. *Had I not been there myself, I would never believe that he killed a man last night.*

Mr. Haber did a double take when he noticed Alexis still observing him. "Is there something that I can help you with? Or are you here for the science club meeting?"

Alexis began wondering if she had gotten her instructions mixed up. "I came here because Noah said that you had an assignment to review with me?"

"Ah, yes. Of course." Mister Haber nodded with recognition. "You forgot to fill in a question on the last page of today's assignment. Your paper is on my desk, if you would like to complete the question before I grade it this afternoon."

Alexis searched Mr. Haber's face for some clue that he understood the real reason she had come.

There was none. "Great. Um, thanks," she finally replied, totally perplexed.

With the science club members scrutinizing her, Alexis headed for the supply closet. She reached the door and checked behind her. Mr. Haber was still at the podium, engrossed in sorting though a stack of papers. With a confused shake of her head, Alexis pushed the door open and stepped inside.

"So how good are you at climbing?" someone inquired.

Alexis nearly screamed in surprise as the door shut behind her. Noah was seated at Mr. Haber's desk, waiting for her.

"Climbing?" Alexis moved closer to him. "What are you talking about? What's going on, anyway?"

"This was the best way to get you in here without being obvious." Noah gestured past her. "We don't know if Doctor Gaige suspects that Ben is part of The Organization, but either way, it's likely that operatives are watching him, since it was in this classroom where you fought off that light attack."

"Watching Mister Haber?" Alexis shivered.

His eyes remained on hers. "Probably."

It was a moment before Alexis found her voice. "But I'll still be going to Headquarters today, right?"

"Yeah. Soon, in fact."

Alexis clasped her hands, her sense of hope returning. "Alright, then let's get going! What's the plan?"

"For starters, do you know where the girls' bathroom is on this floor?"

Alexis crinkled her nose. "Eww, the infamous first floor bathroom that's always closed for repairs?"

"That's definitely the one."

"Yes, I . . . hang on, how come you know about it? Actually, don't answer that question. I don't think I want to know."

The corners of Noah's mouth turned up slightly. "You might want to know, since it has something to do with The Organization."

"You're joking."

"I'm not joking."

Alexis resignedly dropped into a chair. "Okay. Tell me."

Noah lowered his voice. "Leave here, acting as though you finished your assignment. Head directly to the first floor bathroom. As usual, Ralph has made sure that the 'Out of Order' sign is posted. Go inside, confirm no one else is in there, and lock the door." Noah extended his hand, in which he held a white key that shimmered in the light. "Unlock the bathroom closet. You'll find a ladder, which you need to set up near the middle sink. Climb the ladder and push aside the ceiling panel that—"

Alexis laughed. "Okay, come on. You're kidding, right?"

"I'm not kidding."

Alexis's giggles promptly died away. She sighed. "Fine. Keep going."

"Climb the ladder, push aside the marked ceiling panel, and get up in the crawl space. Don't worry about the ladder; Ralph will get it taken care of. Just crawl this direction." Noah stood on Mr. Haber's desk, reached up, and slid a ceiling panel out of place, letting light shine into the dark crawl space above. "Once you get here, we'll help you down and go from there."

Alexis eyed the ceiling warily. "You want me to do all of that only to come back here? Why?"

Noah jumped athletically to the floor. "It's the best we can do before leaving for Headquarters, in case an operative is watching you. If you're seen coming in here before you disappear for a long time, it'd be too suspicious. But if you're last seen going into the bathroom, the operative won't know where you went from there." He motioned to his device, which was on the desk. "And if an operative somehow breaks past our security and enters the bathroom in an attempt to go after you, we'll have plenty of warning and take care of it."

"Watch me? Go after me?" Alexis's voice caught. "You think that operatives are watching me, too?"

Noah seemed to take his time before responding. "Alexis, they're after you, and what happened yesterday proved that they will do almost anything to get you. So, yes, I think that they are watching you. But we're watching you, too, and you're going to be okay."

For the first time, Alexis noted that Noah's eyes were bloodshot. Then the realization struck her.

"Noah, you stayed up to help guard my house overnight, didn't you?"

Noah only held out the key. "You'd better get going. We need to be on the move soon."

Alexis took the key and made her way to the door. "Thank you," she told him, hoping that he understood how much she meant it.

He only gestured to the ceiling. "I'll see you in a couple of minutes."

TEN

'OUT OF ORDER. DO NOT ENTER.'

Standing outside the first floor bathroom, Alexis eyed the dingy sign that hung on the door. She glanced uncertainly over her shoulder before entering. The door swung shut behind her with a loud creak from hinges that were in dire need of oil. After confirming that the bathroom was empty, Alexis secured the bizarre-looking lock.

It's like I'm on a scavenger hunt. A super weird scavenger hunt.

Using the key that Noah had given her, Alexis opened the bathroom closet. As promised, the rusty ladder was there. She carried the ladder across the bathroom and placed it in front of the middle sink, and then she looked up. A faded purple thumbtack had been pushed into one of the ceiling panels.

Here goes . . . I guess.

Alexis hoisted her bag onto her shoulder and climbed the ladder until she was high enough to push the marked panel out of place. Taking a breath, she peered into the crawl space looming over her.

I can't believe that I'm about to do this.

Balancing on the wobbling ladder's top step, Alexis pulled herself up into the crawl space. The stale air smelled of dust, and she could hear muffled sounds coming from the surrounding classrooms underneath. Far to her right, Alexis spotted a small patch of light. She repositioned her bag and began crawling in the direction that Noah had marked for her to go.

Since when did this become my life, anyway? Getting kidnapped by a man with red eyes, learning my chemistry teacher is an undercover science superhero, sneaking around in the crawl space of my high school, deciding that Noah Weston is—

Alexis gasped when a piece of the ceiling snapped under her knee.

"What was that?" asked a guy in the classroom below.

Alexis did not move. Beneath her, she heard people talking and what sounded like a desk being slid across the classroom floor. Then someone started pounding on the ceiling directly below Alexis, trying to push the broken panel back into place.

"The whole school's falling apart!" the guy joked, giving the panel another whack that nearly knocked Alexis over.

"Get down. I'll have Ralph Fox come take care of it," belted a militant voice that Alexis recognized as that of Ms. Hinshaw, the biology teacher.

Alexis waited until the noise underneath her subsided, and then she cautiously resumed creeping forward. As she got close to the supply closet, Mr. Haber popped his head up into the crawl space, smiled, and ducked out of sight once more. Alexis reached the edge of the opening and looked down. Mr. Haber's desk was directly below her, and Noah and Mr. Haber stood next to it.

I sure hope Dad doesn't ask what I did at school today.

Alexis rolled onto her stomach and lowered herself onto the desk, feet-first. Reaching up, Noah took Alexis by the hand and helped her to the floor.

"Thanks," Alexis told him, very aware of how strong Noah's hand felt holding hers.

His expression was unreadable as he let her go. "You're welcome."

Mr. Haber got onto the desk, replaced the ceiling panel, and then spoke into his device. "Ralph, you are clear to clean up the bathroom."

"Copy," was Ralph's reply. "Then I'll head to Hinshaw's room. Apparently, she heard a large rat in the crawl space."

Alexis could not help giggling.

Mr. Haber got down from the desk and put his device away. "Miss Kendall, I apologize for the detour. I hope it was not too inconvenient."

Alexis bent forward and brushed the dust off her jeans. "Nah, it was great. After all, while you guys enjoy that high-tech secret passageway behind the bookcase, I get to masquerade as a giant rat in the ceiling. It's cool."

There was no response. Alexis lifted her head. Mr. Haber had a confused expression on his face, and Noah was observing her with one eyebrow slightly raised.

Alexis grinned. "So now what?"

Mr. Haber motioned to the far wall. "Now we use that high-tech secret passageway."

Alexis's heart skipped a beat. It was finally time to go to Headquarters. She would soon meet the scientists who would fix her. With the prospect of returning to her normal life within reach, Alexis had to summon all her patience while Mr. Haber moved to the far wall and pushed a button on his device. Like before, the center bookcase slid down into the floor, revealing the dark opening of the tunnel behind it.

"Ladies first," Mr. Haber told her.

Alexis did not need to be asked a second time. She hurried to Mr. Haber's side, slid past him, and entered the tunnel. As she crossed the threshold, there was a flash of white light.

"Entry approved," announced a robotic voice.

Noah and Mr. Haber stepped into the passage after Alexis. As they did so, the entryway flashed with royal blue and then bright yellow.

"Entry approved," the same voice repeated.

A light overhead flickered on, and the bookcase behind them rose up to seal off the passageway. A second later, Alexis felt everything start to descend, and she realized that they were actually in an elevator. The elevator soon came to a stop, and on the wall opposite where they had entered, another door slid open. Alexis checked over her shoulder. Mr. Haber gestured for her to exit.

Nearly bursting with anticipation, Alexis hurried off. She let out a cry of amazement. "Are you kidding me? All of this is under the school?"

She was standing at one end of what appeared to be a huge, brightly lit warehouse. Row after row of tall shelves stretched out before her. Towering like skyscrapers, the shelves were packed full with textbooks, jars of chemical powders, electronic gadgets, medical supplies, and countless unmarked crates. As she took in the incredible sight, Alexis heard soft swooshing noises that made her crank her head back. Suspended from the high ceiling was an intricate maze of glass tubes; each tube lit up with a different color whenever a small canister zipped through it.

"Come with us," Alexis heard Mr. Haber say.

Astonished into silence, Alexis followed Mr. Haber and Noah through the rows of shelves. Eventually, they emerged into a large open space at the opposite end of the warehouse.

"Miss Kendall, welcome to our command station," Mr. Haber stated.

For Alexis, things were getting more and more astounding. The wall before her was covered with flat-screen monitors that showed a dizzying display of satellite pictures, live video feeds, news broadcasts, satellite trackers, GPS maps, and rotating three-dimensional images of chemical structures. Underneath the monitors sat a long desk with several computers sitting upon it. Alexis dazedly took in the sight, rendered speechless by the further proof that there really was a secret world of scientists risking their lives to protect important discoveries from evil— and meanwhile, most people had no idea it was happening literally right underneath their feet.

Noah came up beside her. "It looks like Ralph is taking care of Hinshaw's rat problem."

Alexis tracked his line of sight to a monitor that showed the floor plan of what she recognized as the high school itself. In the space representing Ms. Hinshaw's classroom, there was a flashing green dot marked with the letters 'RF'.

"Wow." Alexis managed to find her voice. "You guys track everything."

"Not everything." Noah kept scanning the monitors. "We failed to identify what you ate for breakfast or what Molly said to you prior to first period."

Alexis snapped her head in his direction. "What? You've been spying on what—"

"I'm kidding." Noah looked sideways at her.

"Oh." Alexis let out a nervous laugh. "I knew that."

"I'm sort of kidding," Noah amended under his breath, returning his full attention to the monitors.

Mr. Haber walked to the desk and placed his palm upon a flat glass panel that sat by one of the computers. The panel flashed bright yellow, and a woman's voice was heard over a speaker:

"Agent, please code in."

"Three-two-nine valance," Mr. Haber replied.

"Hello, Ben," the woman said. "How are you?"

"Well, thank you." Mr. Haber leaned casually against the desk. "I was curious to hear how the carbon dating is coming along for the fossil from Angola."

Alexis whispered to Noah, "What is he talking about? What about Headquarters?"

"Don't worry," Noah whispered back.

"Things are going as planned," the woman was telling Mr. Haber. "We're ready to analyze the results."

"Excellent. I will wait to hear the report. Over." Mr. Haber began typing briskly on a keyboard and said to the others, "They are waiting for us, as scheduled."

The whirring sound of a motor filled the air.

"You'd better step back," Noah told Alexis, putting his arm out in front of her.

Alexis complied. Seconds later, the section of floor that had been underneath her split into two panels and opened downward, revealing a staircase to yet another level below. Mr. Haber walked to the edge of the opening and started down the stairs, pausing to address Alexis:

"There are several people who are extremely anxious to meet you. Are you ready?"

"Sure." Alexis kept her watch on the opening. "I think."

With a nod, Mr. Haber continued down the stairs and was soon out of sight.

"It's alright," Noah assured her. "You'll like this part, I promise."

Noah hurried down the staircase, soon becoming lost from Alexis's view. Alone, she scurried to the opening and peeked over the edge. Furthering her shock, she saw Mr. Haber and Noah waiting on a platform of an underground train station.

Since when did this city have a train system? Alexis marveled, going down the stairs to join the others.

Mr. Haber checked his watch. "Ten seconds," he announced, gesturing to their right.

Exactly on cue, the tunnel began rumbling with the sound of an approaching train. Two headlights soon shone out of the darkness, and then a single sleek white train car appeared and came to a stop on the tracks in front of them. Its doors slid open.

"After you, Miss Kendall," Mr. Haber invited.

Alexis stepped with wonderment into the empty car. Taking a seat on one of the big, comfortable chairs, she peered curiously out the front window, but she could see nothing except for the tracks vanishing into the blackness of the tunnel ahead. Mr. Haber entered the car next and sat across the aisle. Noah took a place beside Alexis. As soon as everyone was settled, the car doors shut. A moment later, the train started rolling forward, accelerating so rapidly that Alexis was thrown against her chair.

"How fast is this thing going?" Alexis asked, pulling herself upright.

Mr. Haber smiled slightly. "Very fast."

Alexis gripped an arm rest as the train car maneuvered a curve. "And where is it that we're going, exactly? Where is Headquarters located?"

"The location is a secret."

Alexis was not sure whether to be impressed or offended.

"It's better if we don't tell you, Alexis." Noah seemed to read her thoughts. "That way, if anyone asks you where Headquarters is located, you can honestly say that you have no idea."

"Oh." Alexis swallowed hard. "I see."

They settled into silence other than occasional, brief conversations spoken between Noah and Mr.

Haber. Rocked by the motion of the train, Alexis felt her tired eyes getting heavy. She leaned her head against the cool glass of the window, listening to the hum of the train as it moved rhythmically along the tracks. Before long, Alexis drifted to sleep.

ELEVEN

"End of the line," Mr. Haber announced.

Alexis opened her eyes. As her sleepy thoughts came into focus, she realized that the train had come to a stop. Then she realized that her head was resting on Noah's shoulder. Alexis sat up and brushed her hair from her face, not quite looking at him. Noah quietly put back on his jacket, which—Alexis spied out of the corner of her eye—he had rolled up under her head like a pillow.

The train car's doors slid open. Noah got to his feet and stepped aside, letting Alexis out first. She scrambled off the train and immediately began gazing in awe at what she decided was the most beautiful building she had ever seen. The walls and floor of the enormous, brightly lit station were shiny and white, just like the cube in Mr. Haber's supply closet. At the center of the station stood an ornate fountain, which had water that changed color. Sparkling light fixtures hung down from the ceiling. And the air echoed with the sounds of people hurrying by and train cars moving along the station's many tracks.

Still admiring her surroundings, Alexis noticed a short, balding man who was approaching through the crowds. The man was dressed in an immaculately pressed dark suit and tie, and he walked in a hurry.

When he got close, he set his eyes on Alexis and put on a plastic smile.

"Miss Alexis Kendall, welcome to Headquarters for The Organization. My name is Albert Oppenhall."

Alexis glanced at Mr. Haber before reaching out to shake the man's hand.

Albert next tipped his head to Mr. Haber. "Welcome, Ben. It's nice to have you here, as always."

"Thank you, Albert," Mr. Haber replied politely.

Albert turned to Noah. "And how are you, young man?"

"I'm good," Noah answered with an uncharacteristic edge to his voice.

"That is fantastic to hear." Albert smiled even more broadly. "Now, everyone, please come with me. The group has already gathered for the meeting."

Albert scurried away, his polished shoes clacking on the floor as he went. Alexis looked uncertainly again at Mr. Haber, who motioned for her to follow. So Alexis charged forward, dodging around the throngs of people to catch up with Albert as he moved across the station with his brisk, short strides. Once Albert reached an elevator, he stopped with his chest puffed out importantly. When the others joined him, Albert pushed the elevator call button with dramatic flair. The glass doors of the elevator opened, and the four of them stepped inside.

"Forgive my curiosity, Alexis." Albert observed her as the elevator began to ascend. "I admit that I'm wondering how you're feeling. I can only imagine that it has been very difficult to deal with such a remarkable change."

Alexis opened her mouth to respond when Noah let out an odd cough. Peeking past Albert, she saw both Noah and Mr. Haber watching her closely. It was clear that they were trying to tell her something. They wanted her to be cautious about what she said.

Eyeing Albert once again, Alexis shrugged with indifference. "I'm doing alright."

Albert's smile faded slightly. "That's certainly good to hear."

Unobserved by Albert, Noah's expression relaxed, and Mr. Haber gave Alexis a slight nod. She looked down at her feet to conceal her smile.

The elevator stopped, and with a musical sound, its doors slid open. Alexis heard shuffling papers, throats being cleared, and chairs sliding slightly on a wood floor. She raised her head, and her mouth went very dry. There were several hundred people turning around in their seats to stare at her.

The elevator had opened at the back of a massive lecture hall, which appeared filled to capacity. A wide aisle running through the middle of the audience led to a stage at the front of the room. On the stage was a podium with a tall woman standing behind it. The woman raised her hand and motioned for them to approach.

"Walk to the stage. Promptly now, promptly," Albert whispered, shooing the others out of the elevator.

Unruffled, Mr. Haber started down the aisle. Noah gave Alexis a reassuring look before he did the same. Alexis timidly went after them. She could almost feel the audience's collective gaze sinking into her as she made the long walk to the front of the room. When Mr. Haber reached the stage, he climbed a short set of stairs and went to the woman's side. Noah's face was expressionless as he did the same. Taking a deep breath, Alexis scampered up the stairs to join the others.

"Welcome, Ben. It's good to see you," the woman said to Mr. Haber. She smiled at Alexis and Noah. "Why don't you all take a seat behind me, and I'll get this meeting going."

"Very good." Mr. Haber led Noah and Alexis to the empty chairs behind the podium.

Alexis sat and peered out at the sea of unfamiliar adults before her. *There's got to be someone here with an answer. Someone will know how to fix me.*

A sound from the podium caused Alexis to revert her attention to the woman who stood behind it. The woman had a few gray streaks in her light-colored hair, and she was wearing jeans with a casual shirt and jacket. After adjusting the microphone, the woman began speaking:

"Thank you, everyone, for coming, especially on such short notice. I apologize for the surprise that you must have experienced upon finding so many of us gathered here today. As you have undoubtedly discovered, you were each invited here under a false pretense. For security purposes, we could not disclose the true nature of this gathering until now." The woman bent closer to the microphone. "Ladies and gentlemen, this is an official Priority One assembly."

There was a moment of shocked silence, and then commotion filled the room as everyone began speaking intensely to their neighbors.

"Priority One?" Alexis questioned over the din.

"A scale from one-to-ten, used to designate the urgency of issues that arise," Mr. Haber explained. "A Priority One is used for issues of maximum importance. We have not called a Priority One assembly in years, hence all the fuss."

Alexis observed the audience, totally stunned. "This isn't all because of me, is it?"

"Yes, it is. After what occurred at the football game yesterday, Doctor Caul did not hesitate to set up a Priority One gathering."

"Doctor Caul?" Alexis repeated, noticing a somber-appearing man who was seated in the front row and watching her.

"Doctor Rachel Caul." Noah motioned to the woman at the podium. "President of The Organization."

Alexis sat up in surprise. *She's the president? She seems way too cool to be the leader of a bunch of science nerds.*

Dr. Caul raised her hand, and the audience promptly hushed. She continued:

"Ladies and gentlemen, several weeks ago, some of our agents discovered a new element. Unfathomable to the scientific world at large, this element was stable, naturally occurring, and made up of 407 protons."

Once again, everyone began talking. Dr. Caul had to tap on the microphone several times before the noise ceased and she could proceed.

"Unfortunately, soon after making this amazing find, reports indicated that Doctor Gaige was already on Its trail. We had no choice but to hide the element with one of our most experienced Protectors, Benjamin Haber. I now hand the time over to him for further discussion."

Mr. Haber went to the podium. "Good morning. For any who may not know me, I am Ben Haber, currently stationed as a high school chemistry teacher. I am assisted by my trainee, Noah Weston, whom, no doubt, many of you have heard of."

A rumble of new conversations filled the room. Several people stood up while others leaned into the aisle, all trying to get a better view of Noah on the stage. Confused, Alexis also peeked at Noah, but he kept his attention on Mr. Haber as if unaware of the fuss.

Mr. Haber went on, "Noah and I received the element on very short notice. While we rushed to prepare the storage chamber, I made one grievous mistake: I left the element unattended. The young woman on the stage behind me, Miss Alexis Kendall, found It and . . . actually, Miss Kendall, you should come up and explain what occurred."

Alexis was certain that her stomach dropped to the ground. Every eye in the room had become fixed on her.

"It's okay," Noah said to Alexis in a low voice. "All you have to do is tell them what happened."

Alexis shakily got up from her chair. No one in the crowd seemed to move or breathe as she took her place behind the podium.

"Um, hi," she said, jumping when her voice reverberated over the sound system. "Um, I saw a shiny white cube with lots of colors shooting out of it. I opened up the cube, and bright lights shot into my hands."

Mr. Haber leaned down to speak again. "We believe that is when the element transferred into Miss Kendall and became part of her DNA." He nodded to Alexis. "Please continue. You are doing excellently."

"Well, the next day, I woke up floating in my bedroom, I knew a car was about to hit us, and I made Crystal's drink tip over without touching it. Later, I went to talk to Mister Haber when . . ." Alexis could not finish, her throat catching at the terrifying memory.

"When Alexis spotted an operative outside the classroom who attempted a light attack on her."

Alexis heard Noah's voice and raised her head. He had come to her side. He glanced at her and then continued speaking steadily into the microphone:

"Alexis not only managed to defend herself but also protected me from being struck."

"An operative attempted a light attack on Alexis?" a man in the audience demanded, sounding both angry and horrified.

Mr. Haber was solemn. "Unheard of, I know. The motive for such a horrendous act is still something that I do not understand."

Dr. Caul stepped to the microphone. "At that point, agents had detected the operative and were moving in. However, the assailant was evacuated by the squad that was with him."

Mr. Haber spoke next. "Later, Miss Kendall was abducted by an operative who—"

"Wait, after all that, Doctor Gaige's operatives managed to break through Protector security and abduct her?" a woman interrupted, incredulous.

"That was my fault," Alexis admitted, feeling small and pathetic. "Mister Haber and Noah tried to warn me about the danger, but I didn't listen. I . . . anyway, it was my fault."

"The incident happened while Alexis attended a school football game," Mr. Haber elaborated. "Operatives jammed our communications and utilized a dark shield to get to her. Noah managed to hold the abductor off until I arrived, at which point I was forced to use a light attack to save their lives."

No one spoke.

"And that leads us to where we are today." Dr. Caul was all-business. "First, this newly discovered element may have the potential to increase scientific understanding far beyond anything we can imagine. Second, the element has become part of Alexis's chemical makeup. Third, as best as we can determine, this transfer into Alexis has increased the element's power while bestowing very unique abilities to her. Finally, Doctor Gaige has proven that he will stop at nothing to get his hands on the powers that Alexis possesses."

"So Alexis will be hidden here, I assume?" a woman seated near the doors called out. "At least until we figure out what to do?"

"We can't lock her away like she's a chemical powder," a man retorted.

Another man scoffed. "Are you suggesting that we just let Alexis run around and hope everything turns out alright?"

A few more people shouted, and the room erupted into a flurry of heated discussions.

Alexis shrank back. *This is all my fault. All of it.*

Miserable, she returned to her chair, hunched forward, and stared at the ground.

"Hey, you did a good job up there."

Alexis raised her head. Noah was taking the chair next to her.

"Are you alright?" he added, sounding concerned.

"Yeah, I'm alright." Alexis motioned to the audience. "Look at this, though. Look at the mess I created. This is my fault."

Noah breathed in sharply. "No, this is not your fault. This is because of Doctor Gaige and the evil people who work for him."

Alexis paused, searching his face. "Thanks, Noah," she told him, surprising herself by the emotion that she revealed in her voice. "Thank you for everything."

The hard line of his jaw relaxed, and there was a flicker of movement in his hand as if he was going to reach out and take hers. But the next instant, Noah's expression clouded over. "You don't need to thank me, Alexis. This is my job. This is what I do."

Noah turned away and faced the podium. But Alexis did not move. Her heart was beating distinctly while her mind replayed what had just happened between them. Try as she might, she could not decipher Noah's feelings . . . or her own.

Meanwhile, at the podium, Dr. Caul was tapping again on the microphone. Finally, the audience hushed, allowing her to go on:

"Ladies and gentlemen, we all agree that this is an incredibly difficult situation. However, we are dealing with a fifteen-year-old young lady. We cannot hide her away. Not only would that be cruel to her family and unfair to her, but it is kidnapping, no matter how well-intentioned it may be."

"I think this issue goes far beyond the touchy-feely and even the law," a lady declared.

"Yet the law would play a role, nonetheless," Mr. Haber insisted. "Imagine what would happen if Miss Kendall were assumed to be kidnapped or a runaway. A missing child alert would go out. The region would be filled with police, FBI, volunteers, and news crews. The chaos would provide perfect cover for Doctor Gaige's operatives. Police searches of the school might lead to our command station and all that we have worked so hard to protect. Finally, should a battle be necessary, our identities would be compromised and the safety of countless civilians threatened."

Everyone was quiet.

Dr. Caul scanned the crowd. "Another thing to note: because of the element's increased and almost uncontrollable power, we must assume that It is now potentially detectable wherever Alexis stays for a long period of time. We would not be able to definitively hide her presence—Its presence—here, anyway. So until we can figure out how to restore the element to Its original form, Alexis will keep living her normal life under our guard."

"Which is really not much different from what we initially planned," Mr. Haber pointed out. "We always intended to maintain high security around the element, and so we will. The only difference is that the element is inside of Alexis rather than in a storage chamber."

"It is not the same," a woman argued. "Doctor Gaige knows where It is located. He has a clear target. If the element had been in a storage chamber when Its location was compromised, It would have been hidden in a new location."

"And that is precisely the catch. We can't simply hide Alexis somewhere. This is why we're still working out how best to deal with this extremely unique situation." Dr. Caul waited a moment. "I understand this is uncharted territory and concerning for everyone here. After much deliberation, though, we have determined that this is our best plan for now. As we proceed, we will contact you individually as necessary. Unless there are more questions, this assembly is adjourned."

The conference hall again filled with noise as the attendees got up to leave. From the stage, Alexis watched with sinking heart and fading hope as the members of The Organization filed from the room. It was clear that no one—not even Dr. Caul—had any idea of how to fix her.

I'm going to be stuck like this forever.

"Miss Kendall," Mr. Haber said, coming over to her, "I do apologize for putting you on the spot, but it was very helpful for everyone to hear what you had to say."

Alexis sniffed. "No problem."

"Ralph Fox was right, Alexis. You are a brave young lady." Dr. Caul took a chair and checked her watch. "We can't leave you here much longer, but before you go, I want to make sure that I answer any questions you might have for me."

"Questions?" Alexis actually laughed. "Yeah, I have questions. First of all, who is this jerk, Doctor Gaige, anyway?"

Dr. Caul took a moment before she answered. "Doctor Gaige was my former lab partner. Many years ago, we were both recruited to become agents for The Organization. Doctor Gaige was a brilliant scientist, dedicated to his work, and a good man." Dr. Caul's eyes grew distant. "Tragically, those who used science for evil also recognized his brilliance, and their promises of power and wealth were extremely persuasive. Eventually, Doctor Gaige began working as a spy—an operative—for a group called The Domanorith. When his betrayal was discovered by The Organization, Doctor Gaige disappeared. He now leads The Domanorith, working against everything he once stood for."

Alexis observed her, remaining quiet.

Dr. Caul gave Alexis a sad smile and then addressed Mr. Haber. "We investigated the signal jamming that The Domanorith used at the football game. I am assured such a thing will not happen again."

"That is good to hear." Mr. Haber motioned toward Noah. "It was certainly an unwelcome surprise."

Dr. Caul let out a troubled sigh. "Undoubtedly so. I can only imagine what The Domanorith will try next. But at least it won't be an attack."

"What?" Alexis demanded. "They won't attack me anymore?"

"Not like that," Dr. Caul replied. "Because of what happened at the football game, they must be aware that we know they're on your trail. They will also conclude that we're guarding you closely, which means they will not be able to abduct you again. They will have to change strategies."

Suddenly, Alexis was struck by an idea. "So we should catch them off guard before they try something else. Since I'm going to be stuck like this, I might as well learn how to use my powers to fight them."

A surprised expression came over Dr. Caul's face, and she shifted her eyes to Mr. Haber. "Training Alexis to control and use her powers? It's an interesting idea, don't you think?"

Mr. Haber seemed shocked. "And terribly risky, Rachel. We do not really know what her powers are nor understand the element that made them possible."

"But we can figure that out," Alexis insisted. "After all, you have a gazillion top-notch scientists at your disposal. We should start trying to understand my powers so I can fight The Domanorith."

Mr. Haber's expression became firm. "Miss Kendall, there is no need for you to fight or put yourself at other unnecessary risk. There are trained Protectors watching over you."

"But you trained Noah to fight." Alexis threw up her hands. "Why can't I be trained, too? It's me they're after, so I should be able to fight them like Noah does. I—"

"Alexis, our situations are completely different," Noah interrupted. "You're not going to fight. No way."

Dr. Caul watched Alexis apologetically. "I greatly admire your desire to help, but if my best Protector and his trainee feel that it is both unnecessary and risky, I must listen to them. I'm sorry."

"But I . . ." Alexis dropped back in her chair, her frustration, exhaustion, and fear reaching a tipping point. Before she could stop them, tears began falling down her cheeks.

Dr. Caul put a hand on Alexis's shoulder. "We are going to figure this out, I promise. It may take some time, but we won't rest until this is resolved."

Mr. Haber knelt in front of her. "And although it will often seem like I am treating you as any other student, please know that everything I do is to keep you safe. Like Rachel, I am here for you."

Alexis used her sleeve to wipe her eyes. "Thanks."

Dr. Caul motioned toward the exit. "I regret to say this, but due to the amount of time you've been here, we need to be getting you on your way."

The four of them headed down the staircase and began moving toward the elevator. As Mr. Haber and Dr. Caul conversed in hushed tones, Alexis walked behind them, lost in thought. Then she noticed that Noah had come up beside her.

"And for whatever it's worth," Noah said quietly, "I'm here for you, too."

TWELVE

"Is everything in place for tonight?" Xander asked over his communicator.

"Don't worry," the new operative responded. "I'll take care of it."

"Very well. Keep me informed."

Static indicated that the operative had ended the conversation. Xander set the communicator down on his desk, his mind troubled. But his thoughts were soon interrupted by the sound of someone approaching his office. Quickly, Xander turned to his computer and closed the high school blueprints that had been up on his monitor.

If this new operative gets us to Alexis, Xander told himself, *I'll have all the information I need.*

***

"Look out!" the driving instructor shouted.

Alexis slammed both feet on the brake pedal, screeching the car to a stop.

"You forgot to put the car into reverse." The instructor flared his nostrils.

Alexis attempted a smile. "Sorry."

With an expression of disdain, the instructor pulled a pen from his shirt pocket and began writing on the evaluation card that was attached to his clipboard. "Alright, let's try this again." He made an exaggerated click of his pen before he put it away. "Please back out, Alexis. Care-ful-ly."

Alexis nodded. Shifting the car into reverse, she maneuvered out of the Drive-N-Ride parking lot. She sat up proudly as she started driving down a quiet residential street.

My first driving lesson, and I'm already—

"You aren't maintaining a safe following distance," the instructor snapped. "Didn't you learn anything in lecture today?"

"I listened to the whole lecture and—"

"You are approaching an intersection." He gestured out the windshield. "Let's see if you can manage a right turn, alright?"

Don't let him rattle you. Alexis gripped the steering wheel. *Focus on the road.*

"Not utilizing the turning signal soon enough." The instructor scribbled something else on the evaluation card. "I recommend that you try to get something correct, little lady, or this lesson will be your last."

Alexis narrowed her eyes. *I don't like this guy.*

Suddenly, the car radio turned on, blaring country music.

"Shut the radio off! No distractions while driving!" the instructor barked.

Alexis obediently reached for the radio, pulling on the steering wheel in the process and causing the car to drift into the next lane. There was a loud honk from an SUV that nearly had to drive off the road to avoid getting hit.

"Drive! Leave the radio alone and drive!" The instructor pushed Alexis's hand from the radio and shut off the music himself.

Alexis hastily re-established her hold on the steering wheel and corrected the car's path. Out of the corner of her eye, she saw the instructor make another note on the evaluation card.

"You're marking me down for that?" Alexis was incredulous. "That's not fair. I didn't turn the radio on."

"Of course you didn't. It was the invisible person in the backseat." The instructor snorted. "You know, they really should do I.Q. tests before allowing kids like you to get behind the wheel."

Alexis clenched her jaw. *I really, really do not like this guy.*

The wipers started swishing rapidly across the windshield.

The instructor tossed the clipboard to his feet in exasperation. "Are you a total klutz? Why are you using wipers when it's not—"

His rant was drowned out when the radio lit up again. Rap music pounded from the speakers. Grunting with irritation, the instructor hit the radio's power button, but the music kept playing.

"What's going on?" the instructor growled.

While the instructor sparred with the radio, Alexis clung to the steering wheel and squinted to see past the dizzying motion of the wipers. In the rearview mirror, she noted a growing line of tailgating vehicles, and soon, cars began passing with horns honking and lights flashing.

The instructor gave up on the radio, reached over, and tugged on the wheel. "You're swerving all over the place, you imbecile! I—"

There was a whooshing noise as the instructor's door swung open, causing his clipboard to fly out of the car.

"Stop this car!" the instructor bellowed, his greasy hair flapping in the breeze.

Alexis stepped on the brake. But instead of slowing, the car sped up and accelerated toward an on-ramp.

"It won't stop!" Alexis screamed.

"Not the freeway!" cried the instructor at the same time.

The car flew up the on-ramp and merged into heavy traffic. It made a brisk lane change to the left, which swung the instructor's door shut with a resounding slam.

The instructor reached up with unsteady hand to loosen his tie. "Slow this vehicle down and get into the right lane to exit."

Before she could react, Alexis felt the wheel move gently under her hands. She sucked in a sharp breath. *Is it possible?*

Finger-by-white-knuckled-finger, Alexis cautiously released her hold on the steering wheel.

"What are you doing?" the instructor screeched. "Steer! Steer!"

Alexis ignored him, watching with amazement as the wheel continued to adjust itself, smoothly moving the car through traffic.

Change to the right lane, she silently ordered.

The car's turn signal flipped on, and the vehicle switched lanes.

"I do not believe this! I do not believe this!" the instructor panted, tearing his tie off completely.

Alexis broke into a smile. *Go to Drive-N-Ride.*

The car took the next exit and proceeded through the residential streets, even stopping to let a child and his mother cross the road. Before long, the car pulled itself into the driving school and came to a stop. The engine shut off.

"So is that all for today?" Alexis innocently blinked her eyes at the instructor.

Pasty white, the instructor stared out the windshield and barely nodded in the affirmative.

"Would you like the keys?" Alexis inquired with exaggerated sweetness, holding them out.

The instructor recoiled. "No! I mean, you can leave them on the seat."

"Okay." Alexis opened her door and waved. "See you next time."

Alexis strolled a distance down the sidewalk before peeking behind her. The instructor was still seated rigidly in the car, muttering to himself. With a chuckle, Alexis sent a text message to her mom, letting her know that the driving lesson had ended early. Then she went to the park across the street to wait for her ride. She found a bench tucked under some trees and sat down, watching the autumn sunlight filter through the branches over her head. Alone in the quiet, her thoughts drifted from driving lessons to the bonfire party in the canyon that evening.

*I need to call Molly and ask what I should wear.
The blue shirt? Maybe I—*

"So do we need to put out a warning that says you shouldn't operate heavy machinery?"

Alexis realized that someone had spoken to her, and she checked over her shoulder. A guy with a scraggly blond goatee was seated on a bench nearby and watching her through dark sunglasses. He wore a ripped camouflage jacket and long shorts. There was a skateboard at his feet.

"I'm sorry?" Alexis questioned.

The guy stood up. "Man, Alexis, you sure make it hard to keep up with you."

Alexis peered at him closely. "You look ridiculous, Noah."

"Tell me about it," Noah agreed. "Speaking of ridiculous, though, that was some pretty interesting driving you pulled out there. Way to get us moving. We dispatched three squads just to make sure you weren't going to drive off a bridge or something. What were you thinking?"

Alexis hung her head. "Sorry. The driving instructor was a real bully, but I didn't mean for that to happen—at least, not most of it."

"You should be sorry. While you were enjoying a drive around the city in that ancient Dodge Diplomat, all I got to do was ride this lousy skateboard."

Alexis raised her eyes. Noah's stern expression relaxed. Before she could stop herself, Alexis broke into a laugh. Soon, she heard Noah laughing, too, and she stopped in surprise, observing him. Noah met her gaze, letting his own laughter die away.

There was a pause.

"Lex? Hi, Lex! We're here!" Nina's shout filled the park, interrupting the silence.

Alexis turned. Through the trees, she saw her sister running down a flower-lined path toward them. As Nina got close and spotted Noah, she reduced her pace, eyeing him suspiciously.

Alexis got to her feet. "Nina, I know his goatee his hideous, but you shouldn't stare at the crazy skateboarder. It's not polite."

"Sorry," Nina muttered. After another glare at Noah, she spun around and ran off while shouting, "I get the front seat going home!"

Nina disappeared, and a tranquil hush settled over the park once more.

Alexis faced Noah. "I think that was the first time I've ever heard you laugh, Noah Weston."

Noah watched her steadily. "I guess I really haven't had a reason to laugh, until now."

Alexis could not deny the impact that his words had on her heart. She longed to say something more to Noah—something she did not fully understand herself—but instead, Alexis only glanced away and added:

"I guess I'd better go."

"Yeah, you should get out of here." Noah's tone was businesslike. He hopped on the skateboard. "By the way, are you really going to that party tonight?"

The party. Tanner. I'm meeting up with Tanner.

Alexis cleared her throat. "Um, I think Molly and I are going."

"Just checking," Noah stated before he rode off.

***

"The Organization has agents swarming the city. The girl is going to be protected no matter where she goes."

Xander nodded. "Yes, Peter. Exactly as we knew would happen."

"All the more reason it's good that we're proceeding with Xander's plan," Jackie pointed out, glancing in Gerard's direction.

Gerard tipped his head graciously. "I agree. Xander has proven to be spot-on with his plans for tonight's operation and using the new operative. You must forgive my recent outbursts. I was only trying to help."

Xander immediately put his complete attention on Gerard. Again, Xander's instincts were telling him that something was amiss, yet he could not discern exactly what was wrong.

"I, too, am glad that you're running the show, Xander." Jacob chuckled. "After all, if Gerard is deemed too old to understand teenagers or lead this operation, I could only be classified as ancient!"

There was polite laughter throughout the room until, from the dark corner where he sat, Dr. Gaige spoke:

"So we can assume, Xander, that everything will go as discussed?"

Xander replied, "Yes. Our new operative will contact Alexis at the party tonight. This should lead to further interactions over the next few weeks and, hopefully, to Alexis ultimately being willing to join us."

"And you guarantee that this delay in getting to her—these anticipated weeks of wasted time—will not hinder our objective?" Leslie demanded.

"If anything it will benefit us," Jackie emphasized. "The longer that the girl interacts with The Organization before joining us, the more information she will have to share when she does come."

Dr. Gaige stroked his chin. "Very well. I expect a detailed update after tonight."

"Of course," Xander told him.

Gerard looked around the table and smiled. "I, for one, will be quite interested to hear the report."

THIRTEEN

"We're leaving no later than midnight, alright?" Marcus instructed sternly. "Mom will have my head if we get home after curfew."

With a roll of her eyes, Molly opened the car door. "Don't worry. We'll meet you here on time."

Marcus was clearly not convinced. He turned to the other backseat. "Don't let her forget, Lex. I don't want your dad suing me for keeping you out too late or something."

"I'll keep her on schedule," Alexis assured him with a laugh, sliding out after Molly. "I promise."

Marcus seemed satisfied. He pulled his keys from the ignition, grabbed his jacket, and got out of the car. Giving the girls a quick wave, he jogged off toward a fire pit where his friends were waiting.

Molly let out an exasperated sigh as she watched him go. "Sorry Marcus is being so strict nowadays. He thinks that he has to be all responsible because he's sending out college applications."

"It's alright. I'm glad he was willing to drive us up here at all." Alexis shivered in the night breeze and pulled her coat around her. "My parents never would have let me out of the house if they had known I was coming up the canyon—especially not for something like this."

Molly checked her makeup in the car's side mirror. "My mom thinks we're at a birthday party at some friend's home."

"I told my parents the same thing," Alexis admitted guiltily.

Molly observed her. "Geez, don't worry. What our parents don't know won't kill them. We'll still get home when they're expecting us."

Alexis managed a half-smile as she straightened her shirt and tossed her hair. She wished she could be as relaxed as Molly, but she knew there was no chance of that. It was her first time attending a party with the popular kids from school—not to mention, she had never before gone anywhere without telling her parents.

Molly reapplied lip gloss. "How about we leave Marcus with his geeky friends here at the campground and go find the real party? After all, Tanner is waiting for you, and I fully intend to flirt with Drake all night."

Alexis answered with a jittery nod. "Sounds good."

Molly confidently linked arms with Alexis, and they started up a narrow, moonlit path toward music and laughter in the distance. A brisk wind stirred the trees and blew fallen leaves across the shadowed trail as they continued upward. Finally, the path reached a bend and opened onto a massive grass field.

"Wow!" Molly came to a halt, beaming with excitement. "Look at this, Lex!"

Hovering next to Molly, Alexis observed the scene, overwhelmed. Lit by scattered campfires, the field was packed with people, most of whom she did not recognize. At the far end of the field, close to the edge of a forest, a giant bonfire crackled brightly while more party-goers danced beside it, the beat of the music echoing off mountains that towered in the distance.

Molly kept gazing with awe. "There are college students here!"

"I . . . I didn't expect the party to be quite this big," Alexis admitted.

"Neither did I! It's amazing!" Molly grabbed Alexis's wrist, tugging her forward into the fray. "Do you see Drake anywhere?"

"No," Alexis replied, attempting to keep up. "Maybe he's hanging out over by . . . the . . ."

Molly took another few steps before realizing that Alexis was holding back. She spun around. "Are you alright? You look totally freaked out right now."

Alexis could not respond. A terrible, familiar icy sensation was taking over her body, and her neck had begun to prickle.

Someone is here. An operative is after me.

"Lex?" Molly repeated.

Alexis ignored her friend and spun around, growing dizzy as the petrifying reality of her situation sunk in: it was late, she was far from home, no one had any idea where she had gone, and she was surrounded by strangers.

I need to leave. Now.

"Alexis?" Molly sounded genuinely concerned. "What is it? What's wrong?"

Growing lightheaded, Alexis barely managed a weak response. "Sorry to change plans, but I'm starting not to feel well and—"

"There you are, Alexis Kendall," someone said. "I was wondering when you'd get here."

Alexis never thought she would cringe to hear Tanner's voice. But reluctantly she turned and spotted him making his way toward her. As he got close, another pulse of alarm shot through Alexis's body.

Tanner smiled at her. "Really glad you could make it."

Alexis felt Molly nudge her in the flank.

"Wh-what?" Alexis sputtered. "Oh, um, I mean, thanks, Tanner. Thanks for inviting us."

Tanner motioned to the dancing. "They've got some pretty good music playing over by the bonfire. Do you and Molly want to go—"

"Hey, Tanner, where'd you go, man?" another voice called out.

Alexis saw Drake approaching. He stopped in his tracks when he noticed Alexis.

"Ah." Drake gave Tanner a dry look. "Apparently, you're busy now. I should have guessed."

Tanner chuckled. "Sorry I ditched you. I guess you could say that I've been on a mission to find Alexis."

Alexis staggered as the awful coldness in her body intensified.

Molly slid close to Drake, batting her eyes playfully. "Hey, Drake. What's up? Great party."

After another scrutinizing look at Tanner and Alexis, Drake faced Molly. "Hey. Nice of you to come."

As Molly and Drake continued talking, Tanner held out his hand to Alexis. "What do you say? Wanna dance?"

Alexis cringed. *This cannot be happening. Not when I need to get out of here. But if I leave, Tanner will never ask me out again. I can't lose this chance. Besides, didn't Doctor Caul and Mister Haber specifically say that I should keep living my normal life?*

Ignoring the way her body surged with fear, Alexis reached out and put her hand in Tanner's. With a widening smile, Tanner guided her toward the dance party by the bonfire.

"You look great tonight, by the way," Tanner said as they began moving to the music.

Alexis blushed. "You don't look too bad yourself."

As Tanner put one arm lightly around her waist, Alexis was hit with another spike of nausea. She jumped away from him.

"Sorry, Tanner. I . . ."

Alexis trailed off. Over Tanner's shoulder, she glimpsed Noah among the crowd. Flooded with relief, she instinctively took a step toward him. But Noah only glanced between Alexis and Tanner before disappearing into the throng. Alexis stared after him.

He doesn't know. Noah doesn't know an operative is here. I need to warn him.

Alexis set her eyes on Tanner, thinking fast. "I've gotta find Molly and tell her something. I'll be right back, okay?"

Tanner's expression faltered. "Sure. Okay."

Without another word, Alexis darted past Tanner and started pushing through the fray in a desperate search for Noah. As she dove deeper into the crowd, Alexis spotted Molly and Drake on the opposite side of the dance party, laughing and standing close together. As if he sensed her watching, Drake turned and looked at Alexis.

For one instant, Drake's eyes flashed red.

Alexis was too stunned—too horrified—to move. Smirking, Drake turned back to Molly and whispered something in her ear. Molly nodded. Then Drake led her away, headed toward the forest beyond the bonfire. Alexis clenched her fists, her shock changing swiftly into fury.

I am not going to let you hurt my friend, Drake.

Alexis charged after them, getting jostled back-and-forth by the dense crowd as she fought her way forward. Over the music, Alexis began hearing what sounded like someone calling her name, but she ignored it and kept pushing onward. Again she heard her name, and then someone grabbed her by the hand. Alexis looked up with a start. Noah was at her side.

"Something's wrong, isn't it?" Noah searched her face. "What's going on?"

"Drake is an operative!" Alexis blurted out hysterically. "Drake took Molly to the forest! She's in danger!"

Noah expression stiffened. He reached into his jacket pocket and pulled out his device. "Which way did they go?"

Too distraught to speak, Alexis could only point at the trees beyond the bonfire. Noah raised his head and squinted into the blackness. His eyes narrowed. Then he put a hand firmly on Alexis's shoulder.

"You stay here, Alexis. Right here."

Noah bolted off, leaving Alexis behind. Through the crowd, she saw him break free of the dance party and sprint for the forest, rapidly becoming lost from view within the darkness of the trees.

Tears stung Alexis's eyes, and her heart galloped furiously. *Molly is in danger because of me! I have to help!*

Everything around her became a blur as Alexis started shoving her way after Noah. When she finally escaped the dance party, Alexis halted to take in the sight of the dense forest that loomed before her.

"I'm coming, Molly," Alexis whispered. "I'm coming."

Alexis rushed into the trees without looking back, and soon, the sounds and firelight from the party faded into nothing. Enveloped by the damp forest, Alexis continued running as fast as she could, recklessly sweeping aside the heavy branches that flicked at her face and caught her clothes. The air grew colder and her breathing became labored as she stumbled blindly over unseen rocks and roots in her way. She had no idea how far she had gone before she finally halted to catch her breath.

By the light of the moon, Alexis saw that she had reached the perimeter of a large circular clearing, which was surrounded by trees. Other than her own breathing, all she heard was the ghostly sound of branches rocking in the wind. Alexis shivered as she scanned the deep shadows, realizing that she was totally lost.

A twig snapped. Alexis had no time to react before someone's strong arms were around her and she was tackled to the ground. As Alexis hit the leaf-covered dirt, a hand swiftly clamped over her mouth so she could not scream.

"Shh!" someone said in her ear. "You're alright."

The hand lifted from her mouth. Alexis rolled onto her back and saw Noah over her.

"You were supposed to stay at the bonfire," Noah whispered, obviously alarmed.

Alexis sat up. "But I need to help find Molly."

"No, you need to evacuate. I had agents coming for you." Noah lifted his device and spoke tensely into it. "Alexis is with me."

"Copy. Receiving your updated GPS signal now," came a woman's voice over the device in response. "Redirecting the evacuation team to your current location."

"Copy." Noah lowered his device and addressed Alexis once more. "Turn off your phone."

"What?"

"Turn of your cell phone. Hurry, before someone calls you and the sound gives away our location."

Alexis fumblingly reached into her pocket. She found her phone and powered it down. "Okay, it's off." Shoved her phone into her pocket again. "Now what?"

"Now we're going to run."

Noah leapt up, grabbed Alexis by the hand, pulled her to her feet, and led her deeper into the cover of the trees around the clearing. He crouched down and motioned for her to do the same.

"But what about Molly?" Alexis demanded, still standing.

"Shh!" Noah tugged her to the ground. "Agents tracked Molly. She's safe. After she left the bonfire with Drake, Molly's brother called her. It didn't take long for Marcus to hunt Molly down. Drake returned alone to the party." Noah breathed out slowly. "Look, Alexis, it's not Molly they want. Doctor Gaige's operatives want you. They knew you'd go after Molly if you thought she was in trouble. This was some sort of trap to lure you into their hands."

"So I'll fight them!" Alexis proclaimed irately. "Those cowards put my best friend in danger!"

Alexis tried to stand, but Noah reached out and gripped her arms.

"You have to trust me, Alexis." He spoke with his face close to hers. "Stay quiet and stay down."

Alexis stared back at him and remained still.

"Hey, Drake, it's me. I think Alexis is looking for Molly. Give me a call, okay? Thanks."

The unexpected sound of Tanner's voice echoed through the forest like an explosion. Alexis leaned away from Noah and looked toward the noise. Deep within the trees beyond the opposite side of the clearing, Alexis could see a light that was steadily growing brighter.

"It's Tanner. That light is coming from his cell phone," she told Noah. "He's coming this way."

Noah muttered something under his breath before he spoke into his device. "Alert: we've got a civilian approaching the scene."

"Copy. We will take precautions for the additional civilian. Continue with evacuation. We need to get Miss Kendall out of there," came the recognizable voice of Mr. Haber in reply.

"Copy. Proceeding with evacuation, and initiating precautions for additional civilian," added the same woman who had spoken earlier.

Concealed in the shadows, Alexis and Noah waited in agonizing quiet. It was not long before Tanner stepped out from the trees on the far side of the clearing with his cell phone in hand. Alexis's body went ice-cold.

"Something's wrong, Noah." Alexis shivered. "I think Tanner's in trouble. We've got to—"

Tanner's phone started ringing.

"Hey, Drake. Where are you?" Tanner put his phone to his ear while strolling toward the center of the clearing. "Alexis is looking for . . . no, she ran into the woods and . . . yeah, I'm here now."

"Tanner is leading Drake right to us." Noah grabbed his device and barked an update in a low voice. "At least one operative is headed our way. We'll need a full response. I repeat: we will need a full response."

"Full response initiated," came the woman's succinct reply.

Out of the corner of her eye, Alexis saw Noah change his grip on his device. She did a double take when she realized that he was aiming it at the clearing.

"What are you doing?" Alexis put a hand on his arm, her eyes wide. "You're not going to use that thing to attack, are you?"

Noah tracked Tanner's movements. "Only if I have to."

"But . . ."

Another unexpected sound caused Alexis to hush. Someone else was approaching. Alexis ducked lower. Soon, Drake, too, appeared out from the trees on the opposite end of the clearing. As the moonlight fell upon Drake's face, Alexis was hit by another rush of fear. She clapped her hand over her mouth to stop herself from screaming.

"Hey, Drake." Tanner turned to his friend.

Drake put on a smile, although his eyes were darting agitatedly about the clearing. "Hey. Any sign of Alexis?"

Tanner shook his head. "I was hoping she might have found you. She—"

A sound from a cell phone interrupted the conversation. Drake pulled his phone from his pocket and appeared to check a text message. His posture went rigid. When Drake raised his head and spoke again, his voice was not quite steady:

"Tanner, I'm sorry, but it looks like I need to improvise a Plan B."

Tanner seemed confused. "What are you talking about?"

"It's complicated." Drake put his phone away. "But let's just say that you might help me even more than Molly would have."

Alexis's whole body was pulsating. "Noah, we have to do something!"

"Not yet." Noah kept his device aimed toward the clearing. "We have to wait for reinforcements."

"We can't wait! Tanner is—"

"Alexis, my job is to keep you safe," Noah whispered harshly. "We don't know how many operatives are out there. So until I have reinforcements, or I know how many operatives I would be fighting against, we stay here."

Alexis looked back out at the clearing as Drake took another step toward Tanner. She narrowed her eyes angrily.

Drake already put Molly at risk. If Drake tries to hurt Tanner, too, I swear that I will—

A cracking noise sliced through the air. Alexis looked up and saw a thick branch that was hanging over the clearing snap off from its tree and fall. An instant later, the heavy branch crashed down onto Drake, knocking him to the dirt. Drake let out a weak moan and did not move.

"Drake!" Tanner shouted, hefting the branch off his friend's body. "Drake, can you hear me? Drake?"

Noah sharply nudged Alexis. "You made that happen, didn't you?"

Alexis did not answer and kept her eyes on the clearing. Her body remained cold. Something still was not right. Then a tiny flicker of movement caught her eye. Drake was reaching for something in his pocket.

"Tanner!" Alexis scrambled to her feet. "Run!"

Tanner's head shot up, and he scanned the trees until he spotted her. "Alexis, is that you? Drake's hurt! He needs—"

"Tanner, get out of here!" Alexis sprinted impulsively from the cover of the forest toward the middle of the clearing. "Go now!"

Before Tanner could respond, Drake pulled an object from his pocket and pointed it at him. A flash of red filled the night, forcing Alexis to stop and throw her hands over her face. She heard a moan as someone hit the ground. Alexis dropped her arms and saw Drake staggering to his feet. To her horror, Tanner was motionless on the dirt beside him.

"Drake, what did you do to him?" Alexis screeched.

Pale and breathing strangely, Drake said nothing as he aimed the object that he held at Alexis. Alexis felt her arms get hot and, like a reflex, put them out in front of her. Stunning white light shot from both of her hands.

At the same moment, a burst of royal blue flew in from behind Alexis, also coursing rapidly in Drake's direction. The beams of white and royal blue crashed into Drake simultaneously, the impact hurling him backward. He landed hard several feet away.

"Alexis, get down!"

Noah ran up from behind, throwing himself on top of Alexis as a streak of red came blasting from the trees toward her. The red light struck the ground only inches from them, violently tossing rocks and dirt into the air. Alexis screamed and covered her head with her arms. Getting to his knees, Noah fired a shot of royal blue back at the trees from where the light attack had come. A man's cry of pain filled the night and then echoed away into nothing.

For one moment, the forest was eerily quiet. Then a barrage of red streaks began raining down upon the clearing.

"There are too many of them!" Noah fired at the unseen attackers. "Run while I try to hold them off!"

"No!" Alexis yelled. "I'm not going to leave you to . . ."

Alexis's voice caught when she saw a flash of yellow light in the forest where she and Noah had been hiding.

"Noah!" Alexis pointed. "The Organization is here!"

Another blast of yellow light soared over Alexis and Noah's heads and exploded within the trees on the opposite side of the clearing. Before the yellow light had even faded away, streaks of orange, turquoise, pink, and countless other hues started illuminating the sky, all coursing toward Alexis and Noah's hidden assailants. Within seconds, the darkness of the night was taken over by color, while shouts and explosions resonated among the trees.

"The evacuation team is positioned in the forest behind you!" the barely audible sound of Mr. Haber's voice came over Noah's device. "Get over here now! Now!"

Still using one arm to fire his device as he stood up, Noah used his other hand to yank Alexis to her feet.

"But what about Tanner?" Alexis yelled while another flash of red slammed into the dirt by where she stood.

Noah put one arm around Alexis's waist and began pulling her away from the center of the clearing. As they raced for cover, beams of color continued flying over them and red flashes scorched the ground at their feet. When they got close to the trees, a pair of blinding headlights turned on, illuminating the shadows. Then Alexis heard the deep rumble of a massive engine.

"Get in the evacuation vehicle!" Noah shouted, releasing his hold on Alexis and firing again toward the far end of the clearing.

But Alexis stopped and checked behind her. The clearing was empty. Tanner and Drake were gone.

"Alexis, go!" Noah ducked out of the way of another strike. "Get—"

A terrible flash of red exploded right next to Noah, forcing him to lunge to the ground to avoid getting hit. Alexis spun around and aimed her arms at the source of the attack. Blistering white flew from her hands, and someone in the shadows let out a shriek.

Back on his feet, Noah grasped Alexis by the wrist and tugged her into the trees. Silhouetted against the headlights were two men and a woman standing by an armored vehicle. One of the men, who had a buzz cut, opened the back door of the vehicle and motioned for Alexis to get in.

"Go! Go!" Noah shouted, pushing her forward.

Alexis resisted. "Aren't you coming?"

Noah shook his head. "This evacuation isn't for me."

"You've been risking your life for me out there! I'm not going to leave you!"

Noah nearly had to lift Alexis into the vehicle. "This is my job. I'll see you soon. I promise."

Before Alexis could protest, Noah had shut the door hard. The man with the buzz cut, who appeared to be in his late twenties, took his place behind the wheel. The woman got in the front passenger seat. The other man, his face concealed by a stocking cap and a giant pair of night vision goggles, hopped into the seat next to Alexis. The driver then began backing the armored vehicle away from the scene. All Alexis could do was watch tearfully out the windshield as Noah ran to rejoin the fighting.

<u>FOURTEEN</u>

Xander stormed into the meeting room and slammed the door.

No one spoke. Seeing Xander so upset was almost as shocking as the report of that evening's events. Everyone knew that Xander's anger was justified; Gerard had nearly cost them the girl, Number 407, more operatives . . . potentially everything.

Xander fumingly made his way to the front of the room. He jabbed at the projector's control panel, threw the remote down, and faced the group while the computer warmed up.

"Let's discuss the little fiasco that occurred tonight, shall we?" he quipped. "Of course, obtaining all the information has been a tad difficult since our new operative, Drake, is in the infirmary with critical injuries; Gerard and the other rogue operatives sit in detainment awaiting questioning; and the teenage civilian, Tanner, is also in our infirmary and recovering from an overdose of a paralytic that nearly caused him to stop breathing."

The group remained uncomfortably quiet. Once a video started playing on the projector screen, Xander rubbed his forehead and went on:

"As you know, due to the heightened protection around Alexis, we changed our strategy for how to get her. We agreed to place an operative close to Alexis—one who would befriend her and ultimately convince her to join us. This was deemed the best way to get to Alexis, learn more about The Organization, and safely study Number 407.

"We also determined that a new operative would be needed to carry out this strategy. The plan was to recruit a high school student for the task—specifically, a young man named Drake Spencer. Drake was exactly what we were looking for: he attended the same school as Alexis, he and Alexis had mutual friends, and Drake demonstrated strong tendencies for rebellion and defiance. He was a perfect choice and, as predicted, easily recruited for the task."

Xander motioned stiffly to Gerard's empty chair and kept speaking:

"Apparently, however, Gerard decided that our plan was not to his liking. After we recruited Drake, Gerard met with him secretly. Gerard bribed Drake to carry out a different plan at that bonfire party tonight."

Jacob spoke up. "No doubt Gerard hoped to capture the girl, become a hero, and prove he should still be Head of Intelligence."

"Gerard was reckless! Stupid!" Peter exclaimed.

"Whatever he was or thought, Gerard destroyed our plan." Xander's voice was calm though his face pale with anger. "Gerard instructed Drake to reveal to Alexis that he was an operative, convince Alexis that her friend was in danger, and lure Alexis to a place where Gerard and the other bought-off operatives were waiting."

Leslie defiantly tossed her head. "What was so wrong with that? Gerard was only trying to obtain the girl, and his plan would have worked if—"

"His plan nearly got Alexis killed," Xander seethed. "Gerard gave no consideration to the fact that Drake was new, young, and reckless. Gerard had no business giving Drake a weapon."

Peter gaped. "Gerard gave the boy one of our weapons? An actual telron?"

"Yes." Xander's eyes flashed fiercely. He flicked his hand toward the video of the battle in the forest playing on the screen behind him. "And at some point tonight, Drake was apparently forced to change plans. When that happened, Drake impulsively used the telron to launch a stun attack on Tanner. And he nearly launched a light attack on Alexis."

"Had Drake been a trained shot, the fool might have killed her," Jackie added harshly.

Xander had to take a moment before he spoke again. "When Alexis defended herself, one of Gerard's minions hiding on scene fired at her. Before my company of operatives got there to stop what was going on, The Organization's agents arrived. A battle between the agents and Gerard's cohorts ensued. In the end, several operatives were killed or injured, Tanner was unnecessarily taken hostage, and Drake was injured and his cover blown. Not to mention, we were forced to waste precious time afterward rounding up Gerard and the other traitorous operatives."

"But what about Gerard now?" Leslie's nasally voice quivered. "What will happen to him?"

Xander did not look at her. "That's not my decision."

"It will depend on the answers he provides during his interrogation," Dr. Gaige responded calmly. "The same goes with the other operatives who defied orders and assisted him tonight."

The woman with black hair raised her hand. "And Drake? What about him?"

"His injuries are serious, Daria." Xander almost could not bring himself to say the words. "Drake was actually struck by two attacks. The uncontrolled attack from Alexis was not intended to kill, but it caused injuries. The other was a stun attack from someone else at the scene. The prognosis for Drake is unknown. Our medical personnel will keep me informed."

Peter appeared astonished. "You say that one attack came from the girl?"

"Yes." Xander's eyes darted to Jackie. "The footage taken by one of Gerard's accomplices shows that Alexis again generated some sort of energy without being armed."

Leslie curled her lip. "Well, from all the footage that was obtained by Gerard's assistants and your company tonight, Xander, were you at least able to figure out who the Protector is at that high school?"

"No." Xander looked unflinchingly at her. "As you can obviously see, the footage is extremely distorted. The energy Alexis creates takes its toll, but I have people trying to restore the video as we speak."

"In the meantime, what about the other boy?" Jacob inquired. "The civilian? Who is he, and what is the plan for him?"

"We think that Tanner is Alexis's boyfriend," Xander explained. "From what we can see in the video, Tanner literally has no idea what hit him. Since the battle, he has been given a dose of an amnestic. He will have no memories of what occurred, and we will be able to return him without compromising anything. If Alexis should disclose information to Tanner in the future—if he even believes her—Tanner will have no meaningful way to help The Organization or to harm us. It will be no different than before."

Dr. Gaige clasped his hands with exaggerated patience. "Xander, are you sure that returning the civilian is the best course of action?"

Xander kept his affect indifferent. "I see no reason to keep Tanner here any longer than necessary."

"You have a different opinion, Doctor Gaige?" Leslie prompted, clearly interested.

"Perhaps." Dr. Gaige assumed a casual air. "Our plan for getting the girl has again been thwarted, and we need new options. So before we give away our one bargaining chip, I wonder if we can think of a way to use the civilian to our advantage."

"Bargaining chip?" Peter cocked his head. "You mean, use the civilian as a means of luring the girl to us?"

"In other words, essentially do what Gerard intended?" Leslie smugly added.

Xander ignored Leslie, his mind focused on trying to circumvent the disaster that he knew Doctor Gaige was contemplating.

"Why not?" Dr. Gaige went on. "This blunder will possibly end up working to our benefit. It may bring us what we ultimately want, after all."

"It is an interesting idea." Jacob shrugged. "What do you think, Xander?"

Xander replied, "It will be futile to try and use Tanner as bait. After what occurred tonight, The Organization is not going to allow Alexis out of their sight. She would never be able to come for Tanner, even if she wanted to."

Dr. Gaige looked at Xander. Xander's unfazed demeanor did not waver. Finally, Dr. Gaige addressed the others:

"Does anyone else have a better suggestion?"

Xander took a step forward. "Doctor Gaige, this is not their area of—"

"We should keep the boy and question him," Daria voted. "If we think of a better plan, we will get him home. Until we come up with an alternative, however, we should hold on to the one potential advantage that we have."

"Absolutely not." Xander was no longer able to keep his emotion totally in check. "My job is not to arrange an interrogation of innocent civilians or hold teenagers hostage. My—"

"Your job, Xander, is to lead this operation." Dr. Gaige interrupted pointedly. "I'm sure you can see the advantage of questioning a civilian who knows the girl so intimately. You were just bemoaning the loss of the new operative, were you not? Well, this boyfriend will know far more about the girl than a rookie operative learned during his few hours on the job."

Xander was about to argue further when Jackie caught his eye. She gave him a look. Xander understood and kept quiet, letting Jackie address the group:

"I agree with Doctor Gaige. We should keep the boy, and Xander should do the interrogation himself. After all, he knows far more about this operation than the rest of us."

Xander made an exaggerated sigh of annoyance. "Fine. I will personally conduct the formal questioning of Tanner. Then, as discussed, after we prepare our new strategy, we will get him home. Agreed?"

"Of course," Dr. Gaige replied.

FIFTEEN

Head in her hands, Alexis was staring despondently at the floor when the armored vehicle came to a stop. Although the engine was still running, Alexis noted that the vehicle no longer made a sound. Looking up in surprise, she saw the driver push one of the buttons on the dashboard. The streetlamps outside shut off.

Straining to see in the darkness, Alexis watched curiously as the woman in the front passenger seat checked a small screen that was attached to her sleeve and then flashed a thumbs-up sign. In response, the man seated by Alexis opened the door and got out of the vehicle, motioning for her to follow. Alexis obeyed and peered around. They were standing in the bus zone of her high school's parking lot.

Still without a word, the man headed toward a side door that led into the school. He unlocked the door and held it open, gesturing again for Alexis to come along. She stepped past him and into the empty, unlit hallway. Letting the door shut behind them, the man began jogging down the corridor, his feet somehow not making a sound. Alexis uncertainly headed after him, trying to stay concealed in the shadows like he did. The man led her to Mr. Haber's room and used a shimmering key to unlock the door.

They went inside. Drapes over the windows blocked out the moonlight as Alexis trailed after him past the desks and workstations to the closed door of the supply closet. The man pulled off one glove and placed his thumb on the wall beside the doorframe. Yellow light flashed under his thumb, and then there was a clicking sound as the door unlocked. The man ushered Alexis into the supply closet, closed the door, and turned on a small flashlight.

"Miss Kendall, you need to make some phone calls."

Alexis started. "Mister Haber?"

The man pulled off his goggles and stocking cap, revealing his scraggly black ponytail.

"Mister Haber, what are we doing here?" Alexis demanded. "Tanner was captured, and Noah is still fighting! We have to go help them!"

"No, we have to keep moving. Before we go to Headquarters, though, you need to call Molly and also your parents. Molly will be leaving the party soon, and your parents are going to be expecting you home. They all must know that you are safe so they do not worry about you tonight. Quickly, Miss Kendall."

Alexis's hands shook as she searched her pockets to find her phone. Her heart ached when she saw that the phone was turned off, exactly how Noah had asked her to leave it. Suppressing her tears, Alexis pushed the power button and dialed Molly.

"Hey!" Molly shouted over the music at the bonfire party. "I've been trying to call you!"

Alexis breathed out with relief when she heard her friend's voice. "Hi, Mol."

Molly went on ecstatically, "Guess what? Drake asked me to dance at the bonfire a little while ago! Can you believe it?"

"That's . . . that's great."

"And did you see the fireworks that someone set off in the forest? Weren't they incredible? No one has any idea who did it, which is hilarious! Where are you, anyway? Marcus and I have been looking all over the place!"

"I've, um, been with Tanner."

Molly sighed. "I would still be with Drake if Marcus hadn't felt the need to play babysitter."

Alexis could not help smiling a little when she heard Marcus mumble something in the background.

"Anyway, Marcus says it's time to go home," Molly explained with annoyance. "Where should we meet you?"

"Oh, actually, I have a favor to ask." Alexis cleared her throat. "Some people are going to Tanner's house after the party, and he invited me to go along. I don't want my parents to know, though. So is it okay if I come to your place later and stay the night? I'll tell my parents that I'm sleeping at your house."

"What did Lex say?" Marcus sounded as though he had moved closer to Molly's phone. "She is not gonna go hang out with a bunch of jock morons at some guy's—"

"No prob, Lex!" Molly yelled over her brother's protests. "I sure wish Mister Responsible would let me go, too!"

"Thanks. Talk to you later."

Alexis hung up quickly. After a moment's pause, she dialed her dad's phone. She was glad when it went to voicemail. It would be easier to lie to a recording.

"Hi, Dad. I'm gonna spend the night at Molly's. I'll see you in the morning. I . . . I love you."

When Alexis ended the call, Mr. Haber nodded approvingly. "Good work, Miss Kendall. Now we must go."

For Alexis, the next several minutes went by in a blur. She knew that she was going with Mr. Haber into the passageway behind the bookcase . . . through the warehouse toward the command station . . . down the stairs . . . onto the train . . . and yet nothing seemed real. As the train raced toward Headquarters, Alexis sank low in her seat and leaned against the cold window, consumed by the gut-wrenching emotions coursing through her body and the terrifying images in her mind.

Molly was in danger, Tanner has been captured, and Noah is still out there putting his life at risk. All because of me. Noah might get . . . he could be . . . Noah . . .

Alexis's thoughts were interrupted by a soft musical sound when the train car came to a stop. The car doors opened. They had arrived at Headquarters.

"Exiting now," Mr. Haber said into his device as they stepped out of the car. "Start time twenty-three-thirty."

"Start time?" Alexis almost had to run to keep up with Mr. Haber's rapid strides.

"We have to track how long you are here. The more time you spend in one place, the more likely that The Domanorith will detect where you are."

The glass doors of the elevator up ahead were open. Mr. Haber and Alexis stepped in, the doors swiftly closed, and the elevator began to descend. After a long time, the elevator settled to a stop. The doors slid aside, revealing that Dr. Caul was waiting for them.

"It's a relief to see you both here safely." Dr. Caul's brow was furrowed with worry. "Please come with me."

Alexis lagged behind the others as they headed down a long, warmly lit hallway—the soothing quiet making a jarring contrast to the violent battle she had so recently left behind. Dr. Caul and Mr. Haber spoke in soft, succinct tones until they reached the door at the far end of the hall. Dr. Caul broke off from what she was saying and pressed her thumb on the wall adjacent to the door. The area of wall under her thumb flashed magenta, and the door opened slightly.

"Alexis, this is The Lounge." Dr. Caul pushed the door open wide. "Please go in and sit down. You need to rest."

Alexis mutely did as she was told. Inside, she found a modern kitchen to her left. On her right was a large sitting area with a big couch and several recliner chairs. All the seating faced the same wall, which was covered with monitors. The monitors were dark, mirroring how everything at that moment felt terribly somber and still. Alexis drifted over to the couch and sank down upon it. Only then did she realize that she was completely exhausted.

"Take this, Miss Kendall."

Mr. Haber brought her a glass of water. She accepted the drink but set it at her feet without taking a sip.

Dr. Caul stepped into The Lounge and let the door shut. "Alexis, this has been an awful night for you. How are you doing?"

The question only drove guilt into Alexis's heart like a knife. "It doesn't matter how I'm doing. Molly could have been hurt, Tanner is a prisoner of The Domanorith, and Noah is fighting for his life even as we speak. All because of me." Alexis stood up. "I should be out there helping. I need to help somehow. Please let me go."

"Molly is safe with her brother," Dr. Caul reminded her. "As for Tanner, our initial analysis of the battle suggests that he was only temporarily paralyzed when he was captured—the operatives had no desire to hurt him then, and there is no reason to think that they will hurt him now. We will find Tanner and get him home safely."

Alexis looked away. "And . . . and Noah?"

"Noah is also safe," she heard Mr. Haber say. "By getting you out of the forest, Miss Kendall, we eliminated any reason for the battle to continue. The fight is over, and Noah is here."

"What?" Alexis spun to face him, trying to process what she had heard. "Noah is safe? He's here? Right now?"

Mr. Haber gestured to his device. "Noah just sent notification that he has arrived at Headquarters. He will be coming down to join us."

At first, Alexis could not move. Then she ran across the room and yanked the door open, desperate to see Noah with her own eyes. As she rushed out of The Lounge, there came a sound from the elevator at the other end of the hall. Alexis halted, barely able to breathe as she waited. After what felt like an eternity, the elevator doors slid open. Limping and covered in dirt, Noah stepped out into the corridor. Raising his head, he did a double take when he saw Alexis and stopped in his tracks.

"Hi, Alexis."

Alexis swallowed hard. "Hi."

Noah started coming down the hall.

"You're . . . you're alright." Alexis's heart was pounding in a strange way.

"I'm alright," he echoed.

Alexis blinked, fighting the urge to run and embrace him. "That's good. That's good, Noah."

Noah kept approaching until he was right in front of her. "I promised that I'd see you soon, didn't I?"

"Yes . . . yes, you—"

The door behind them was flung open.

"Noah, are you hurt?" Mr. Haber hurried out of The Lounge. "Do you need anything?"

Noah cleared his throat, took a step back from Alexis, and shook his head. "No. I'm okay."

"Noah, come in," Dr. Caul encouraged from the doorway.

After a last glance at Alexis, Noah walked into The Lounge with Mr. Haber on his heels. While Noah, Mr. Haber, and Dr. Caul moved into the kitchen and began talking, Alexis made her way to the other side of the room. Dropping again onto the couch, she lowered her aching head and closed her eyes. As her breathing steadied, she tried making sense of her thoughts, but the swing of emotions she had experienced over the past few hours seemed to render her unable to think . . . or understand her heart.

"Hey, are you sure that you're okay?"

Alexis saw Noah approaching with concern evident in his gray eyes.

"I should be asking you that question," she told him guiltily.

"Don't worry about me." He sat beside her. "I'm fine."

"But you could have been hurt. Or worse." She reached out and stroked a bruise on his cheekbone.

"Like I said, don't worry about me. This is my job." But Noah's resolute demeanor seemed to relent at her touch, and he brushed her hand in return. "I want to know about you. Seriously. Are you alright?"

For a single moment, Alexis could concentrate on nothing except Noah's touch. But the awful memories of that evening swiftly returned to her mind, and she shook her head. "No, I'm not alright. I'm relieved that Molly is safe and you're safe. But until we get Tanner, I'm not going to be totally alright."

The hint of softness that had crept into Noah's expression faded. "Don't worry. We'll get him back for you."

"For me?" Alexis repeated, confused. Then realization struck her. "Hang on, this isn't about . . . I mean, I'm not worried about Tanner because . . . I mean—"

"Miss Kendall. Noah." Mr. Haber came toward them. "I am sorry to interrupt. Unfortunately, our time here must be limited, and we must push on."

With a nod, Noah leaned away from Alexis, his expression as aloof as ever. Alexis cleared her throat, her hand still warm where he had touched her.

Mr. Haber took a chair. "Now, our immediate concern, of course, is—"

"Getting Tanner back," Alexis finished for him, her mind refocusing.

Dr. Caul also sat down. "Yes, and on the surface, it would appear that we have two options. The first is to coordinate a mission to discover Tanner's whereabouts and rescue him. The other option is for me to attempt to contact Doctor Gaige and negotiate a trade for Tanner's safe return."

"Trade? Trade with what?" Noah's eyes flew to Alexis. "There is nothing that we would give The Domanorith."

"I agree," Dr. Caul stated. "Not to mention, locating Doctor Gaige and the base of The Domanorith has proven to be an impossible task. I don't know if we could send him a message, even if we wanted to. And if we did somehow find him, I know Doctor

Gaige would not negotiate. He goes after what he wants, no matter the cost."

"In other words, neither option is really an option." Alexis drummed her fingers on the arm rest. "We would never trade with Doctor Gaige, but we also have no way to locate the base of The Domanorith in order to rescue Tanner."

"Precisely." Mr. Haber commenced cleaning dirt off his glasses with the corner of his plaid button-up shirt. "This means that we have to come up with a third option."

"Like what? What are we going to do?" Alexis slid to the edge of her chair.

"Well, for starters, there won't be any 'we' about it, Alexis," Noah said. "You're not going to be involved."

Alexis stared. "What are you talking about?"

"Miss Kendall, you will not be asked to play a role in the rescue mission," Mr. Haber told her kindly.

"But that's not fair!" Alexis protested. "I want to be involved. This whole mess is my fault!" She nudged Noah. "You saw me out there tonight. I fought, and I didn't even need a weapon. I could help!"

"Yeah, you fought. You fought well. But you were also put in immense danger," Noah countered, sounding deeply bothered. "That's not going to happen again. Not on my watch."

Alexis set her eyes pleadingly on the others. But Mr. Haber shook his head, and Dr. Caul remained quiet. In a surge of frustration, Alexis stood up and stomped for the door.

"Fine, then I'm going to go out there and find Tanner myself!"

Noah jumped to his feet. "What? Where are you going?"

"Miss Kendall," Mr. Haber also called after her. "Please wait and give us time to figure this out."

Alexis spun around."Time? Mister Haber, we might not have time. Who knows what terrible things they're doing to Tanner right now?" She took a breath to calm herself before continuing. "Look, we know that Doctor Gaige wants me captured, right? So I bet that if I just go wander around somewhere, an operative will come after me within ten minutes. I can hand myself over, and you guys can secretly follow my captor. It'll lead you right to Tanner."

Alexis spun away from the others and opened the door. But Noah jogged up from behind and leapt in her path, blocking the exit.

"Get out of my way." Alexis glared and tried stepping past him. "You don't know what this is like, Noah. Doctor Gaige is trying to harm the people I care about."

"I do know what it's like," Noah snapped. "I know better than anyone. Doctor Gaige killed my parents."

Alexis froze, and everything around her seemed to become horribly still. Slowly letting go of the door, Alexis raised her eyes. Noah shook his head and walked off into the kitchen.

Mr. Haber came to Alexis's side and spoke quietly. "Miss Kendall, please give us a chance to sort through this."

Doctor Gaige killed Noah's parents. Noah is an orphan because of Doctor Gaige.

Sickened, Alexis could not move. She just kept watching Noah, who stood with his back to the others and his head bowed. Then she heard Dr. Caul ask:

"Alexis, despite what you witnessed tonight, would you really be willing to face the risk?"

Alexis peered over her shoulder, looking Dr. Caul in the eyes. "Yes."

Dr. Caul spoke next to Mr. Haber. "Her idea is not a bad one. What if we use Alexis to draw The Domanorith in so we can trail them to their base?"

Mr. Haber was clearly taken aback. "We cannot use Miss Kendall as bait. We do not know what they would do to her. We could not guarantee her safety. It would also require a rescue mission for both of them. This would not—"

"Can you think of a better solution for finding Tanner?" Alexis interjected.

Mr. Haber did not reply.

Noah yanked off his baseball hat and tossed it onto the kitchen counter. "No way. We're not going to put Alexis at risk to find that guy. We'll think of something else."

"But this would work," Alexis insisted. "Train me to use my powers so I could fight if I needed to defend myself. Once I'm ready, you can use me as bait. I'll learn fast, I promise. Besides, if what's in me is so important, The Domanorith won't harm me."

"Won't harm you?" Noah angrily threw up his hands. "Then what would you call what nearly happened tonight?"

"I don't know," Alexis admitted. "A fluke? Maybe Drake didn't know what he was doing?"

"Okay, but what about the operative who was outside Ben's classroom and very intentionally launched a light attack on you?" Noah challenged.

"Well, what about the operative who kidnapped me from the football game? He really could have hurt me if he had wanted to."

Noah's face stiffened. "No way. You're not fighting, and you're not going to be used as bait."

There was a tense break in the dialogue as Alexis and Noah frowned at each other.

Eventually, Dr. Caul spoke. "Alexis's idea does seem to be the best option we have."

Mr. Haber began pacing. "If we were to proceed with such a scheme, we would need some time—and your patience, Miss Kendall—while we came up with a detailed plan."

"Hang on, you can't really be considering this." Noah looked between Mr. Haber and Dr. Caul. "You're not actually going to train Alexis to fight, are you?"

"No, we're not," Dr. Caul replied.

Noah seemed to relax slightly. "Good."

"We're not going to train Alexis," Dr. Caul repeated. "But you are, Noah."

"What?" Noah and Alexis exclaimed together.

<u>SIXTEEN</u>

All of this because of Gerard's reckless disregard . . .

Xander stood by Tanner's infirmary bed, reviewing the medical chart. The notes indicated that Tanner had been heavily sedated to keep him comfortable until the paralytic was out of his system.

"How is he doing?" Xander eventually asked, putting the chart down.

"He's doing quite well," the doctor answered. "The paralytic will leave no lasting damage. We'll soon begin weaning him off of the sedation. I anticipate that he'll be back to baseline in one or two days."

Xander eyed the bags of fluid and medication that were infusing through Tanner's IVs. "How much of this experience will Tanner remember?"

"I don't think we can say. The medications will provide at least some short-term amnestic effects, but we won't really know how complete the amnesia will be until he is awake and talking."

"I see." Xander moved for the door. "Thank you, doctor."

Xander left the room. His fists clenched as he strode down the corridor. *I don't have much time left to make this work.*

***

Where am I?

Alexis sat up with a start. She was lying on a bed in an unfamiliar room. To her right, hints of early morning sunlight streamed in through a tiny window high up on the wall. Opposite the foot of her bed, a small dresser sat next to a closed door.

As her head cleared, the memories of the night before came back in a rush: the bonfire party, dancing with Tanner, the battle in the forest, Headquarters, and the decision to train her to use her powers. Then Alexis relaxed; she knew that she was safe. By the time the meeting in The Lounge concluded, it had been nearly two o'clock in the morning. Given how long she had been at Headquarters, Mr. Haber and Dr. Caul determined that Alexis needed to be moved to a different location while she got a few hours of rest before returning home. Alexis remembered exhaustedly leaving Headquarters with Noah, getting on the train for a destination he never disclosed to her. After that, Alexis's recollection was spotty. Her last memory was going in-and-out of sleep as someone carried her off the train.

Alexis yawned, rubbed her eyes, and reached down to the floor at her left to find her cell phone. But she stopped in surprise. On the far side of the room, Noah was asleep on another bed, which was floating near the ceiling. Alexis clapped a hand over her mouth to prevent herself from laughing out loud.

Oh boy. He's gonna love this.

Sleeping deeply and breathing steadily, Noah lay on his stomach with one arm hanging off the floating bed. Alexis observed him, realizing that it was the first time she had ever seen him appear totally at peace.

Doctor Gaige killed his parents.

The nauseating thought struck her hard, and Alexis's smile disappeared. She quietly picked up her phone to check the time. It was five-thirty in the morning. Her parents would be expecting her to return in a few hours, still believing that she had spent the night at Molly's. Wondering how long it would take to get home, Alexis hurriedly found a rubber band in her jeans pocket and pulled her hair into a low ponytail. Then she slipped on her mud-covered shoes.

Noah stirred at the noise. "Alexis? Are you okay?"

"Hang on, Noah!" Alexis jumped to her feet. "Don't move!"

"What?" Noah sat up fast but froze, eyes wide, when he spotted her on the ground below. "Alexis! What in the heck is going on?"

"It's nothing to worry about!" Alexis rushed over to his end of the room. "I'm, um, all over it!"

Noah peered over the edge of the bed. "You're all over it?"

She cranked her head back to see him. "Yeah. This has happened before."

"What?"

"Well, it's been a bit of a recurring problem for me. When I wake up, either I'm floating or some of the objects in the room are in the air. I don't exactly know why. It looks like your bed got affected this time. Um, sorry."

After another incredulous look at her, Noah started positioning himself to jump off of the bed.

"Wait!" Alexis shouted.

"What?" Noah gripped the mattress. "What? What is it? What's wrong?"

"I want to practice using my powers to get you down."

"Practice?" Noah's voice cracked.

"You are my personal trainer now, aren't you?"

Noah dropped his chin to his chest. "I did not sign up for this."

"Shh. I need to concentrate."

"Great."

Alexis gave him another look, and then she pushed up her sleeves and shut her eyes. *Put the bed down. Put. The. Bed. Down.*

"Yeah. You totally have this mastered," she heard Noah say in a tone that was deadpan.

Alexis excitedly opened her eyes. Noah's bed was back on the floor, but he remained hovering in the air.

Alexis could not contain her laughter. "Whoops. Hang on."

"I don't think I can do much else at the moment."

Ignoring his quip, Alexis closed her eyes once more. *Noah needs to get down. Put Noah down, too.*

But when Alexis peaked, Noah was still suspended near the ceiling.

"Hmm." She scrunched her nose, perplexed.

Noah twisted his body, changing his position. "Maybe you should—"

"No, I've got this," Alexis insisted.

"But I think you—"

"I said that I've got this, Noah."

"I know, but I'm also getting altitude sickness."

Alexis cracked a smile. "Fine. I'll bring the bed back up to you, and you hold onto it this time."

Alexis caused the bed to rise up off of the floor until it came within Noah's reach. He grabbed the bed frame and held on while Alexis guided it to the floor.

"There. You see?" Alexis declared proudly. "Totally mastered."

Noah stood very still for a few moments. Then he examined his watch, picked up his jacket, and headed for the door. "It's time to move."

Alexis followed. "Agreed. Where are we, anyway?"

"Somewhere we've been for too long, that's where." Noah pulled the door open. "We need to get on the train and get you home."

Alexis trailed him into another stark room with cement walls. She continued toward a narrow staircase but noticed Noah veering toward a short cabinet that stood against the side wall. Alexis waited, watching curiously as Noah pressed a button on his device. To her shock, the cabinet started rising out of the floor, becoming taller than Noah before it came to a stop. Noah opened the cabinet door, revealing the entrance of a dark tunnel behind it.

"That's impossible!" Alexis proclaimed. "How'd you do that?"

Noah grinned. "Your chariot awaits."

***

Jackie slipped into Xander's office and shut the door. "They still have Gerard in detainment. I don't know if he's been through his full interrogation yet or not."

"And Drake? Did you hear anything about him?" Xander rubbed his aching head. He had no idea how many hours it had been since he had slept.

"Last I heard, he was still in the infirmary."

Xander looked away. "They're only teenagers."

"Hey, this was not your fault." Jackie came closer. "You were the one trying to prevent something like this from happening."

"So much good I did."

Jackie put a hand on his shoulder. "Those boys are going to be alright. Drake is getting good care in the infirmary, no one is going to do anything with Tanner without your approval, and you have time to come up with a new plan for Alexis." Jackie checked her watch. "I've got to go, but I'll let you know if I hear anything else."

"Jackie?"

She looked back. "Yes?"

"Thanks."

SEVENTEEN

"So do I get a costume?"

Noah raised an eyebrow. "A costume?"

"Yeah." Alexis shrugged playfully. "You know, a costume like all superheroes get to wear. Maybe a unitard with my initials on the front, or a piece of fabric across my eyes that somehow conceals my identity."

"Oh. Right. A cape, too." Noah set a cantaloupe on top of a steel crate. "Okay, try to aim at this . . . but wait until I'm out of the way."

"Aim? How am I supposed to aim? I can barely see in this thing."

With a chuckle, Noah walked across the command station and tapped his finger on the thick welding mask Alexis wore. Then he put on a mask of his own. "These are only precautionary, until you've got things under control." He motioned toward the cantaloupe. "Alright. Give it a shot. Uh, no pun intended."

Stretching out her fingers, Alexis faced the cantaloupe that rested on the crate several feet in front of them. She had no idea what to do.

"Just try," Noah prompted again.

Alexis held her arms out in front of her, waiting. But after a while, she dropped her arms to her sides. "I don't know how to make a light attack happen. They've been occurring on their own."

"Hmm." Noah tipped his head thoughtfully. "I guess looking at a cantaloupe doesn't quite generate the same fearful response in your body as when your life is in danger, does it?"

"Um, no. Not quite."

"So maybe you have to somehow simulate fearful emotions in your mind. Try to make yourself feel the way that you did when you were able to generate a light attack."

Alexis pushed her mask up slightly. "Huh?"

Noah took his mask off completely and ruffled his hair. "I was giving it some thought after I got you home this morning. I think that—"

"You were supposed to sleep after you got me home this morning." Alexis narrowed her eyes. "You haven't been up this entire time, have you?"

"Not the entire time."

"Noah, seriously, I appreciate all you did to prepare, but you also need sleep and—"

"Anyway, I had this thought," he interrupted. "This morning, you really had to concentrate to get my bed down when it was floating in the air. So I bet you have to channel even more concentration into generating a light attack. You'll really have to focus, even if it requires creating some tough emotions in your head."

"Tough emotions," Alexis echoed. "Got it."

She put her mask into place and saw Noah hurriedly do the same. Shaking out her arms, Alexis peered at her target once more.

*Okay. That isn't a cantaloupe. That is someone
with evil, red eyes.*

The terrifying images of the operative hiding
outside Mr. Haber's classroom flashed through
Alexis's mind, and she felt her throat tighten. Glaring
at the fruit, she kept talking to herself.

*That's an operative who wants to kidnap me. The
operative even wants to hurt my friends.*

Alexis's heart punched her chest as she
recalled being dragged away from football game.
Then her hands began to burn.

It's an operative who's holding Tanner captive.

Her palms throbbing, Alexis instinctively held
out her arms toward the target and braced herself.

"You can do it, Alexis," she heard Noah say.

*Noah. Noah's parents were murdered. Operatives
tried to hurt Noah last night. They could have killed him.*

A rush of furious energy shot down Alexis's
arms, which was followed by a blast of bright white
light from her hands. Alexis let out a cry as the force
knocked her flat on her back. She heard the clatter of
metal and a splat.

"Ouch," Alexis muttered, sliding the mask off
and staring up at the color-filled glass tubes that hung
from the ceiling.

"Are you okay?" Noah crouched down near
her, his mask askew.

"Yep." Alexis sat up and looked down range.
She saw splattered cantaloupe dripping down the wall
and a large scorch mark on the tipped-over crate.
"Your idea worked, Noah."

He sat beside her and admired the mess. "Yeah, whatever you thought about definitely got your emotions churning."

Alexis did not reply.

Noah's expression changed. "Hey, I understand. Like I said before, we'll get him back safely."

"What?"

"We'll get Tanner back for you." Noah stood up a little too quickly. "I'll go set up another one."

Before Alexis could say anything else, Noah had grabbed an orange from a pile of fruit in the corner and started to set up the next target. Alexis watched in silence while emotions that made her feel far too vulnerable rose close to the surface of her heart.

Don't be stupid, she chided herself. *I can't tell him how I feel—I don't even know how I feel. I'd embarrass myself, and Noah would never want to talk to me again.*

Remaining on the floor, Alexis pulled her knees to her chest, observing Noah as he worked. At times, she thought she glimpsed something like pain buried beneath his aloof expression, which made her recognize that there was one thing she did want to say to him. She got to her feet.

"Noah, I want you to know that I'm sorry about your parents. I can't imagine how . . . I'm really sorry."

Noah stopped what he was doing. Time passed before he replied. "Doctor Gaige killed my Dad in a battle ten years ago. I was told he died in a car accident. When my mom died two years ago, people said it was from a heart attack. She was only fifty-five."

Alexis said nothing, waiting. Noah looked her way and continued:

"In my parents' will, it said that Ben was to become my legal guardian should anything happen to them. After I moved in with Ben, he told me about The Organization, Doctor Gaige, the truth of my dad's death, and that my mother had died protecting something Doctor Gaige wanted. That's when I joined The Organization. I'm going to fight Doctor Gaige one day."

"So that's why you're Mister Haber's T.A.?" Alexis dared ask. "And why you were his T.A. last year, too?"

"Yeah, I do mostly homeschooling, so I'm ahead. But as a registered student, I'm still able to work as Ben's T.A. and . . . wait a second, how do you know what I did last year?" Noah peered quizzically at her. "You were in eighth grade at the time. You were still attending middle school."

Alexis blushed. "People talk about you."

"Ah, I see. People are still talking about the weird T.A., huh?

"No! People talk about you in a good way!" Alexis rushed to clarify. "Don't you know that there lots of girls at school who have crushes on you? They call you mysterious and hot and . . ." Alexis's voice faded when she saw the strange way that Noah had begun watching her. She cleared her throat. "Um, but that's not what I think about you, of course. I think you're a science nerd and . . . wait, that's not what I meant, either." Alexis could feel her face getting very warm. "What I mean to say is that I used to think you were a science nerd, but I don't think that anymore. Now I think that . . . I think that . . ."

Noah had not taken his eyes off her. "Now you think what?"

The conversation was interrupted by the sound of footsteps approaching. Then they heard Mr. Haber's voice:

"Noah? Miss Kendall? How is it going down here?"

Mr. Haber emerged from the maze of shelves, peered around, and continued:

"From the noise I heard upstairs in the supply closet, I am guessing that you two are making progress down here?"

Noah coughed.

Alexis hastily motioned to the wall. "I blew up a cantaloupe. And Noah's been helping me get better at making stuff move with my mind, too. Watch this." Alexis put her eyes on an apple that was resting on the ground. *Slide to the right.*

The apple began rolling across the floor, precisely as Alexis had intended.

"Incredible," Mr. Haber remarked with genuine awe. "Truly incredible."

"Thanks. I think I'm getting pretty good." Alexis smiled proudly. "I could fight an operative."

Noah spun around. "You think you're that good? Then move me."

"What?"

"Move me," Noah repeated sharply. "Make me slide five feet forward."

Alexis blinked. "Is this some sort of challenge?"

"Yes. It's a challenge."

"Fine. Challenge accepted."

Noah kept watching her and said nothing.

Alexis widened her stance, clenching her jaw with determination. *Slide Noah forward. Slide him five feet forward right now.*

Noah did not move.

Alexis shut her eyes and tried again. *Noah needs to move. Move him toward me.*

Alexis opened her eyes. Noah remained in the same place, still watching her with a look that was infuriating.

"Okay, okay. You win, Noah," Alexis snapped. "I'm not as good as I thought."

Noah relented. "Winning is not my point."

"Really? You could have fooled me."

"Really. My point is that I want you to know— I want us all to know— your limitations. The stakes are too high for you to get in over your head. Frankly, the thought of you having to fight makes me . . ." Noah trailed off and looked away.

Alexis's bitterness melted. "I'll be okay."

Noah gave her a slight nod but said nothing.

It was a while before Alexis spoke again. "I don't understand, though. I made myself get down the first time I was floating in my bedroom—at least, I think I did. But I couldn't make Noah move. I haven't intentionally controlled anyone since that first morning, come to think of it. I wonder why?"

"I do not think we can say." Mr. Haber seemed similarly bewildered. "Perhaps your ability to move people is not as refined or reliable as your ability to move objects. Perhaps it is a skill you have yet to develop, or perhaps you never will. Only time will tell."

"Which is all the more reason to keep working on perfecting the skills that we do know you have," Noah stated. He walked to Mr. Haber and handed him an extra mask. Then he addressed Alexis while motioning to the orange on the crate. "The orange is obviously a smaller target, but I think you can do it."

Alexis heard the return of the unemotional tone to Noah's voice and, for some reason, became extremely irritated.

Noah wants to know what I think of him? He wants to know? Well, tough! I don't know what I think!

Glaring, Alexis spun around and stared at the orange.

My feelings were totally sorted out until Noah came along and started messing things up! This is his fault! He—

The orange unexpectedly popped up into the air and flew like a bullet directly at Noah's head. With a shout of surprise, Noah ducked. The orange sailed over him and smashed into the wall. As the sound from the impact echoed away, Noah cautiously stood back up.

"Oops," said Alexis.

"That was interesting, Miss Kendall." Mr. Haber's eyes were large. "You made that orange attack Noah just by thinking about it?"

Alexis lifted her mask. "I wasn't trying to make it attack Noah. Not exactly, anyway."

Noah glanced at her.

"But I really do think I'm getting the hang of it. Watch." Alexis put her mask down and zeroed in on the smashed orange. *Go back to the crate. Oh, and don't do anything to Noah.*

The dripping remnants of the orange rose up from the floor, floated across the room, and settled on top of the crate. Satisfied, Alexis steadied her footing and closed her eyes.

Doctor Gaige wants to hurt my friends. He wants to hurt me. In fact, operatives are probably plotting how to kidnap me right now.

Alexis felt a familiar burning in her arms moments before a blast of white light flew from her hands and collided into the already-splattered fruit.

"Well done." Mr. Haber applauded. "Very well done, Miss Kendall."

"Yeah, your aim was perfect. You hit the orange, and I don't think the crate was even touched." Noah went closer to inspect the damage.

Alexis pulled off her mask and shook out her hair. "So what's the plan from here?"

"I'm sort of making this up as we go along," Noah admitted. "But for now, I can't think of anything more important than continuing to help you learn how to protect yourself."

"Agreed," Mr. Haber stated. "Meanwhile, I am coordinating with Headquarters for a Monday evening meeting. We will leave after school."

Alexis did not hide her disappointment. "Monday evening? That's over twenty-four hours away."

"We are moving as fast as we can," Mr. Haber counseled. "Taking a little time to establish a good plan is better than rushing in without a plan at all."

Alexis sighed and started to nod. But a new thought struck her. "Mister Haber, you said before that a reason you didn't want me hidden away was because of what would happen if someone reported me as missing—the police, searches, operatives hiding in the chaos, and all that. So what if someone reports that Drake and Tanner are missing? Won't the same thing happen?"

"It already has."

"What?" Alexis realized that, since the bonfire party, she had been completely unaware of what was happening in the outside world.

"Yes, it is as we feared." Mr. Haber motioned past her. "Come with me and see."

Stunned, Alexis set down her mask and trailed Mr. Haber and Noah through the rest of the shelves to the command station. Every monitor was on. Alexis anxiously set her attention on one monitor and fell quiet upon finding herself watching a news report of police officers with search dogs scouring the scene of the bonfire party. She shuddered and checked another monitor; it was playing footage of volunteers gathering in the canyon to look for Tanner and Drake. Frantic, Alexis scanned the rest of the screens only to be met by a barrage of videos showing crying family members, flowers and candles being placed near the canyon's entrance, and law enforcement personnel giving press conferences to reporters. Alexis also started catching pieces of what news reporters were saying:

". . . were at a party last night. When neither of them returned home, their parents contacted authorities."

"Searches of the canyon are currently underway. The FBI is expected to be arriving soon . . ."

". . . those interested in volunteering to help can sign up at the community church . . ."

". . . we expect the police to be making regular announcements, updating the public."

Alexis finally had to turn away.

"This is why we have to be very careful," Mr. Haber told her. "With the chaos that has ensued since Tanner and Drake were declared missing, our ability to quickly identify operatives in this area is going to be greatly hampered."

"I don't believe it." Alexis wrung her hands. "Why didn't anybody call to tell me?"

She pulled her phone from her pocket. It was still on mute, the way she had left it after she returned home that morning and went to sleep. There were several new voicemails waiting. With a gulp, Alexis pushed a button to listen.

"Lex, it's me," came Molly's frightened voice. "It's about nine-thirty on Sunday morning. Have you seen the news about Tanner and Drake? It's awful. Why didn't you come to sleep at my house after the party last night? Did you go home, instead?"

Alexis bit her lip, waiting for the next voicemail.

"Lex, it's me again. It's about noon. Where are you? Please call. I need to know that you're okay."

The third message played:

"Lex, it's about one o' clock in the afternoon. I called your mom. She told me that you got home this morning and you've been sleeping since. She still thinks that you were at a birthday party and then spent the night at my house. Lex, what really happened? Where did you go when you left the bonfire? Were you out with the guys all night?"

Yet another message, left only minutes before, played in Alexis's ear:

"Lex, I called your mom again. She said that you just had her drive you to the school for an extra cheer practice. She asked why I wasn't at cheer practice, too. I didn't know what to say! Cheer practice? On a Sunday? Anyway, your mom realized that you had lied, and she's driving to the school now to find you. She's really worried, and I am, too. Where are you? What's going on? Call me ASAP."

Alexis put the phone down, not even wanting to hear the next voicemail, which she knew would be from her mother.

"This is bad," Alexis announced. "My mom figured out that there wasn't really a cheer practice here at the school today. Now both she and Molly are worried. Not to mention, Molly is wondering where I went last night."

Mr. Haber did not seem concerned. "This can be easily fixed. Call your mother and explain that you were mistaken. You thought there was an extra cheer practice today, but after you got to the school, you discovered that you were wrong."

"But use this to make the call. It's not traceable." Noah held out his device to her. "There's no doubt The Domanorith have the entire area under close surveillance. The last thing you want to do is allow an operative to track your cell phone activity. The only place your regular phone can't be tracked is at Headquarters. So keep your phone off unless you're at Headquarters or it's an absolute emergency."

Alexis hastily turned off her phone and took Noah's device from his hand. "But what do I tell Molly?"

Mr. Haber remained unruffled. "Tell Molly that after you got off the phone with her at the party last night, you could not find Tanner or Drake. Since Molly had already left with her brother, you got a ride home with someone else."

Alexis peered at Mr. Haber. "How come you're so good at making up excuses?"

"Because I have been trained by the very best, Miss Kendall," he replied with a smile. "Remember, I teach high school students for a living."

EIGHTEEN

"Now that the paralytic has completely worn off, we're letting the sedatives metabolize out of his system," the doctor explained. "It will take time before he's fully lucid, but he is making steady progress."

"How long do you estimate it will take for the sedatives to clear?" Xander asked, watching as Tanner stirred.

"Another twelve to twenty-four hours. Please forgive me for asking, Xander, but you are Head of Intelligence. Why do you have such an interest in the medical condition of this boy?"

Xander stood up straight. "He was injured during one of our operations. I monitor all civilian casualties."

"I understand. I will certainly keep you posted on any developments."

"Thank you."

The doctor stepped from the room. While Tanner fell back into a medicated sleep, Xander leaned down and spoke in his ear:

"Tanner, you're going to be alright. I'm going to make sure of that."

***

Marcus groaned. "Great. We're being invaded."

Alexis stared through the car window, astounded. The scene in front of their high school looked like something out of a movie. Police cars with lights flashing lined the road. News vans were parked across the street while reporters and camera operators set up nearby. Bystanders clustered together along the sidewalk, many of them talking to reporters, crying, and holding posters that displayed pictures of Tanner and Drake. Yellow tape kept the crowds from advancing while law enforcement personnel directed students past the chaos and into the school.

"This is horrible," Molly whimpered.

"It's ridiculous. They're turning this place into a circus," Marcus muttered, maneuvering the car into the parking lot. When he brought the car to a stop, he pulled the keys from the ignition and turned to the girls. "Look, a lot of people know that you had a connection with Tanner and Drake. So stay away from anyone asking questions or who suddenly wants to be your friend. Lay low until this blows over. Okay?"

Molly twirled her hair thoughtfully. "But isn't it weird that we were some of the last people who saw them? No one has any idea what happened to them after the bonfire party. Doesn't that creep you out a little bit?"

Alexis cringed.

"It is weird, Mol. Really weird." Marcus sighed. "But weird or not, it doesn't make you more involved than anyone else. So don't let idiots who are desperate to get on television drag you into something."

Molly shrugged in apparent agreement and got out of the car.

Alexis slowly climbed out after her, feeling sick. *No one has a clue what happened to Tanner or Drake. But I do. I know, yet I can't tell anyone. And would anyone believe me even if I did try to explain?*

Alexis and Molly parted ways with Marcus and entered the school together. Inside, the atmosphere was completely different than the Friday before. A tense stillness had settled over everything. Teachers stood somberly outside their classrooms. Students passed one another with looks of confusion and fear on their faces.

"I'll see you in algebra, okay?" Molly's voice quavered as she walked off.

"Alright," Alexis softly called after her. "I'll see you soon."

Shivering, Alexis turned and went the other direction toward Mr. Haber's room. As she rounded the corner, she halted. A man and a woman in police uniforms stood outside the door, talking to a man who had 'FBI' written in yellow lettering on the back of his jacket. Alexis did her best to appear nonchalant as she proceeded past them and went inside.

"Hi, Alexis," Julia greeted her as she took a seat. "How are you doing?"

Alexis put her bag down. "I'm alright. What about you?"

"I'm awful. This is all so sad."

Sam reached out and gave Julia a pat on the arm. Then he leaned forward and addressed Alexis. "Did you see those three goons outside? I heard they're here to conduct interviews of teachers and students today."

Before Alexis could answer, Mr. Haber stepped in from the hall. Everyone stopped what they were doing, waiting as Mr. Haber walked to the podium and laid out his things. He raised his head, looked out over the class, and addressed them:

"Good morning. As you undoubtedly know, today is going to be rather difficult as we grapple with our concerns regarding Mister Tanner Ricks and Mister Drake Spencer. I . . ."

While Mr. Haber spoke, Alexis heard a sound from the back of the room. She peeked over her shoulder. Noah had come out of the supply closet and taken an empty seat. Wearing earbuds and looking straight ahead, Noah did not seem to notice her. Alexis faced forward again.

". . . modifying our schedule today," Mr. Haber was saying, "since I am sure that many of you did not do your homework over the weekend due to the news."

No. Please no.

Alexis gasped when a recognizable, terrifying coldness took over her body. She immediately checked out the windows but saw nothing.

"I have been informed that there will be brief interruptions in all classes by law enforcement today," Mr. Haber went on. "This will be quite disruptive, but do your best. We will use today as a study hall so you can do the homework that . . ."

Fear expanding within her, Alexis rubbed her aching palms against her jeans, desperately trying to figure out what to do.

How can I warn Mister Haber and Noah without blowing their cover?

The classroom door was opened once again, and the male police officer whom Alexis had seen in the hallway poked his head inside.

"'Scuse me, are you Ben Haber?"

Mr. Haber tipped his head curtly. "I am."

"I apologize for the interruption. My name's Officer McGlashan. Wonderin' if we might start our interviews for the day in here. We'll be as quick as we can."

Mr. Haber did not hide his annoyance. "Not at all."

Officer McGlashan stepped into the room. "Good mornin', everyone. You'll be seein' us around campus today because we need your help. We'd like to chat with anyone who was at the bonfire party on Saturday night or who might have other information 'bout Tanner Ricks or Drake Spencer." He motioned to the supply closet. "We'll hang out in there, so as not to be too disruptive. If anyone has somethin' to tell us, even if you don't think it's important, come on over and chat."

Officer McGlashan began making his way toward the back of the classroom, motioning for the other law enforcement personnel who had remained in the hallway to join him.

"Students, if anyone would like to speak with our visitors, please do so one at a time," Mr. Haber added succinctly. "Otherwise, begin your homework. As always, let Noah or myself know if you have any questions."

"Or ask Alexis," Sam whispered. "She's like having a personal tutor."

Alexis forced a laugh, though she was barely able to open her textbook because of the way her hands shook. The alarm coursing through her was still increasing. She needed a plan.

"Geez, what's with the entire posse coming in here?" Sam mumbled, glancing up from his homework. "Why do they need two cops and two FBI agents in one classroom?"

It took a second before Alexis processed what Sam said. "Did you say two FBI agents?"

Sam continued working. "Yeah. They just went into the supply closet."

Alexis felt her mouth go dry. *There was only one FBI agent in the hallway before class started.*

Leaning out to get a better view, Alexis peered through the open door of the supply closet. She observed Officer McGlashan and the female police officer conversing casually. The FBI agent she had seen earlier was strolling back and forth while making a phone call. A fourth person, another man who was also wearing an FBI jacket, was standing with his back to the others and examining the contents of one of the bookcases. Alexis's stomach lurched.

An operative is here.

Her eyes leapt to Mr. Haber, who was walking between students' desks and answering questions. Shifting her position, Alexis cleared her throat loudly in the hopes of catching Noah's attention. But Noah continued setting up an experiment. Finally, she blurted out:

"Mister Haber, may I please use the bathroom?"

"Hmm?" Mr. Haber did not even look up from the assignment that he was reviewing. "Oh, yes. Certainly, Miss Kendall."

Noah cast Alexis a pointed glance. For Alexis, it was enough. She knew that they had understood her meaning.

Alexis slid back from her desk. At the same time, Noah causally began walking toward the front of the room, taking a path that would bring him by her. When Noah got close, Alexis brushed her elbow against her chemistry homework, causing the paper to fall to the floor.

"I'll get that," Noah mumbled with convincing aloofness.

He bent down, grabbed the paper, and gave it to Alexis. As he did so, Noah slipped her the shimmering key for the bathroom closet.

"Thanks." Alexis set the paper on her desk while tucking the key under her shirt cuff.

Noah continued past. Alexis got up and left the room. Hurrying as fast as she dared, she went to the first floor bathroom. She found the 'OUT OF ORDER' sign on the door, as usual. After a check behind her, Alexis entered the bathroom, surveyed the scene, and secured the lock.

"Sorry, Ralph, you're about to get notified that the rats in the ceiling have returned," Alexis said aloud while using the key to open the closet.

Moving fast, Alexis hefted the ladder out from the closet and placed it near the sink. She climbed up the rungs until she could push the marked ceiling panel out of place, and then she boosted herself into the dusty crawl space above.

Here we go again.

Holding back a sneeze, Alexis began creeping on hands and knees through the darkness, doing her best to guess her way toward Mr. Haber's supply closet. She heard Ms. Hinshaw lecturing her biology class as she passed over. Once Alexis reached what she believed to be her target, she lowered herself onto her stomach and pressed her ear against the ceiling panel. Alexis could hear people walking in the supply closet below and faint sounds from Mr. Haber's classroom in the background.

"You guys okay with continuin' in here while my partner and I go chat with the teacher?" came Officer McGlashan's recognizable drawl.

"Sure," was another man's reply.

Two sets of footsteps passed under Alexis and faded away. Someone coughed. Then there was silence.

I need to see what's going on down there.

Alexis pried her fingers under the edge of a ceiling panel beside her, sliding it just enough to create a gap to watch through.

"Hey, I can stay in here if you want to go join the two cops," stated a man with a smooth voice. "It might speed things up if you give them some assistance."

The FBI agent whom Alexis had seen earlier in the hall walked into her view. "Good idea. At the rate we're going, we'll be here all day. What's your name, anyway? I don't think we've ever been on assignment together."

"Kevin," replied the man with the smooth voice whom Alexis still could not see. "I recently transferred here from another office."

"Welcome. I'm Tony," the FBI agent replied. "Anyway, I'll head out to help the police while you stay here in case any more students want to chat. And while you're at it, maybe you'll find some really valuable evidence among these old textbooks, eh?"

"I certainly might," Kevin replied.

Alexis was sliding herself forward for a better look when the man named Kevin stepped directly beneath her and paused. Alexis held her breath, watching as tiny flecks of dust and white paint from the ceiling crumbled down onto the shoulder of his jacket. After several seconds, Kevin continued past and was soon again out of view.

New footsteps entered the supply closet.

"Yo. Mr. Haber wanted me to ask if I could get you anything."

Alexis almost giggled. *Was that Noah? Did he just say 'yo'?*

"Nah. Thanks, kid. I should be out of here in a minute or two."

"Whatever," Noah replied before he walked away.

Alexis inched forward. Through the tiny opening in the ceiling, she spotted Kevin walking past the bookcases and examining them carefully. Alexis bit her lip.

He's getting too close to the entrance of the command station. I need to create a distraction.

Her eyes darted around the room, stopping when she noted the fire sprinklers.

Perfect. Let's make it rain.

She closed her eyes and concentrated.

"Hey! What in the . . ?"

Kevin threw his arms over his head, shielding himself from the water that had started pouring on top of him. Meanwhile, in the main classroom, students shrieked in surprise at the unexpected shower. As the water continued falling, Kevin let out an exasperated grunt and dashed from the supply closet. Once he was gone, Alexis replaced the ceiling panel and hustled to the opening above the bathroom. She spun onto her stomach and dropped her foot down onto the ladder. Someone grabbed her by the ankle.

"I received another call from Ms. Hinshaw about rodents above her classroom," a familiar voice remarked. "I figured that I might find you here."

Alexis looked below. Ralph was grinning up at her.

"Geez, you scared me!" she exclaimed, climbing down. "There's an operative in Mister Haber's room right now. I—"

Ralph's walkie-talkie squawked. "Ralph, the fire sprinklers were triggered in Ben Haber's classroom. There's no evidence of any fire. Must be a malfunction. Do you mind seeing if you can shut them off?"

"I'll head there right now," Ralph answered and then hooked his walkie-talkie onto his belt. "You should get going, Alexis. I'll clean this up."

With an appreciative smile, Alexis exited and jogged toward Mr. Haber's room. As she turned the corner, she was met by the sight of her drenched classmates evacuating into the hallway. Meanwhile, teachers and students from other classes were coming out to see the cause of the commotion.

Alexis shoved through the fray until she could see into Mr. Haber's room. Water continued cascading down from the sprinklers. The last students were making their way out when one girl slipped and fell, pulling the others down with her amid bursts of laughter. As Mr. Haber went to assist them, Alexis charged in and made a show of also helping the girls to their feet. While she did so, Alexis leaned in and whispered to Mr. Haber:

"The tallest guy was not a real FBI agent."

Mr. Haber gave her a single, slight nod.

"Well, Mister Haber, we'll be clearin' out." Officer McGlashan splashed across the room, wiping water off his face. "Appreciate you takin' the time to chat with us. Nothin' like a little indoor rain to make a Monday mornin' even more exciting, eh?" He turned to the other police officer and Tony. "Time to move on to drier pastures."

"Where'd Kevin go?" Tony peered around in confusion.

Office McGlashan shrugged. "Thought he was with you."

"Nope." Tony shook his head. "He stayed in the supply closet when I came out here."

Officer McGlashan laughed and moved for the door. "Land's sake! You guys come into a room with four walls and still manage to get lost!"

"But we would have seen him go . . ." Tony's voice trailed off as he departed with the others.

"Miss Kendall, please go join the other students. Noah and I will be right behind you," Mr. Haber told her.

Dripping wet, Alexis returned to the hall to wait with the rest of her class. Before long, Ralph strolled upon the scene with a mop in his hand. When he reached the classroom door, he chuckled and said:

"My, my, what on earth could have happened here?"

He gave Alexis a wink before stepping into the room.

NINETEEN

"Xander, when are you going to get some sleep?"

Xander spun around. He was so focused on his computer that he had not noticed Jackie enter his office. He coughed and gestured to the monitor.

"As soon I finish this."

Jackie came closer. "What are you doing?"

"Reviewing the video that our first operative obtained while undercover at the high school today. Kevin managed to record a lot with his lapel camera, though much of it is distorted."

"Really? Can I watch?"

Xander almost hesitated. "If you want."

Jackie walked around the desk to get a view of Xander's computer. The video was paused on a frame of a tall young man who wore a baseball hat.

"I recognize him," Jackie stated. "He's the boy who helped Alexis when Victor attempted the light attack, right?"

"I believe so."

Xander pushed a button on his computer mouse, and the video resumed playing:

"Yo. Mr. Haber wanted me to ask if I could get you anything," the young man had said to Kevin.

After Kevin responded, the young man glanced at the ceiling and walked away. Then the video paused, and the same clip played again.

"Hmm. Not sure why that segment is on loop." Xander made a few clicks on his keyboard. "I guess I really am getting tired. I'll start the footage from the beginning."

Jackie gave Xander a pat on the shoulder and resumed watching the monitor. After a few seconds of black, the video began. It showed Kevin's perspective when he had approached two police officers and an FBI agent who were standing outside a classroom. After some conversation, Kevin followed the others through the door. As Kevin passed a row of desks where students were working, the video became more distorted.

"Alexis was in there, wasn't she?" Jackie's eyes scoured the monitor. "Could you see her at all, or was the picture too messed up?"

"Too messed up. Alexis must have been close for the distortion to be this bad."

The footage cleared enough to show Kevin standing with the others in a large supply closet.

Jackie leaned forward. "What was Kevin doing in there?"

"Trying to spot anything that will help us figure out who the Protector is at that school. I'm taking advantage of all the chaos around campus by stationing undercover operatives there throughout the day."

"Then what?"

"Then, hopefully, I'll know who works for the other side. With our options for getting Alexis being eliminated one by one, I may have no choice but to contact someone to negotiate."

Jackie pointed to the screen. "There she is."

The footage cleared again, showing that Kevin was hiding in bushes outside the classroom, similar to what Victor had done days before. There were now drops of water were on the lens of Kevin's lapel camera. Through the windows, Alexis could be seen. She and the teacher were helping other students off the floor.

"What on earth happened? It looks like it's raining in there!" Jackie exclaimed.

"The fire sprinklers went off."

Jackie laughed and resumed watching the video. The police officers and FBI agent spoke with the teacher before leaving the room. Alexis exited, too. The young man with the baseball hat went to the teacher's side as a janitor walked in. The footage faded to black.

Xander shut the video off.

Jackie leaned against the desk. "So what do you make of all that?"

"Not much on its own." Xander ran a hand through his hair. "Especially since we already saw that room when Victor was there previously. But what will help is comparing this footage with what comes in from the other operatives over the rest of the day. We'll see if anyone acts atypically toward Alexis or if something unusual happens—"

"More unusual than an indoor rainstorm, you mean," Jackie joked.

"Yes. More unusual than that."

Jackie studied Xander for a moment. "I should let you rest. Our next meeting isn't for several hours. Get some sleep. I'll let you know if there are any updates from the school or the infirmary."

Jackie slipped out and shut the door. Once he was alone, Xander breathed out and looked again at his computer.

The fire department never came to the school, which means that the fire alarm didn't go off. Something—or someone—else triggered those sprinklers. On purpose.

***

"Hey, girl-ie!"

Crystal Lark eagerly sat down next to Alexis and displayed her plastic smile.

"Um, hi, Crystal," Alexis replied, casting a questioning look across the cafeteria table at Molly, who only shrugged in return.

"Isn't this the saddest thing about Tanner and Drake?" Crystal began setting out her lunch. "By the way, I've got a great new move for our routine. I'm super excited for cheer practice after school today!"

"Fabulous," Molly remarked dryly.

Alexis began snickering but stopped. *Cheer practice. Cheer practice is after school today, but I'm supposed to go to Headquarters. What am I going to tell Molly? Another lie?*

"Can you girls get over all the television crews around campus?" Crystal munched on a celery stick. "How many interviews did you do?"

Alexis snapped to attention. "Interviews? You mean, with news reporters? None."

"Real-ly?" Crystal emphasized. "Hmm. I'm sure the reporters didn't see you, or they would have asked. I mean, you'd probably look okay on camera."

Alexis peered at Crystal. "How many interviews did you do?"

"Four." She sat up proudly. "I happened to be walking past the news crews this morning and—"

"You happened to be walking past? You happened to be walking down the road right where the news crews were stationed?" Molly interrupted.

Crystal tossed her hair. "Mmm-hmm. One of the reporters asked if I knew Tanner or Drake, and I obviously said yes. I mean, Tanner and I are, like, practically almost dating. Once I mentioned that, everyone wanted to interview me."

"Really. You and Tanner are practically almost dating." Molly pursed her lips. "Tell me, were you at the bonfire party on Saturday? I didn't see you there, but Tanner seemed to be having a great time dancing with Alexis."

Crystal's eyes narrowed. "Tanner is always nice to spend time with anyone who's lonely." She let out flippant laugh and propped her chin in her hand. "But tell me more about the party. What was Tanner saying and doing? How was he acting? I mean, if you saw him right before he disappeared, maybe you noticed something unusual?"

"Tanner was fine," Molly snapped. "So was Drake. In fact, we were—"

"Why do you ask, Crystal?" Alexis cut in.

Crystal smiled again. "I'm just wondering."

***

"That's all he got?" Leslie scoffed. "A few seconds of video footage showing the girl going into her history classroom?"

"Our operative had to change his cover at the last minute because the real school janitor was nearby," Xander spoke bluntly. "Unfortunately, posing as a parent who was searching for the school office proved to be more limiting in terms of where he could go and still be believable. Remember, all operatives are under strict orders to be observing and data-gathering only. Nothing more."

"A fine effort, given the circumstances," Jacob declared. "So will there be any more information coming in from the high school today?"

"Yes." Xander shut the computer off. "There's an operative watching Alexis in her sixth period class as we speak. Another operative is set to monitor her at cheer practice after school."

"With the end goal of all this surveillance being what?" Daria questioned. "What's the objective?"

Xander replied carefully, "The objective is to determine who the Protector is at that school. It's vital to know this before we try again to get Alexis."

Peter raised a hand. "Rather than all of this sneaking around, why don't we contact The

Organization and offer to hand the civilian boy over in exchange for the girl?"

Leslie retorted, "Even if we found a way to contact The Organization, there's no way that they would give over the girl—give over Number 407—for an unimportant teenage boy."

"We will offer nothing," Dr. Gaige cut in. "The boy is only our insurance plan, should we run into difficulties when we move to obtain the girl our way."

Xander remained quiet. He knew Doctor Gaige wanted him to react, and Xander was determined not to give him the satisfaction.

Dr. Gaige spoke directly to Xander. "What do you make of the fire sprinkler fiasco this morning?"

"What do you mean?" Xander spoke calmly.

"It seemed a bit odd, did it not?" Dr. Gaige noted in a pleasant tone. "Is it possible that it was a calculated deterrent? Is it possible that Kevin was getting too close to something that The Organization wanted to hide?"

Xander tipped his head politely. "The idea is being considered. However, there was nothing about the event to suggest that it was anything but an accident. Of course, I'm saying this before the analysis is completed, and I will update the group if something of note is discovered."

Dr. Gaige did not reply.

"Speaking of video footage, Xander, I have a question." Leslie did not temper her patronizing tone. "What about that footage from the battle in the forest the other night? Surely you must have finished reviewing it by now. Any leads?"

"Why yes, Leslie. Thank you for reminding me. I might have forgotten." Xander barely contained his sarcasm. "I first need to point out that the majority of the footage was useless due to massive distortion. However, after extensive video reconstruction, we discovered that Alexis once again generated her own light attack—"

Leslie cut him off, "And you feel it is important to tell us something we already know because . . ?"

Xander let his steel-gray eyes fall right on her. "Because Alexis's light attack was intentional, not simply reactionary. More importantly, it was more powerful than the attack that severely injured Victor. Therefore, we must conclude that Alexis's powers are getting stronger and she is learning how to use them. So yes, Leslie, I feel it important to tell you."

Leslie's mouth fell open in surprise. But her expression swiftly changed to a scowl, and she slumped back in her chair.

"This is important, indeed." Dr. Gaige motioned toward Jackie. "I assume you're working on some way to quantify the increasing strength of the girl's powers?"

Jackie nodded. "As we speak."

Dr. Gaige addressed Xander again. "So the next time we meet, can we expect to hear your new plan for getting the girl?"

"Yes, I will definitely have a plan," Xander replied.

TWENTY

"Police and FBI are continuing their exhaustive investigation into where the two young men may have gone, and volunteers from all over the region are assisting in daily search efforts. But so far, the boys' disappearance remains a mystery. Right now, we are waiting for an update from the police department's Public Information Officer. Until she arrives to provide her statement, let's watch more interviews of friends of the missing boys."

The news broadcast was suddenly shut off, and the monitor went dark. Noah tossed the remote control onto the couch beside him with a look of disgust.

"What are you doing?" Alexis objected. "Turn it back on."

"Why? It's not like the police will have anything helpful to say," Noah grumbled.

Alexis reached for the remote. "Well, if you don't mind, I would still like to see it."

"I do mind, as a matter of fact." Noah slid the remote out of her reach.

Alexis narrowed her eyes. "What's wrong with you, anyway? You've been like this ever since we left after school to come to Headquarters."

"It's none of your business." Noah got off the couch. "I'm going for a walk."

Alexis stood, too. "But we were told to wait here in The Lounge. Where are you—"

Noah stepped out and slammed the door.

Exhaling with frustration, Alexis dropped onto the couch, snatched up the remote, and hit the power button. When the news broadcast came back on, Alexis groaned: it was another replay of an interview Crystal had done that morning.

"Tanner and I were really close," Crystal was saying to the reporter, posing as if she stood on the red carpet. "We were talking about going to homecoming together this weekend and . . . I'm sorry, this is so hard for me." Crystal faced the camera, her eyes glistening with tears.

"I understand, dear," the reporter said in a voice dripping with sympathy.

Alexis heard footsteps coming down the hall, and she shut the monitor off again. Soon, there was a click as the lock on the door released, and then Dr. Caul entered The Lounge with Mr. Haber and Ralph.

"Hello, Alexis. I heard you had quite a morning," Dr. Caul greeted her.

"She sure did." Ralph smiled proudly. "Setting off those fire sprinklers was fast thinking on her part."

Dr. Caul nodded. "And how are your parents? How are you handling things with them today?"

"Mom and Dad are fine. They think I'm going to cheer practice and then to a friend's house to work on an assignment." Alexis sighed. "So far, I've been able to keep them from realizing that anything weird is going on . . . not that they'd believe the truth, anyway."

"Excellent." Mr. Haber adjusted his glasses. "And now that you and Noah are here, we . . . wait, where is Noah?"

Alexis shifted. "I, um, think he went for a walk."

"Odd." Mr. Haber reached for his device. "I will call him."

"Don't bother. I'm here," Noah announced sullenly from the doorway. He jammed his hands in his pockets and moved to the kitchen.

Dr. Caul watched him. "Noah, I understand that you're doing an excellent job training Alexis."

"Right," Noah said dryly. "And did you also hear what a lousy job I'm doing actually protecting her?"

Alexis went slack-jawed with surprise. "Noah, what on earth are you talking about?"

"I'm talking about the fact that an operative was able to get within a few feet of you in class this morning," he snapped.

"But that wasn't your fault." Alexis got back to her feet. "There were so many strangers around school today that—"

Noah faced her squarely. "Of course it was my fault. My job is to protect you, and I failed. How is that not my fault?"

Alexis had no idea what to say. She glanced at Mr. Haber for help.

"Miss Kendall is right. It was not your fault," Mr. Haber concurred. "This was a prime example of why we feared a missing child alert. There were too many unfamiliar people at school this morning. By the time our agents identified the operative, he had already infiltrated the classroom." Mr. Haber observed Noah for a few moments before speaking again. "You have more natural talent as a Protector than anyone I have ever worked with. And you are handling more responsibility than many of twice your age or experience. I sometimes forget that you are still in training. I am sorry that I ask more of you than I should."

Noah said nothing.

Alexis went to his side. "Noah, don't you realize how much you've done for me? You've saved my life. Not to mention, you've put yourself at risk, lost sleep, and almost been knocked out by a flying orange because of me. Thank you."

The hard line of Noah's jaw softened. "You're welcome, Alexis."

Alexis wanted to say more. But afraid of revealing how she felt, she instead turned away and returned to the couch. Dr. Caul looked between them before sitting nearby. Mr. Haber also took a chair, keeping an eye on Noah, who finally came over and sat by Alexis.

"Alexis, I have a question for you." Dr. Caul changed the subject, still pensive. "This morning, you were able to sense that an operative was in the classroom before our agents indentified him. How did you do that?"

Alexis shrugged. "For some reason, every time an operative gets close, I get this really horrible feeling."

"Every time?" Dr. Caul glanced at Mr. Haber.

"Every time," Alexis repeated.

Dr. Caul breathed in deeply. "That is interesting."

"I've also noticed that the operatives' eyes turn red," Alexis added. "It's creepy. Why does that happen?"

"That is something we don't understand for sure," Dr. Caul acknowledged. "However, we think that . . . well, have you noticed anything interesting about our magtros?"

Alexis snickered. "Your what?"

"Our magtros." Mr. Haber held up his device.

"Oh, is that what they're called?" Alexis let a smile spread across her face. "Hmm. Let's see. Other than the fact that they're apparently a phone, GPS unit, computer, walkie-talkie, and gun that shoots colored lights to kill people, no, I haven't noticed anything interesting about your magtros."

Noah ducked his head, his shoulders shaking with silent laughter.

Dr. Caul was smiling, too. "Good point. Let me explain where I was going with that. You see, magtros provide several options for deterring an assailant, a few of which you have unfortunately already had to witness. What you may or may not have noticed is that each agent's magtro fires a unique color."

"Royal blue," Alexis thought aloud, peering at Noah. She next motioned to Mr. Haber. "And yours is yellow."

"Right," Mr. Haber said. "The interesting part is that we agents do not choose our magtro's color. The color, one could say, chooses us. It is based on genetics."

"But the weapons that the operatives use always fire red," Alexis noted.

Dr. Caul responded, "Exactly. We don't know why. Perhaps their weapons—their telrons, as they call them—do not require any genetic link. However, given the red eyes that you have seen, it is troubling."

Before Alexis could say more, there was a click from the door, which swung open. Albert Oppenhall rushed in.

"I apologize for the interruption, but I felt it important to show you something that we recorded off the national news just now," he announced, turning on one of the monitors.

The news broadcast promptly began, showing a female reporter standing in front of the high school with a group of onlookers nearby. When the camera shot widened, Alexis's stomach dropped: Crystal and Molly were at the reporter's side.

"With me are two brave young women who have been dealing with this tragedy on a particularly personal level," the reporter stated dramatically. "Crystal and Molly, please tell us how you know Tanner and Drake."

Crystal pushed herself close to the microphone. "I'm Tanner's girlfriend, and Molly is Drake's girlfriend. The four of us are, like, best friends."

Alexis gaped. *Best friends?*

The reporter continued, "Molly, we understand that you and another friend, Alexis Kendall, were with the boys on the night they disappeared. What can you tell us about that?"

Molly's posture was stiff. "Well, Alexis was with Tanner, and I was with Drake. We were—"

"But Tanner is actually my boyfriend," Crystal emphasized.

The reporter pulled the microphone out of Crystal's reach. "Molly, please go on."

"I said goodnight to Drake and went home." Molly peeked nervously at the camera. "The next morning, I heard that he was missing."

"But what about Alexis Kendall?" the reporter pressed, sounding hurried.

Molly blinked. "She told me that she couldn't find him, and so she got a ride home with someone else."

"Really?" The reporter went on in a way that seemed abrupt. "Alexis Kendall wasn't concerned that she couldn't find Tanner?"

Crystal shoved her face into the shot. "I would have known that something was wrong. Tanner and I were so close that I could tell whenever—"

"So where is Alexis Kendall now?" demanded the reporter.

"We don't know." Crystal was gloating. "She should have been at cheer practice this afternoon, but she never showed up. Alexis is not exactly a team player, if you know what I mean."

The reporter's expression fell. "So you have no idea where Alexis Kendall is now?"

"No," Molly replied, her voice barely audible.

"I see. Thank you, ladies." The reporter turned coldly to the camera. "Back to you."

The footage ended, paused on the final frame.

Alexis was sick with shock. *I forgot to tell Molly that I wasn't going to be at cheer practice, so now she's best friends with Crystal and insulting me on the national news?*

Albert straightened his jacket. "Again, I apologize for the interruption. But given the increased publicity this will surely draw to Alexis, I felt you would want to know immediately."

"Yes. Thank you, Albert. This is important," Dr. Caul told him, her eyes flicking in Alexis's direction.

Humiliated to feel tears rising, Alexis dropped her head, the image of the news reporter still burning in her mind. But then, with a gasp, Alexis looked at the monitor again.

"Alexis?" Noah sounded concerned. "What is it? What's wrong?"

Alexis pointed fiercely. "She's an operative."

Everyone turned. In the paused video frame, the news reporter's eyes were unmistakably red.

Dr. Caul sat up. "Replay it, Albert. Half-speed."

Scrambling, Albert cued up the footage. The video began playing once more. As the reporter slowly turned her head toward the camera, a flash of red filled the iris of her eyes.

"So that is why the reporter was so interested in learning Alexis's whereabouts," Mr. Haber uttered, sounding more annoyed than surprised.

Albert immediately spoke into the tiny microphone on his suit lapel. "We need a full check on that news reporter. Now."

"Copy that," came a reply.

"Please excuse me." Albert was already moving to the exit. "I'll make sure that everyone is working on this new lead." He left the room, the door shutting behind him.

Alexis continued observing the image that was frozen on the monitor. "I don't understand. Why would an operative bother posing as a news reporter?"

"To watch you, Miss Kendall," Mr. Haber told her. "Once we discovered that an operative had snuck into my classroom this morning, we were certain others would stalk you throughout the day. We kept agents near you to assess the situation, and our assumption quickly proved to be correct."

"My favorite was the operative posing as a student's father who couldn't find the school office. Worst cover I'd seen in a long time." Ralph chuckled. "He was hanging out near Alexis's fifth period classroom. He got skittish when he saw me and left."

"I should have known there were more operatives around," Alexis nearly whispered. "That awful feeling I had during first period never really went away. But why would they stalk me like that. What was the point?"

Dr. Caul remained deep in thought. "They're clearly trying to glean more information about you. For what purpose, though, we don't yet know."

Alexis motioned to the monitor. "So why bother posing as a reporter when I wasn't even around?"

"It is likely that she intended to watch you during your cheer practice," Mr. Haber guessed. "When you did not show up, I suspect she pretended to be a reporter in the hopes of finding out where you had gone."

Alexis was skeptical. "And somehow that footage actually got on the news?"

"No station would refuse to air a dramatic interview like that, whether it's credible or not. Trust me," Noah remarked with unmasked cynicism.

Alexis massaged her head, which had begun to ache. "Okay, so now that operatives are stalking me, my best friend made a fool out of me on national television, and my parents might kill me when they hear that I went to that bonfire party, what do we do from here?"

Mr. Haber slid to the edge of his seat. "We move ahead with our plan. We lure an operative to a designated location and allow him or her to capture you. Then we follow. This will lead us to Tanner."

"Okay." Alexis let the idea sink in. "And how, exactly, have you decided that this is going to go down?"

Dr. Caul answered, "Tomorrow, you'll go to the community church and volunteer to join a search party. One of our agents, Elise, will be stationed at the church as a volunteer organizer. She'll be wearing a heart-shaped pin on her t-shirt and a navy cap."

"Elise. Hat. Heart pin," Alexis echoed. "Got it."

"Search parties have been consisting of fifty volunteers," Mr. Haber added. "Elise will ensure that twenty volunteers assigned to your search party are actually our agents. Additionally, another of our agents, Jason, will be posing as the search party leader."

Mr. Haber pushed a button on his magtro, and a map appeared on one of the other monitors on the wall. He pointed to the map as he continued:

"Jason will take your search party to Planter's Field. The field consists of thirty acres of grassy, flat land. It is bordered by foothills on the north, a lake on the west, forest on the east, and a small highway to the south. We chose this location because it is remote enough to tempt an operative to come after you, yet it provides plenty of cover for our agents, including Noah and myself, to hide. We will move in and follow, should the need arise."

"You mean, should an operative find and capture me," Alexis stated bluntly, looking Mr. Haber in the eyes.

Mr. Haber slightly bowed his head. "Miss Kendall, you are another young person we are asking a great deal of. Are you sure that you want to do this?"

"Alexis, you don't have to." Noah's words were almost pleading. "We can find another way."

But Alexis did not flinch. "Yes. I'm sure. I want to do this."

***

"That was quite the interview." Jacob chuckled with amusement. "I think our operative missed her true calling in life—she should have been a news reporter."

Leslie nodded. "Yes, it was brilliant of her to make that last-minute decision to pose as a reporter and interview the girl's friends."

"It would have been even more brilliant if she hadn't lost track of Alexis." Xander shut off the projector.

Leslie glared at him.

Peter raised his hand. "So are you assuming that the girl slipped away after school with the help of The Organization?"

"Yes." Xander adjusted his suit coat. "And so we must also assume that The Organization has met and planned its next move. Therefore—"

"We must act first," came Dr. Gaige's voice from the doorway.

Businesslike, Xander turned to greet him but froze. Dr. Gaige had Gerard standing beside him.

"Gerard, what a surprise to see you . . . out of detainment . . . unannounced," Jacob stated uncomfortably, glancing at the others.

"Thank you." Gerard deferentially entered the room and took his usual chair near Leslie.

With a pleasant smile, Dr. Gaige went to the head of the table. "We apologize for being late."

Xander could do nothing but watch in furious silence. *Doctor Gaige let Gerard out of detainment. This could ruin everything.*

"Forgive me, Doctor Gaige," Peter ventured, "but as this is completely against policy, I must inquire how it is that Gerard is with us this evening?"

Dr. Gaige responded in a tone that was gracious. "No apology necessary. It was my decision to release Gerard from detainment and restore him to his previous position."

"So we're not worried about the fact that Gerard sabotaged Xander's plan and caused that battle in the forest?" Daria frankly asked.

"The explanation for his actions Gerard gave during his interrogation was adequate." Dr. Gaige remained calm, though a hint of impatience was returning to his tone. "Gerard knows he acted without order, and he has been reprimanded for doing so. However, as his actions were not intended to harm our group or our ultimate goal, I deemed Gerard eligible to return."

Gerard held up a hand. "Xander and everyone, I'm sorry for what is, undoubtedly, quite a surprise. I know that none of you were expecting to see me, especially not at a committee meeting."

"No, we weren't," Jackie muttered, peeking at Xander.

Gerard continued humbly, "Please know that I deeply regret my recent decision to undermine your authority, Xander. I was so worried about obtaining Number 407 that I was brash and impatient. It is a mistake I will not make again."

Xander stayed quiet, revealing nothing.

Dr. Gaige scanned the table, stopping on Xander for an extra moment, before speaking again.

"Now that everything is cleared up, let's not waste any more time. Xander, please resume discussing your proposed plan to get the girl. That is, obviously, what we are interested in."

It took all Xander's willpower to continue speaking unfazed. "For quite some time, Alexis's cell phone has been off, preventing us from listening in on her calls. Minutes ago, however, her phone went live, and she called her friend, Molly. We were able to record the conversation."

Xander clicked a button on his laptop, and an audio recording began to play:

"Hey Mol, it's me."

"Lex, what was up with you skipping cheer practice today?"

"What was up with you insulting me on television?"

"Lex, I'm sorry, okay? That reporter came up after cheer practice and asked if I wanted to be interviewed. Crystal demanded to be included. The next thing I knew, we were both in front of the camera. I didn't know what to say. I guess I was mad at you for lying and ignoring me. I'm sorry."

There were a few seconds of quiet.

"It's alright," Alexis eventually told her, sighing. "I can't go into details, but I'm sorry for missing cheer practice."

"Lex, are you okay?"

"I'm fine."

"Do you want to talk after school tomorrow?"

"I can't. I—"

"You can't? What's going on? It's like you're keeping something from me, Lex."

"Nothing is going on. I promise. I'm just planning to go to the community church tomorrow so I can join one of those volunteer search parties. That's all."

"Oh. Wish I could go, too, but I know Mom wouldn't let me."

There was another break in the conversation.

"Hey, Molly, I gotta go. But I'll see you in the morning, okay?"

"Okay. Bye."

When the recording of the phone call ended, Xander lifted his eyes to the group. "As you heard, Alexis will be taking part in a search party tomorrow afternoon. That's our time to make a move."

"In other words, we'll be abducting the girl after all, eh?" Leslie gave Gerard a victorious look.

"Yes, but only because all of Xander's other plans were either sabotaged or disobeyed, eh?" Jackie retorted.

Peter seemed doubtful. "As we discussed before, The Organization will have security in place to protect her. Abducting her won't be easy."

"It won't matter how much security The Organization has in place." Daria waved her hand dismissively. "They won't engage in battle, even to protect the girl. There will be civilians around the girl tomorrow, and The Organization is simply too opposed to the loss of innocent lives to do everything it might take to keep us from her."

"There will be no need for a battle." Xander turned off the laptop. "I will have at least thirty undercover operatives in Alexis's search party tomorrow. While there will undoubtedly be agents protecting Alexis, they certainly won't be prepared for such a show of force from us. We will have them outnumbered, and once the search party reaches its destination, we'll be able to abduct Alexis without a fight."

"Which will be the best scenario of all, since avoiding a battle will minimize any risk of harming Number 407," Jackie emphasized.

"At least thirty operatives? You're sending at least thirty of our operatives out there?" Leslie gaped. "Seems a little extreme, don't you think, Xander? You might as well send an entire company."

"I am. Four companies, actually," Xander replied without missing a beat. "In the very unlikely chance that the operatives in the search party need backup, those companies will move in on my word. Again, though, we will have The Organization's agents so outnumbered that they'll know a fight would be futile. We'll be able to take Alexis peacefully." He gestured to the laptop. "We were extremely fortunate to intercept this call. The Organization won't be expecting us."

TWENTY ONE

Noah held up a tiny clear object. "You'll wear this while you're out there."

Alexis had to lean in to get a better look. "What is it?"

"An earpiece. It'll allow you to hear us if we need to talk to you."

"Right. Okay." Alexis nodded apprehensively. "Sounds good."

Noah's brow furrowed. "Alexis, you still don't have to do this."

"I know."

Noah said nothing.

"Hey, I'll be fine," Alexis told him after a pause, hoping that she sounded convincing. "It'll be you, Mister Haber, and a bunch of other agents versus one unsuspecting operative. The plan is going to work. So let's get this show on the road."

Noah still hesitated before slipping the object into her left ear. "Okay, you're set."

"Noah." Alexis impulsively grabbed his hand, her voice no longer steady. "You are going to be out there, right?"

His eyes locked on hers. "I'm not letting you out of my sight."

The door to the supply closet was opened.

"It is time, Miss Kendall," Mr. Haber reported, coming inside. "I received word from Headquarters that city bus five-forty will be making its expected stop in front of the school in eight minutes. Two agents are on board, simply as a precaution. After you get on, the third stop will be the community church. That is where you will sign up for the search party. Elise is already in position there, and we have additional undercover agents on site."

Alexis released her hold on Noah's hand and shakily picked up her fake chemistry assignment. "Alright. I guess I'll . . . go turn this in. Um, see you guys later."

Unable to bring herself to look again at the others—especially not Noah—Alexis stepped from the supply closet into the main classroom. She wove past the workstations and empty desks, set the paper near Mr. Haber's podium, and exited into the hallway. The corridor was vacant but for a few students who passed by, laughing as they went. Alexis watched after them, suddenly feeling very alone.

"Hey, Lex! What are you still doing on campus?"

Alexis checked behind her. Her friend from the cheer team, Tessa Raines, was approaching.

"We missed you at practice yesterday afternoon," Tessa went on. "Hey, are you going to homecoming? I've got the best dress and—"

"Keep going, Miss Kendall, you have a bus to catch."

Alexis jumped when she heard Mr. Haber's voice in her ear. She moved for the door. "That sounds great. I've gotta run, but I'll talk to you later, okay?"

Tessa waved. "Okay! Bye! See you soon!"

"Yeah. Soon."

Alexis pushed the door open. Outside, she found the afternoon sun casting golden light onto the trees, which swayed lightly in the autumn breeze. The air was crisp and scented by freshly mowed grass. Birds were singing, and the familiar sounds of the football and soccer teams practicing nearby could be heard. Shivering despite the sunlight, Alexis started toward the front of the school. She closed her eyes, focusing on how the soft wind caressed her face, trying to calm her anxious heart.

Soon, the noise of cars in the distance made Alexis open her eyes. Up ahead, news crews and groups of onlookers remained gathered on the opposite side of the street, and police officers were directing traffic that had backed up as far as Alexis could see.

"Two minutes, Miss Kendall," Mr. Haber informed her.

Alexis shivered again as she reached the bus stop. While merging into the waiting crowd, a sickening sensation crashed over her body, causing her to whip up her head with a start.

An operative is already close!

Frantic, Alexis scanned the strangers at the bus stop. No one even glanced her way. She peered next across the street, surveying the crowd. She gulped when she spotted the same woman who had posed as a news reporter the day before. The woman—the operative with the red eyes—was staring up at the school as if waiting for something. Or someone.

Alexis dropped her head to hide her face. *Does Mister Haber know that the operative is already after me?*

The rumble of an engine caused Alexis to peek down the road. The city bus was approaching. Wiping her sweaty palms on her jacket, Alexis dared to peer again across the street. The operative still had not noticed her.

"Hurry up. Hurry up," Alexis whispered, watching the bus get closer.

The bus began to slow. Alexis pushed to the front of the line and then checked across the street one last time. The operative suddenly turned, catching Alexis watching her. The next instant, the bus pulled up to the curb, blocking Alexis's view. Once the bus doors opened, Alexis had no time left to think. She dashed up the stairs with her heart in her throat.

The elderly bus driver tipped his hat. "Good afternoon, Miss. I'm Jasper."

"Hi," Alexis mumbled, hurrying past him to find a seat.

The doors shut, and the bus lurched forward. Alexis gripped the handrails as she made her way down the aisle past rows of unfamiliar people. She slid into an empty seat and looked out the window. The operative was gone.

***

"The girl is on the move," came the operative's report over the communicator. "City bus five-forty just departed from the bus stop in front of the high school. I watched her get on myself."

Xander lifted the communicator from his office desk and spoke into it. "And four of our operatives are on the bus as planned?"

"Yes."

"How many people riding the bus in total?"

"The report is that twenty-seven people are on the bus, including the girl," the operative informed him. "More than expected for this time of day."

"As we expected, The Organization must have agents on board," Xander noted.

"Given this development, the operatives will refrain from taking any action other than providing surveillance during the bus ride."

Xander banged the desk with his fist. "Was there ever a discussion about those operatives doing anything but providing surveillance?"

There was a pause before the operative replied: "No, Sir."

Xander clenched his jaw. *If anyone—anyone— makes one move without my order . . .*

The operative continued, "The report indicates that traffic is as expected. The girl will arrive at the community church shortly."

"Copy."

Xander set the communicator down, exhaled, and loosened his tie. It was going to be a long night.

***

"Central Command, this is Noah. Do you copy?"

"Central Command copies," Mr. Haber said into his magtro. "Have you arrived at the community church, Noah?"

"Yeah."

"What is the latest from there?"

"Seventy-three people have already volunteered for this afternoon's search party, and more are arriving as we speak. That's in addition to our twenty agents who signed up."

"How many volunteers are there?" Mr. Haber asked, not hiding his alarm.

"Seventy-three so far, and from the looks of it, there'll be more."

Standing nearby, Dr. Caul turned worriedly to Mr. Haber. "That number of volunteers is significantly higher than we anticipated, Ben."

Mr. Haber's brow furrowed. "Indeed. All twenty of our agents checked in with Elise, and yet over seventy other people have signed up for the same search party. This can only mean one thing: Doctor Gaige somehow learned of our plan." Mr. Haber took a moment before talking again into his magtro. "Noah, we suspect that Doctor Gaige's operatives have infiltrated the search party."

"Then we need to abort the mission and evacuate Alexis!" Noah barked. "We planned for one operative to come after her, not several!"

Dr. Caul began pacing. "Ben, if The Domanorith did somehow learn of our plan, who knows where else their operatives are positioned? They could be on the bus, or posing as civilians or reporters around the community church. Our agents may be vastly outnumbered." She removed her own magtro from her pocket and used it to address Noah. "We must assume that you and our other agents at the community church are outnumbered. If we attempt to evacuate Alexis when she arrives there, the operatives will figure out that they have the advantage. They'll start a battle, which would lead to countless casualties and potentially prevent us from tracking Alexis if she's captured. And if The Domanorith block the GPS device that Alexis is wearing, we'd never know where they took her."

"So send reinforcements!" Noah sounded frantic. "Hurry!"

"Our companies are already positioned at Planter's Field; it will take too long for them to get there." Mr. Haber hurriedly surveyed a map on the computer. "Noah, tell Jason that I am dispatching two new companies from here at Headquarters to join you at the community church. Until then, only move in if the operatives create a disturbance."

"But, Ben, we—"

"Noah," Dr. Caul interrupted, "I know that Doctor Gaige will not hesitate to let his operatives act with full aggression if they figure out that they have us outnumbered. The safest thing we can do for Alexis is to get her to Planter's Field where our other companies are ready and waiting. It's the only place we can successfully abort the mission, evacuate Alexis, and engage in battle if necessary."

There was a sharp silence.

"I understand," Noah finally replied. "I'll inform Jason."

***

"The next stop is the church, Miss Kendall."

Alexis heard Mr. Haber's voice in her ear and slid to the edge of her seat, doing her best to ignore the alarm that still pulsed through her body. Once the bus came to a stop, Alexis charged past Jasper and fled down the stairs. Pushing by the news crews that clogged the sidewalk, Alexis scampered up the stone steps of the church, tugged open the heavy door, and went inside.

Alexis found herself in a large square room, which was filled by people who were signing up at various volunteer stations. Banners hanging above each station indicated what service was being coordinated there for the search efforts. Alexis hovered in a corner until she spotted a banner that read, 'SEARCH PARTY SIGN UP' above a table at the far end of the room.

I guess that's my cue.

While sunlight streamed through the church's stained glass windows and made colorful designs at her feet, Alexis wove through the throngs of people to get to her target. As she approached, Alexis noted two women working behind the table. One of them wore a dark blue cap and had a heart-shaped pin on her t-shirt.

That's got to be Elise.

Alexis made a move for Elise's end of the table, but a short man stepped in front of her. Alexis was forced to wait.

"Are you here to sign up, dear?" The other lady behind the table was watching her. "I can help you right here."

Alexis pretended to check a message on her phone. "Thanks, but I'm actually looking for friends."

Sensing the lady still observing her, Alexis moved away. It was a very long time before the short man finally left Elise's end of the table. He gave Alexis a peculiar glance before walking out a side door. Once he was gone, Alexis hurried forward.

"Hello, young lady," Elise greeted her warmly. "How can I help you?"

Alexis searched Elise's face. "I want to join today's search party."

"Let me see if we still have spots available." Elise picked up a sheet of paper and seemed to review it. "There is a group leaving for Planter's Field in a few minutes. You'd be there until five. Does that sound alright to you?"

Alexis spoke deliberately. "Sure. Sounds fine."

Elise still showed no sign of any recognition as she handed Alexis a form. "Wonderful. Please fill out your information here. Once you're done, go out the side exit." She pointed to the same door that the short man had gone through. "You'll see the group waiting near the street. The person in charge is named Jason. He'll give you further instructions."

"Jason. Got it. Thanks." Alexis bent down and scribbled fast on the form.

Only when Alexis handed over the completed form did Elise give her a slight nod. For Alexis, the hint of acknowledgement was enough. Reassured, she retreated from the table and walked out the side door into the sunlight. But then she stopped in surprise.

Mister Haber said there'd only be fifty people in the search party, but there are way more people here than that. He must have added more agents to the group.

Alexis noticed a tall guy with a buzz cut standing at the front of the group. He appeared to be in his late twenties, his eyes were hidden behind reflective sunglasses, and he wore a black, long-sleeved shirt and camouflage pants. It took Alexis only a moment to recognize him as the agent who had driven the armored vehicle when she was evacuated from the battle in the forest. Gathering her courage, Alexis approached him. As she got close, she noticed that he also wore small earbuds like the ones Noah used.

"Hi." Alexis gave him a slight, awkward wave. "I'm Alexis."

He looked down at her, expressionless. "I'm Jason. The bus will be here shortly."

"Great. Um, thanks."

Not sure what to do next, Alexis wove into the still-growing mass of volunteers. Again, she was jolted by a wave of coldness and a prickling along the back of her neck. She rubbed her aching hands together, trying to ignore how nauseated she was becoming.

It's okay. Don't freak out. Even if that operative followed me here, I'm surrounded by tons of agents. I'll be okay.

"Incoming," Jason announced to the group in his low voice.

Alexis saw an old school bus, which was painted light blue, rolling down the road. Once it came to a stop, she boarded along with the volunteers. She deliberately took a seat at the front so she could remain close to Jason, who stood near the driver. Once the bus got underway, Alexis shifted in her seat, trying to identify the agents among the group. She made eye contact with a few people, but they showed no indication of caring who she was. Giving up, Alexis faced forward and slid low in her seat, rubbing the back of her prickling neck. She did a double take when she realized that it was the same elderly bus driver, Jasper, who was behind the wheel.

***

"I don't think our car is the only one that's following the search party's bus, Xander," the operative stated.

Xander loosened his tie further as he talked into the communicator. "What do you mean?"

"Ever since the bus left the community church, there's been a van driving in front of it and a suburban right behind it. Atypical for this country road."

Xander rubbed his forehead. "Understood. It's likely that both the van and the suburban contain agents from The Organization."

"How would you like us to proceed?"

"Continue maintaining an exaggerated distance so as not to draw attention. If there are more agents protecting Alexis than we expected, it's all the more reason to allow the bus to reach its destination before we make our move." Xander stood up. "In the meantime, I'll order our companies to get into place around Planter's Field."

***

Mr. Haber scanned the latest satellite images. "Noah, do you have a visual on the car that is trailing your suburban?"

"Yeah," came Noah's reply over the magtro. "The car is staying pretty far behind us, but it's definitely following." His comment was emphasized by the sound of the suburban he rode in hitting a pothole.

Mr. Haber kept watching the live satellite feed. "This seems to confirm our suspicion that there are more operatives trailing Alexis than we prepared for. Continue with the plan to evacuate Alexis once she gets to the field."

"Copy," Noah replied. "As soon as we get there, I'll join up with Forest Company."

Mr. Haber said, "And I am departing Headquarters now to join Foothills Company. Once I arrive, I will update everyone again on this emergent change in plans. Because we suspect several operatives are after Miss Kendall, we are aborting the mission and evacuating her to safety."

TWENTY TWO

Alexis watched out the window as Jasper made a left turn off the bumpy road and drove the bus through an open gate. The bus continued rumbling down a tree-lined dirt lane, crunching over rocks and splashing through water-filled potholes, until eventually coming to a stop in front of a giant red barn. Two police officers and an FBI agent were waiting nearby.

Jason addressed the group. "File off and listen for instructions."

Alexis sprang from her seat and got off the bus. Moving away from the others, she turned in a circle, surveying her surroundings. Everything appeared just as the Mister Haber had described: behind the barn sprawled a vast field of dense, waist-high grass and green foothills rising up in the distance. A dark forest was to her right. Down a hill on her left, a lake sparkled in the early evening light.

"Everyone over here, please!" one of the police officers called out, standing up on a hay bale and waving her hand in the air.

Alexis joined the others as they congregated in front of the police officer. Just then, she heard Noah's voice in her ear:

"Hey, Alexis, you're doing great. Our four companies of agents are getting into position around the field, and we've got you in our sights."

Alexis lifted her head sharply. She had detected a strain in Noah's voice. Something was wrong. There was something he was not telling her.

"Thank you for coming," the police officer began. "As you know, we're searching for anything that might help us determine what happened to those two boys who disappeared late Saturday night. This afternoon's search area is obviously here at Planter's Field. We're going to have you line up along the near edge of the field, which is directly behind this barn. At our word, you'll begin walking forward through the grass, going north in the direction of the foothills. Your individual area of responsibility is five feet to your left and to your right, and as far ahead as you can see. As you proceed, if you find anything even slightly unusual, stop and hold up your hand. Do not to touch what you have come across until law enforcement has . . ."

Alexis could no longer concentrate, due to the horrible way she felt—the sickening sensation had become far worse than anything she had experienced before. Rubbing her throbbing hands, Alexis kicked the ground with her shoe and distractedly scanned the group. She spotted the short man whom she had seen earlier at the community church. He met her stare. Then his eyes flashed red.

Alexis barely stopped herself from screaming. *There's an operative here, and there was a different operative near the school . . . so how many operatives are actually after me?*

As a dreadful realization sank in, Alexis peered again at the strangers who surrounded her. She had no idea who was on her side and who was not. How many were after her? Who were they? With her throat getting tight, Alexis turned her head and anxiously fixed her eyes on the foothills in the distance.

Does Mister Haber know? Does he know that more than one operative is coming for me? Was The Organization ready for this?

***

"I've joined up with Forest Company, and we're in position," Noah reported over the magtro. "I can see the search party, which has started moving in a south-to-north direction across the field, heading toward the foothills. Alexis is located near the middle of the group."

"Copy that," Mr. Haber replied. "I am moving Foothills Company into position north of the field, but we are proceeding slower than anticipated due to rocky terrain."

"I'm with Lakeside Company, and we are in position," came Jason's report.

Dr. Caul spoke next. "This is Central Command at Headquarters. I've been informed that Roadside Company is getting in position to the south. Once everyone is in place, we'll proceed with the plan to extract Alexis and abort the mission. Remember: we don't know how many operatives are out there. So be careful, all of you."

***

Leaning forward, Xander watched tensely as the live video feed came through on his computer. Though the operatives who were obtaining the video had stationed themselves quite a distance from the field, the footage was still distorted. Xander could barely see Alexis and the search party as they steadily moved northward.

A motion out of the corner of his eye caused Xander to look up. Jackie had entered his office. She gave him a nod as she came over to his desk and started viewing the monitor over his shoulder.

Refocusing, Xander spoke into his communicator. "East Company, are you in position?"

"Affirmative. We're in good cover within the forest."

"West Company?"

"We are in place near the lake."

"North Company?"

"Moving in along the foothills. Progress is hampered by rocky terrain."

"South Company?"

"Our vehicles will soon be on the road by the farm gate."

Xander's jaw clenched. "Everyone, listen very closely. No one moves, unless it is on my order. No one."

***

Alexis's breathing was becoming labored as she continued forward through the tall grass. From the exhaustingly sick way she felt, she knew that the number of operatives around her had to be increasing—and increasing fast.

Mr. Haber's voice sounded in her ear. "Miss Kendall, we suspect that there are operatives in the search party. Be aware that the man immediately to your left and the woman on your right are not agents from The Organization. They may be civilians, but they may also be working for Doctor Gaige."

Shuddering as her worst fears were confirmed, Alexis knelt in the dirt, pretending to check something on the ground while letting the search party continue by her. Alexis knew that with each passing moment, agents from The Organization were getting closer to operatives who worked for Dr. Gaige. Alexis also knew that both sides were ready to fight—to kill, if necessary—because of her. One wrong move, or one anxious person on a trigger, could ignite a battle between the two sides. Innocent people would get injured. Those she cared about might be killed.

"Alexis, hang in there. You're going to be alright," she heard Noah say. "And remember: if anyone tries something, he or she is just a big cantaloupe."

Alexis laughed as she started to cry. *What would I have done without Noah? I can't put him at risk again. Not after everything he's sacrificed for me. It's only me that The Domanorith want. I can prevent a battle from happening. I can keep Noah and the others safe.*

Slowly, Alexis stood up. She knew what she had to do.

***

"What is she doing?" Xander asked sharply, peering at his computer screen.

As best as Xander could tell, Alexis had knelt in the middle of the field while everyone else in the search party continued walking.

Jackie moved close to the monitor to get a better look. "She's getting up, and now it's like she's just standing there."

Xander rubbed his chin uneasily. He knew that Alexis was brave and even proven willing to fight—but he also knew that there was no room for surprises.

Don't try anything, Alexis. The only way this will work is if you—

"She's on the move! She's on the move!" an operative cried over the communicator.

In the grainy video feed, Xander saw Alexis sprinting southbound and away from the search party.

"Request permission to move in!" the same operative yelled.

"Xander, he's waiting for your command." Jackie's eyes were darting between the computer and Xander's face.

"Request permission to move in!" the operative shouted again.

***

"Alexis, what are you doing? We need to get you out of there! Alexis! Stop!"

Though Noah was shouting in her ear, Alexis continued charging toward the barn. Behind her, Alexis heard others in the search party rushing after her, but she did not look back. All she cared about was getting herself as far away from everyone else as she could.

Panting with exertion, Alexis finally reached the edge of the field. Breaking free of the long grass, Alexis picked up her pace and sprinted past the barn. She ignored the police officer who called to her as she flew by. Chest burning, Alexis raced down the dirt lane, splashing though the muddy puddles while heading for the gate that led to the south road. As she ran, Alexis felt her hands start to ache.

She was ready to defend herself.

***

From his position with Foothills Company, Mr. Haber spoke into his magtro. "Miss Kendall is leaving the property! Proceed with the plan to abort the mission. Roadside Company, move in now and take Miss Kendall into your protection. Jason, get Lakeside Company there to provide reinforcement."

"Copy," Jason responded.

"Ben, we're showing that operatives are also moving in from the south and west." Dr. Caul's words were hurried and strained. "They'll converge with our companies on that road. There is going to be a battle."

"I will take my company to the road as additional reinforcements," Mr. Haber announced. "If we are outnumbered and engaged in battle, we will not be able to go after Alexis if she is captured. We must intercept Miss Kendall before The Domanorith get to her, whatever it takes."

***

Alexis reached the end of the dirt lane. She bolted through the open gate, went right, and started running down the two-lane road, her shoes slapping hard against the asphalt. The sun had fallen low on the horizon, forcing her to raise an arm to shield her eyes.

Alexis began hearing vehicles approaching fast, but blinded by the sun's glare, she could not see them. Suddenly, the blaring sounds of car horns and screeching tires filled her ears. Then something rammed into her left hip, throwing her off balance. With a cry, Alexis stuck out her right arm to break her fall. As she hit the ground, an intense pain shot through her wrist. Then her head smacked the pavement. She felt the listening device roll out of her ear before everything went black.

***

"She's down, Ben! They hit Alexis with their vehicle!" Dr. Caul screamed.

"All companies to the south road. Authorized to use full force for protecting Miss Kendall," Mr. Haber ordered. "Noah, how long until Forest Company will get there?"

There was silence.

"Noah?" Mr. Haber repeated. "Noah, do you copy?"

"This is Forest Company," announced a different voice. "Noah moved out alone several minutes ago. We're heading to the south road now to join him."

"Ben, what is Noah doing?" Dr. Caul whispered.

***

Alexis groggily rolled over. Her head ached, and her right wrist was killing her. Through blurred vision, she saw an unfamiliar man standing over her. The man reached down and sat her up. Alexis immediately felt a wave of nausea and vomited onto the pavement.

There was a crackling noise from a walkie-talkie, and Alexis heard a voice ask:

"How is she?"

Alexis raised her head, certain she had heard the voice before. "Noah? Is that you?" she mumbled deliriously.

The man standing by Alexis replied to the voice by speaking into something that he held in his hand. "The girl is awake but concussed."

"Evacuate immediately," she heard the familiar voice order. "We'll have medical personnel awaiting your arrival here at the base."

"Copy."

The man lifted Alexis off the ground. As her head weakly rolled back, Alexis saw a bright flash of orange fly across the sky.

"We're under attack!" The man carrying Alexis broke into a run. "The Organization has companies moving in from all sides!"

Queasy and only half-conscious, Alexis watched as streaks of colors shot overhead. There were screams. More tires screeched. Something exploded in the distance. The scent of smoke filled the air. Then Alexis heard the door to a vehicle being opened, and someone lifted her out of the man's arms and set her onto a stretcher.

"We have the girl secured," the man who had carried Alexis reported as the vehicle's door slammed shut.

"Copy that. South Company will surround you to facilitate evacuation," the familiar voice stated. "North, West, and East Companies will stay on scene to keep The Organization's agents occupied while you get out of there."

The vehicle began to move. The last thing Alexis saw out the window was a flash of royal blue.

TWENTY THREE

Dr. Caul whipped around. "Ben, where do you think you're going?"

"Ben, give me a few minutes to take care of your injuries," Ralph insisted at the same time.

Mr. Haber relented, sinking wearily down onto a chair. "How could this have happened, Ralph?"

"It's not worth asking that right now." Ralph started cleaning the abrasions on Mr. Haber's face. "Right now, it's time to figure out what you're going to do about it."

"I've got Jason on the line," announced a young woman seated at a computer nearby.

"Thanks, Kate," Dr. Caul said to her, stepping to the computer. "Jason, this is Central Command. Do you copy?"

"I copy," Jason replied.

"What do you have so far on the operatives who abducted Alexis?"

"My Lakeside Company tracked their vehicle for approximately thirty miles northeast through rural countryside. We were then engaged by another company of operatives, at which time the vehicle with Alexis got away."

Dr. Caul flinched before continuing. "Copy. And what is the latest casualty count from the battle at Planter's Field?"

"Foothills Company with eight injured. Lakeside Company with fourteen injured and one fatality. Roadside Company with twenty-one injured and three fatalities. Forest Company with three injured and one missing. All of the injured are in transit or have arrived at Headquarters for medical care. Plans for notifying the next of kin of the fatalities are underway."

Mr. Haber stood up, despite Ralph's protests. "Jason, are there any updates on the whereabouts of the missing agent?"

"Not at this time."

Dr. Caul glanced despondently at Mr. Haber. "Copy. Jason, we'll expect the next update in thirty minutes—or sooner, if there are developments. Over."

"Over."

With brisk strides, Albert Oppenhall moved for the door. "Shall I announce another Priority One assembly?"

"No," Dr. Caul and Mr. Haber answered together.

"No?" Albert's jaw dropped. "Two high school boys have been abducted, the girl has been injured and kidnapped, the element is now within Doctor Gaige's possession, multiple agent injuries and fatalities occurred tonight, the famous Noah Weston is missing, and a battle took place out in the open. Yet you don't want to call a meeting?"

Mr. Haber nodded at Ralph and then looked Albert in the eye. "This is not a time for meetings, Albert. This is the time to find those kids."

***

"So this is the girl."

A man's raspy voice caused a shudder to run down Alexis's spine. She kept her eyes shut and remained still on the bed.

"This is Alexis, yes," someone else replied.

Alexis recognized the second person's voice as belonging to the man who had instructed the operative when she was carried from the road. It was the voice Alexis had heard another time before. Somewhere.

"I see she was injured," continued the first man. "What does this mean in terms of our timeline for being able to work with her?"

"We don't know yet," a confident-sounding woman chimed in. "The doctor said her right wrist fracture is non-operative and will heal, and I highly doubt that injury will have any effect on the powers she holds. The bigger concern is the concussion. The doctor said it could be several days before she is feeling well enough for us to start performing tests."

Tests? Alexis felt a pulse of fear.

"So we've turned our base into an infirmary for high school students." The first man's tone had a wickedly amused edge to it.

"But we have Alexis here safely, Doctor Gaige," the familiar voice replied with restraint. "I would say that has moved us much closer to our ultimate goal."

Alexis had to force herself to stay quiet. *It's Doctor Gaige. The man responsible for all of this. The one who killed Noah's parents.*

"True," Dr. Gaige stated after a moment. "Congratulations on your work tonight, Xander."

Xander, Alexis repeated to herself, finally remembering. *He was the man who didn't want me hurt when I was kidnapped from the football game.*

Dr. Gaige spoke again. "While this is all very enthralling, I must be going now."

Slow, steady footsteps started moving away.

"Doctor Gaige?" Xander called out.

"Yes?"

"Now that we have Alexis here, I assume there is no further need to keep the boy?"

"The boy?" Dr. Gaige repeated.

"Tanner. The civilian who was abducted during the battle in the forest."

Tanner! He's alive!

"Ah, our little bargaining chip." Dr. Gaige chuckled. "I can't imagine that I have any use for him now. You may do with him what you would like."

Monster!

"Speaking of high school boys," Dr. Gaige continued with curiosity, "what about the other one? Our recruit?"

"Drake Spencer is also still here in the infirmary," Xander told him.

"Ah, that is a shame, isn't it?"

Alexis listed to Dr. Gaige's footsteps fade away. Several seconds passed, and then she heard Xander speak quietly:

"We need to get Tanner out of here tonight, Jackie. He's healthy and lucid enough to travel safely yet still amnesic to what happened here, thanks to the medications he received. However, if he stays any longer, he'll start forming memories of this place."

"I agree. What time should we arrange for transport?" the woman named Jackie inquired.

"I'll get it coordinated as soon as I know that Alexis is okay."

"I'm okay."

There was a surprised silence. Alexis opened her eyes. Standing a few feet away from where she lay, Alexis saw a tall, handsome man with light brown hair who was dressed in a business suit. She guessed he was in his early thirties. Beside the man was a short woman wearing a white lab coat over her stylish outfit. She had auburn hair and looked about the same age as Xander.

"You were awake that whole time," Xander said more as a statement than a question.

"Yes," Alexis answered. For some reason, he did not frighten her—in a way, he looked familiar.

Xander observed her with an expression that was serious but not unkind. "I'm glad that you're alright."

Alexis eyed him. "I've been kidnapped, my wrist is broken, and I'm apparently concussed. I'm not sure that counts as alright."

"Good point," Xander replied, the corner of his mouth turning up slightly.

Alexis shifted her focus to the woman, who was watching her with interest. "You said tests. What kind of tests are you going to run on me? I'm not a lab rat, you know."

Jackie appeared taken aback. "Of course you're not. I only meant that when you are feeling up to it, we would like to work with you and study your powers."

"That's why I got kidnapped? For tests?"

Jackie looked to Xander for help.

Xander sighed. "Unfortunately, Alexis, yes. You were kidnapped for tests."

Alexis examined the white cast that covered her right forearm. "Will your tests hurt me?"

Xander came across the room and crouched down by the bed. "No one is going to hurt you. That I promise." He motioned to the woman. "Jackie also has your best interests in mind. She is going to help us learn what Doctor Gaige wants to know as fast and as easily for you as possible. The sooner we do that, the sooner we get you home."

Alexis dropped her arm. "When are you going to let Tanner go?"

"Right now." Xander stood and straightened his jacket. "But before I go, Alexis, I must ask one thing of you. No matter what, never tell anyone about Jackie or me. Never mention that you saw or interacted with us. Never tell anyone what we said or did. That is absolutely critical. Do you promise?"

Alexis met his gaze. "I promise."

The conversation was interrupted by a buzzing noise. Xander pulled something out of his jacket pocket, which he held to his ear like a phone.

"Yes?" Xander answered. His eyes flashed angrily. "I will be there immediately. I want him placed in a private interrogation room. Word of this does not get out, do you understand me?"

"What's wrong?" Jackie inquired.

Xander was already going for the door. "As if we don't have enough to deal with, East Company dragged someone in here, accusing him of working for The Organization. They brought him like a prisoner of war or something." Xander stopped when he noticed Alexis still studying him. "I'll take care of this and then get Tanner home. I promise."

"May I come with you to see the prisoner?" Alexis asked.

Xander did not hide his surprise. "No."

Alexis pushed herself up on the bed, ignoring her dizziness. "But if it's someone from The Organization, that person could at least tell the others I'm alright. Then they won't worry so much. Please."

I can't believe I'm about to do this. Xander watched Alexis for a few seconds before gesturing to the exit. "Alright, you can come."

Jackie's mouth fell open, but she helped Alexis climb out of bed and get steady on her feet. Once her nausea faded, Alexis nodded to Xander that she was ready.

Xander opened the door. "Thanks for your assistance tonight, Jackie. I'll be in touch."

"And I'll go update the committee." Jackie reached the doorway and looked up at him. "Be sure to get some sleep."

Jackie hurried out. Xander continued holding the door open for Alexis, who exited into the hallway. She halted abruptly when she saw two intimidating-looking security guards stationed outside. They stopped chatting and scowled at her.

"It's alright, gentlemen." Xander came up beside Alexis. "I'm taking her with me for a few minutes."

Xander continued calmly past the guards. Alexis followed, doing her best to keep up with his determined strides as he headed toward an elevator at the end of a long corridor. They stepped into the elevator, and the doors promptly slid shut. Neither of them spoke as the elevator started to ascend. In the silence, Alexis stole a sideways glance at him. Xander was staring straight ahead, his expression sharp and resolute. There was something recognizable about his profile, Alexis decided.

The elevator came to a stop, and its doors opened. Xander stepped out first. Alexis trailed behind him into a stark room with light gray walls. Hovering near the elevator, she remained quiet as Xander walked over to a metal door on their left and rapidly began punching numbers on the keypad beside it.

"I'll call you in when I'm ready, Alexis. In the meantime, have a seat over there." Xander motioned to a chair against the far wall. Then he opened the door and went into the room, letting the door close behind him.

Alone, Alexis sighed and rubbed her aching head. *What are my parents going to think when I don't come home tonight? They're going to be so worried.*

Miserable, Alexis went to the opposite side of the room and sat down, not sure what was making her the most sick: her injuries, her concern, or the fact that she was undoubtedly surrounded by operatives. Shivering, she pulled her jacket closely around her. As she did so, she felt her cell phone in her pocket.

They didn't take my phone from me when I was captured?

Alexis yanked out her phone and pushed the power button, pleading with it to find reception. Just then, there was a sound from the elevator. Someone else was coming. Alexis stuffed her phone back into her pocket, her apprehensive breathing shallow and quick.

A moment later, the elevator doors slid open. A man with blond hair stepped out, charged over to the metal door, and knocked. The door was opened from the inside only a crack. The blond man reached out and held the door open, and he used his other hand to gesture to the elevator as he spoke:

"Bring him."

A captive was shoved out of the elevator. Two dirt-covered men trailed close behind him, grabbed the prisoner by his arms, and dragged him through the open door. The blond operative went in after the others, letting the door slam behind him. In their haste, no one had even noticed Alexis, who was poised tensely on the edge of the chair.

Noah! They've captured Noah!

Alexis stood, bracing herself against the wall until her head stopped swirling. She moved to the door and set her ear against it, listening furiously to the muffled voices on the other side. Then she focused on the keypad next to the door.

This door needs to unlock. Now.

A click was all Alexis needed to hear. She grabbed the handle with her good arm and pulled the unlocked door wide open.

Everyone inside stopped what they were doing when Alexis appeared in the doorway. Alexis held her ground. She saw Noah seated at a table at the center of the room, hunched over with his back toward her. He did not turn around. The blond operative and his two assistants were leaning against the wall at her left, eyeing Alexis threateningly. Lastly, Alexis looked at Xander, who stood on the far side of the table, facing Noah and the door. Xander's face was pale and his expression shell-shocked. Something, Alexis realized, was very wrong.

"You were supposed to make sure the door was closed," the blond operative barked to his assistants.

"I did," retorted one of the men, who had red hair.

The blond operative did not seem to buy it. "If that's the case, explain to me how some little girl—"

"I unlocked it," Alexis interrupted.

Out of the corner of her eye, Alexis saw Noah sit up. Noah had recognized her voice. He knew she was there.

The other assistant, whose shirt was torn, started coming toward her. "Well, little girl, perhaps you need to take yourself—"

Alexis faced him squarely. "Don't come near me."

Before Alexis knew what was happening, an empty chair at the table rose into the air and flew toward the operative, who looked over just in time for the chair to smack him in the face. The man howled in pain and staggered, gripping his nose. The chair landed beside him.

Xander watched in silence. *If Doctor Gaige learns about what she can do . . .*

While the red-haired assistant tended to the wounded operative, Xander dropped his attention back to the mud-covered young man who remained seated stoically at the table in front of him. The boy seemed to sense Xander watching him, for he slowly raised his eyes. Xander and the young man watched each other for what seemed to Xander like an eternity. The young man's face showed no signs of recognition.

He doesn't know who I am, Xander thought.

Revealing nothing of the torment he felt, Xander walked across the room, picked up the empty chair, and carried it to the table. He sat down.

"What is your name, young man?"

"Noah."

Xander kept his voice even. "Noah, my men tell me that you tried stealing one of our vehicles, which we had at a mining excavation near Planter's Field. Is that correct?"

"That's not what we said," the blond operative spat, stomping up behind Noah's chair. "This boy works for The Organization. He attempted to steal one of our vehicles to pursue South Company when they took the girl. And he left a trail of injured operatives along the way, I might add. He's one of them."

"No, he's not." Alexis angrily took another step into the room.

"Shut up, brat," the blond operative snapped.

Noah stood up fast, knocking his chair to the floor. "Don't talk to her like that."

The blond operative punched Noah in the stomach, causing him to collapse to his knees with a grunt of pain.

"Stop it!" Alexis yelled, horrified.

"Keep your hands off of him," Xander ordered at the same time, barely containing his rage.

The blond operative shrunk back under Xander's piercing stare. Alexis rushed to Noah and knelt beside him. Putting her casted arm gently on his shoulder, she discreetly slipped her good hand into her pocket to find her phone. Noah remained doubled over, gripping his abdomen. After a few moments, Alexis took a deep breath and looked up at Xander.

"He's not part of The Organization," she said firmly.

Xander's set his eyes on hers. "I see. And why should we believe you?"

There was deliberateness in the way Xander waited for her reply. Alexis understood what he was trying to tell her: the response she gave might determine whether or not Noah would go free.

"Because," she told him without wavering, "Noah is my boyfriend. He came with me to help in the search party. Tanner and Drake are his friends from school."

Noah's eyebrow rose almost imperceptibly.

The red-haired operative laughed. "That's the most pathetic excuse I've ever heard. This girl ran away from the search party. Why would she have done that if this boy was only—"

"I ran away because I knew there would be a fight, and I didn't want my boyfriend to get hurt," Alexis interrupted with exaggerated irritation. "I was trying to get you clowns as far away from Noah as I could."

The corners of Noah's mouth twitched.

Still holding his nose, the injured operative snorted. "So how do you explain all of our operatives whom your little Romeo managed to injure before we caught him? Or the fact that he attempted to steal one of our vehicles?"

Alexis rolled her eyes. "He saw me get kidnapped. Of course he would try to help me, you moron."

Xander almost smiled himself as he turned to the other men. "Tell me, did you find any sort of weapon on this young man?"

The three men looked at each other blankly.

"No?" Xander emphasized. "Gentlemen, do you honestly think that an agent from The Organization would enter a battle without a magtro, or without any other weapon or means of communicating?"

The blond operative frowned disgustedly at the other two and then shook his head.

"Like I told you, he's not part of The Organization," Alexis repeated, helping Noah to his feet. "He's only my boyfriend. You can let him go."

Xander observed her, nearly smiling again. *She's going to pull this off.*

"Excuse me, I'm sorry to interrupt," came an unexpected voice from the doorway.

Everyone looked toward the sound. Jackie was entering the room.

"If we're going to get Alexis's boyfriend home from the infirmary, we need to do it now," Jackie told Xander with urgency. "A few members of the committee—perhaps you can guess who—are starting to voice resistance to the idea of letting him go. I suggest you get him out of here ASAP."

The room fell silent. Alexis cringed.

"Get her boyfriend home from the infirmary?" the injured operative finally repeated, blotting the remaining blood from his nose. He gestured toward Noah. "He's not in the infirmary. And how does anyone on the committee even know that this kid is here?"

Xander hastily cut in, "I'm sure this is all a misunder—"

"Because we arranged to release Tanner some time ago," Jackie interrupted, speaking to the operative. A puzzled expression came across her face. "How did you know about the plan?"

"This kid said his name was Noah, not Tanner," the blond man noted suspiciously.

The operative with the red hair peered at Jackie. "Then who's Tanner?"

"Like I said, Tanner is Alexis's boyfriend." Jackie seemed even more bewildered. "He's upstairs in the infirmary."

The blond operative narrowed his eyes at Alexis. "Does this mean that you lied to us? Does this mean that this kid does work for The Organization?" He threw an arm tightly under Noah's neck. "It's time to fess up, boy!"

"What are you doing?" Jackie cried out.

Alexis raised her arms, which were hot and burning.

"No, Alexis, don't!" Noah sputtered, struggling for air.

Xander's frighteningly quiet voice cut through the commotion like a laser. "Let him go."

The blond operative looked up, did a double take when he saw Xander's face white with fury, and pushed Noah free. Alexis tremblingly lowered her arms.

Wide-eyed, Jackie cast Xander a look. "Am I missing something? I thought that Tanner was Alexis's boyfriend."

"We were mistaken," Xander told her, his voice catching.

The blond operative observed the exchange closely. "Xander, you seem quite interested in protecting this prisoner, although there's enough circumstantial evidence to suggest that he works for The Organization. If you let him go, I'll be forced to report to Doctor Gaige that you're being sympathetic to the enemy."

Alexis watched Xander meet the operative's glare. Xander's strong expression faltered for only an instant, but for Alexis it was enough. Xander was in trouble. She had to act.

"For the last time, Noah doesn't work for The Organization," Alexis blurted out. "He's really just my boyfriend. Um, see?"

Alexis pulled Noah toward her and connected her lips to his. She felt a sensation like a lightning bolt shoot through her body.

I'm kissing Noah Weston. I. Am. Kissing. Noah. Weston. Wait. I'm kissing Noah Weston?

Alexis sprang away from Noah, her cheeks scorching. Noah remained very still, staring at her.

The room was silent.

"And, um, regarding the confusion about Tanner . . . I can explain that, too," Alexis heard herself ramble on. "I danced with Tanner at the bonfire party, but he isn't my boyfriend. I was super excited that he wanted to dance, though, especially since I'd never been to a party like that before. Anyway, it's Crystal who has the massive crush on Tanner. Everyone knows that she really wants to go to homecoming with him. Oh, um, Crystal's the cheer team captain, by the way, but she's a pretty lousy dancer, to be honest. I think the only reason she became captain is because she sucked up to last year's seniors who were voting on it. She—"

"Enough! Enough of this ridiculous teenage soap opera!" the blond operative exclaimed impatiently. "Xander, if you want to sort out kids' love lives, that's fine. I have better things to do with my time."

With an exasperated shake of his head, the man stormed out of the room with the other operatives close on his heels.

"So I guess I'm clear to set up some transports home?" Jackie ventured after a pause, still sounding perplexed.

Xander viewed Alexis and Noah. "Yes, but how about you and I step out, Jackie, and discuss travel arrangements."

Jackie and Xander left the room, leaving Alexis and Noah alone in the quiet.

Her face still painfully hot, Alexis did not quite look at him. "Sorry about that, Noah. I, um, didn't know what else to do."

Noah stayed silent.

With a shake of her head, Alexis collected herself and motioned to the door. "Look, we don't have a lot of time. This is important, though: I think those two are on our side, but you can't mention anything about them to anyone. They made me promise. Okay?"

Noah finally spoke. "Alexis, I'm not going to leave you here."

"You have to. Get out of here before Doctor Gaige prevents it. Better that one of us escapes than none."

Noah shook his head.

"Noah, please. You need to trust me. Go while you can. Don't tell anyone about those two, get to Headquarters, and figure out a way to rescue me. They don't want to hurt me. And I can take care of myself. Remember, I've had a good teacher."

Noah smiled faintly.

Alexis heard footsteps beyond the door. "Be sure to let the others know that I'm alright."

Xander reentered the room with Jackie behind him. "Noah, I have a team ready to take you home. They'll want you hooded during the ride simply as part of the precautions taken to maintain our location's secrecy. Don't let it alarm you."

But Noah remained in his place.

"Go," Alexis whispered pleadingly. "Trust me, Noah. Please. Go."

Noah looked at Alexis again, searching her face. His expression changed slightly, and then he turned and walked out behind Xander. When Alexis heard the doors of the elevator open and close, she finally let tears fill her eyes.

Jackie came to her side. "How about we get you back to the infirmary. You should rest."

TWENTY FOUR

"The nearest witnesses, who were approximately five miles away from Planter's Field, told authorities that the brightly colored lights were visible in the sky around four o'clock this afternoon. Many locals believe the lights were of mystical origin. Weather experts, however, explain that the lights were caused by charged electrons colliding harmlessly with the earth's magnetic field. Whatever the cause, the display of lights was said to have been spectacular. From outside Planter's Field, this is Gary Sanchez reporting live for Channel Five Evening News."

Dr. Caul turned away from the monitor. "Do we have our people reviewing this broadcast?"

"Yep. They're working on it right now," Kate responded, typing fast on her keyboard.

"Rachel, the reporter said that the nearest witnesses were five miles from the field," Ralph noted. "Could it really be that every person in that search party who was not one of ours, as well as the other police officer and the FBI agent, were—"

"Working for Doctor Gaige?" Dr. Caul finished for him, sounding equally troubled. "Possibly so. The Domanorith had operatives everywhere."

The conversation was interrupted when the door was opened and Mr. Haber hurried into Central Command.

"Any luck tracking the GPS device that Miss Kendall was wearing?"

Kate shook her head. "No, Ben. The Domanorith must have found and deactivated it as soon as she was captured."

Mr. Haber's expression clouded over even more. "And Noah?"

"Nothing yet," Kate told him softly. "I'm sorry."

Mr. Haber took in a sharp breath. "Then I am taking a squad to begin a search for him. We will start at Planter's Field and circle out from there. Call me immediately if you get any updates. Anything."

Ralph put a hand on his shoulder. "Ben, I'm sure that Noah is alright. He's a smart boy and very skilled at defending himself. He'll be—"

"We have a disturbance," Kate cut in, pointing at her computer screen. "Someone without identification is approaching Central Command. I don't know how he or she possibly got into Headquarters without triggering an alarm."

Dr. Caul grabbed her magtro. "Call for security."

"Kate, bring up the surveillance cameras." Mr. Haber also reached for his weapon. "That person is right outside the door and—"

"Hey, don't freak out. It's only me."

Everyone turned with a start. Noah was standing in the open doorway.

"Noah!" Dr. Caul exclaimed.

Ralph stepped toward him. "Are you hurt?"

"No. I'm fine. I'm okay."

Mr. Haber appeared like a massive weight had lifted from him. "Noah, it is very good to see you."

"Thanks," Noah replied simply. He looked around the group. "I've seen Alexis."

"What?" Dr. Caul exclaimed, astounded. "Where? How? Is she alright?"

Noah took a seat. "She's at their base. Her right arm was in a cast, but she otherwise looked good."

"Noah, are you saying that you actually found and infiltrated the base of The Domanorith?" Mr. Haber was incredulous. "Alone?"

"Sort of. I basically used our original plan for Alexis on myself. I let myself get captured by making an obvious show of trying to steal one of their vehicles. I barely had enough time to ditch my magtro in the field before three operative thugs tossed a hood over my head, threw me into their rig, and drove me to their base."

Dr. Caul dropped her head in her hand. "Noah Weston, if I weren't so happy to see you right now, I'd ground you or something."

Mr. Haber sat down, stunned. "Their base—the actual base of the Domanorith—was close enough to Planter's Field that you were able to reach it by road? How long did it take you to get there?"

"Forty-eight minutes, including what I'm sure was a six-minute detour to throw me off," Noah replied immediately.

"Road conditions?"

"Flat for the first three miles, and then it was packed dirt at about a fifteen percent descent for the rest of the way."

"Kate, get us a map of all roads—paved and unpaved—that could be covered in a two-hour drive from Planter's Field," Dr. Caul ordered.

"You got it," she replied.

Noah met the inquiring stares of the others and continued, "When we arrived at their base, the operatives walked me through what sounded like a heavy set of double doors. We went through a foyer, turned right, and headed down a hallway before entering an elevator. That's when they removed the hood. From there, I was taken into an interrogation room where there . . . was a table and some chairs inside."

"That's when you saw Alexis?" Ralph prompted.

Noah smiled a little. "Yeah. She broke into the interrogation room and took one guy out with a flying chair."

"A flying chair?" Dr. Caul was unable to hide her grin. "You taught her well, Noah."

"Everyone is just a big cantaloupe," Noah replied, grinning himself. "Anyway, Alexis managed to convince them that I was . . . not part of The Organization, and so they let me go."

"They let you go simply because Alexis told them to?" Mr. Haber sounded both amazed and skeptical.

Noah shifted slightly. "Yeah. And a few minutes later, someone tossed the hood over my head and drove me to town. I asked them to drop me off at the community church, claiming it was close to my house. I'm sure that they took several detours along the way, again to throw me off. Once I had been let go and was sure that I wasn't being followed, I went to the school and rode the train here. Sorry I didn't notify you. My equipment is still out near the field."

Dr. Caul stood up, appearing troubled. "Doctor Gaige never knew that you were at their base. Had he known, he wouldn't have allowed his operatives to let you go. In fact, it's almost like someone on the inside is trying to help us. Did anyone approach you as an ally, Noah? Think hard. This is vital."

Noah's expression did not change. "No."

Just then, Albert rushed in. "You must see the news!" he proclaimed, turning on a monitor.

As the monitor lit up, everyone saw Gary Sanchez from Channel Five News smiling at the camera. He stood on a residential street, and there were police cars lining the road behind him. He began speaking in excited tones:

"Breaking news: Tanner Ricks, one of the two missing high school students, is home tonight. He is said to be amnestic to recent events but otherwise healthy and acting normally. Police and psychologists are planning to work with Tanner in the hopes of discovering where he has been since Saturday night. For now, though, the family spokesperson states that everyone is simply thrilled to have Tanner home safely.

"The other missing student, Drake Spencer, has not yet been found. However, Drake's family expressed joy at Tanner's return and that they pray Drake will also come home soon. We will stay on this story as it develops. This is Gary Sanchez, Channel Five News."

Albert shut off the monitor and faced the group. "You must be relieved to hear about such an incredible develop—Noah! I didn't see you here! You're alright!"

"Sorry to disappoint," Noah mumbled.

Dr. Caul was pensive. "Tanner and Noah both returning tonight cannot be a coincidence. It's like we have a sympathizer amid Doctor Gaige's operatives."

"Hmm. Possible." Mr. Haber distractedly checked a map on his magtro. "We need to move quickly to begin our search for where they are holding Miss Kendall. Kate, how are you coming along with your analysis?"

She gave a thumbs-up. "Almost completed."

Noah went for the door. "I'm going to take a team out to Planter's Field to locate my magtro. I'll get back here in time to join the search for . . . hang on, what's this?" Noah pulled a cell phone out of his jacket pocket and turned it over in his hand. "This belongs to Alexis. How did it . . ?"

Noah's eyebrows shot up, and he started pushing buttons on the phone.

Dr. Caul came to his side. "What is it? What are you thinking?"

"I'm thinking that Alexis slipped her phone into my pocket on purpose," Noah spoke fast. "Remember when we told her to keep her phone off because operatives would be able to track her calls? She—"

"That must have been how The Domanorith knew where she was going this afternoon!" Mr. Haber hit his forehead with his hand. "That is how they were able to prepare for us!"

"Exactly," Noah replied while pushing another button on the phone. "This indicates Alexis called Molly late yesterday. No doubt The Domanorith learned of her plans because of that call."

Dr. Caul continued watching Noah. "But that still doesn't explain why Alexis snuck her phone to you tonight."

"Well, yesterday she made a mistake. But tonight, giving away her location was exactly what Alexis wanted to do." Noah gestured to the phone screen. "Looks like she called me earlier this evening. I had already ditched my stuff and didn't answer, yet Alexis kept the call live for several minutes. When I saw her in the interrogation room, Alexis must have put her phone into my pocket to—"

"Tell us that we might be able to identify her location from the call that she made," Mr. Haber finished.

"I'll get working on it," Kate told them. "We'll combine the information gleaned from that phone call with the data Noah provided. We should be able to get a very good idea of where Alexis is being held."

Mr. Haber went to the door. "I will notify the battalion that we will be leaving soon for a rescue mission."

***

Alexis rolled onto her side, letting her casted arm flop onto the infirmary bed. It felt good to be resting, although she knew that she would never be able to fall asleep.

I kissed Noah Weston. I kissed him . . . but it didn't mean anything. It was an emergency. I was pretending. So was he. It's no big deal.

Yet no matter how she tried, Alexis could not stop thinking about Noah—his steady voice, slight smile, and the way he often looked at her. Noah had counseled and trained her with thoughtful dedication. He had even put his own life at risk to keep her safe. As the memories stirred her heart, Alexis let a tear roll down her cheek. She admitted to herself what she had instinctively known for a long time: that she harbored a tender excitement and hope about Noah, which were unlike feelings she had for anyone else. When those feelings developed, Alexis could not say. But they were deep and strong. With a sigh, Alexis closed her eyes, smiling as she finally drifted to sleep.

***

"We've got it, Ben. We know where she's located."

Mr. Haber joined Dr. Caul, who was looking over Kate's shoulder at a satellite image on the computer monitor.

"The call she made on her cell phone came from here." Kate zoomed in on the image. "The coordinates are a great match with the information that Noah gathered when he was captured."

Mr. Haber bent forward for a better view of the monitor. "Can you zoom farther? What is out there?"

Kate clicked the keyboard a few times. "Oddly, we're seeing nothing but small mountains and countryside."

"Could their base be underground?" Dr. Caul wondered.

"It must be." Mr. Haber stood up straight again. "We are leaving in ten minutes. I will contact Noah and tell him not to return here after finding his magtro, but to go instead—"

"Noah already returned from Planter's Field." Kate gestured to the tracking system.

Mr. Haber raised an eyebrow. "How on earth did he get there and back so fast?"

"I believe he took the chopper," Kate explained.

Mr. Haber sighed. "Teenagers."

***

"Security, how is Alexis doing?"

"Fine. She hasn't made a noise since Jackie brought her to the infirmary," one of the security guards replied. "The doctor said she'll be resting in her room for the remainder of the night. I can't imagine that a concussed girl with a broken wrist is gonna cause any trouble. Do you still want us to remain stationed outside her room?"

Xander smiled, the memory of the operative getting smacked in the face by a flying chair still fresh in his mind. "Yes. As a routine precaution, of course."

"Copy that," the security guard stated. "No

complaints from our end. Makes it an easy night for us."

Xander put his communicator down on his office desk and flipped the TV to another channel. The story of Tanner's safe return was being covered by every evening news broadcast. Xander continued watching, deep in thought, until a message came through on his communicator:

```
Noah left at community church, per his request.
                Team at base.
            Transport complete.
```

Another person whose life was put at risk tonight, Xander fumed. Then he paused and read the message again. *Why would Noah ask to be dropped off at the church?*

Too exhausted to think, Xander leaned forward and dropped his head in his hands. He knew that he would never forget his shock at seeing Noah being dragged into the interrogation room. The sight of his younger brother staring at him across the table would haunt Xander forever.

Noah has had to grow up too fast. I could see it in his eyes.

Xander turned toward the mirror on the office wall, staring at his reflection with eyes that were just like Noah's.

I guess we both had to grow up fast after Dad was killed.

***

"What is on your mind, Noah?"

Noah jumped slightly. "Huh? Nothing."

Mr. Haber was watching him. "You have done an incredible job through all of this. Your parents would be proud."

"Thanks." Noah looked away and swallowed hard. "But it's not over yet."

"No, indeed it is not," Mr. Haber replied, bracing himself as the armored vehicle rolled through another deep pothole in the road.

"Approaching rendezvous point," Jason announced from the driver's seat.

The vehicle slowed, allowing Mr. Haber and Noah to jump out. Then Jason sped off, disappearing noiselessly into the night. As a cool wind rustled the trees, Noah and Mr. Haber jogged up the rocky mountainside to their designated lookout point. They peered over the edge of the mountain, which dropped steeply down to the forested valley below.

"We are in position," Mr. Haber reported into his magtro.

"Central Command copies," Dr. Caul replied. "Jason, are you in position?"

"I've reached the valley. I'm joining the battalion now," Jason answered.

"Copy," Dr. Caul said. "And Jasper, is everything set on your end?"

"Yes. The fly-over will be commencing shortly."

"Copy," Dr. Caul replied, ending the communication.

Noah paced. "So what do we do now?"

Mr. Haber raised his night vision binoculars. "We wait for the fly-over to conclude. We need to know what else—if anything—is down there and where the entrance to the underground base is located."

"How long will the fly-over take?"

"It should be complete in twenty minutes."

"Twenty minutes?" Noah impatiently kicked the dirt with his shoe.

Mr. Haber glanced at him. "The fly-over had to start three minutes behind schedule because, for some reason, the chopper was low on fuel."

Noah almost grinned. "Sorry."

***

How long have I been asleep?

Alexis opened her eyes. Her head ached, and she was still nauseated. Reaching out, she used her left arm to flip on the lamp by the bed, which cast a long shadow onto the white walls of the infirmary room. In front of her, a chair was hovering a few feet in the air. The clock that sat on the small desk beside the chair indicated it was eight-forty-two pm.

Maybe there wasn't enough reception for my call to Noah to get through. Maybe he found my phone, but it won't help them. Maybe they'll never have a way to locate me.

Alexis raised her arms in the air, the right one bulky and heavy from the cast.

If I try to fight my way out, how far would I get? Security is outside the door, and there are probably a million operatives in this place.

Alexis dropped her arms and stared despondently at the ceiling. Then she sat up with a start.

If I can be a giant ceiling rat at school, why can't I be one here, too?

Alexis pushed off her blanket, stood up on the bed, and concentrated. With jerky motions, the bed rose off the floor. Soon, Alexis was high enough to rest her left palm against a ceiling panel. She pushed it aside, the scraping noise it made sounding like a bomb going off in the quiet. Alexis froze, listening tensely as the security guards on the other side of the door spoke to one another. Then they went quiet once again.

Convinced she had not aroused the guards' suspicion, Alexis clumsily boosted herself into the crawl space and rolled onto her stomach. Looking down at the room below, she made the bed and chair drift to the floor where they belonged. Satisfied, Alexis pushed the ceiling panel into place and began crawling through the blackness. For a few seconds, she thought that she heard the faint sound of a helicopter somewhere outside.

***

"The fly-over team has completed their assignment, and the crew is returning to Headquarters," came Jasper's announcement.

"Copy. We at Central Command are downloading your surveillance images now," Dr. Caul replied.

"We will wait to receive those images before moving out." Mr. Haber put his magtro away.

Noah restlessly tapped the binoculars in his hand. "Ben, I had a thought: we trained Alexis to defend herself and use her powers, if necessary. So what if she actually tries doing just that?"

"You mean, what if Miss Kendall tries to fight?"

"If she tries to fight or, more likely, attempts to escape and ends up having to fight."

"Miss Kendall will be patient. She knows that we are coming."

"Does she? She has no way of knowing that we found her phone or that we were able to locate her."

"Nonetheless, I am sure that Miss Kendall will give us some time."

Noah remained wary. "Or she'll charge ahead on her own. Like, for example, taking out operatives with some sort of floating furniture."

"Hmm. I see your point." Mr. Haber checked his magtro with more urgency. "The fly-over images have almost finished downloading. We will move out as soon as they come through."

Noah turned to peer out over the dark valley below. "Hang on, Alexis," he whispered. "We're coming. Don't try anything funny down there."

***

Alexis had nearly crawled into a wall before she realized it was there. She was at a dead end. Feeling her way in the darkness, Alexis backed up and was about to move in a different direction when she heard a recognizable sound behind the wall.

It's an elevator shaft.

Working fast, Alexis pried the fingers of her good hand underneath one of the ceiling panels, lifting it slightly out of place. Peering through the opening, Alexis saw another hallway beneath her. There were elevator doors to the right.

Alexis again heard the whirring sound, this time followed by a chime from the elevator. She pulled her head out of view. A second later, the elevator doors below had opened and the hallway became filled by the sounds of people talking and walking away. When the noise finally faded, Alexis closed her eyes.

Keep the elevator doors open.

Everything was still. Cautiously, Alexis slid forward and inspected the hallway. To her right, the elevator remained empty with its doors ajar. To her left, halfway down the vacant corridor, was a set of heavy fire doors. Alexis hurriedly made the doors slam shut, and then she scanned the area once more, confirming that the section of hallway under her was secured.

Alexis changed her focus to a bench that sat against a wall near the elevator. At her bidding, the bench rose until it was hovering underneath her. She lowered herself onto the bench and set the ceiling panel into place. Then, grasping the bench with her good hand, she directed it to the floor.

As the bench touched down, the fire doors started rattling loudly. Someone was on the other side, trying to pry them open. Alexis scurried off the bench and rushed into the elevator. Scanning the panel of buttons, Alexis saw that she was on the third floor. The basement was listed as being a level below, and the second, first, and ground floors were marked above.

I must be underground. I need to go up to the ground floor to get out of this place.

The fire doors were yanked open.

"Hold the elevator!" someone yelled.

Alexis hit the button for the ground floor and threw herself against the side wall of the elevator to hide from view. Alexis caught a brief glimpse of a woman rushing toward the elevator before the doors closed completely.

"How rude. Didn't even wait for me," Alexis heard the woman say as the elevator began its ascent.

***

"Xander, I need you to review something."

Xander shook his head as the operative's voice came through on his communicator. *Just when I thought that I'd be able to lie down for a few minutes.*

With a sigh, Xander finished rolling up his sleeves, got off his office couch, walked over to his computer, and opened an email that was waiting.

"Alright, I'm opening your email right now," Xander replied into his communicator. "What's going on?"

"I've sent you a record of a cell phone call," the operative explained. "Earlier this evening, someone who was in our base used a regular cell phone to place a call to the outside. I don't know why anyone would do that, how anyone managed to get reception, or who would ignore policy, but it happened."

Xander scanned the record, his pulse jumping. *She actually made a call. That's enough for The Organization to track her location. Alexis might lead them right to us.* Xander picked up his communicator and spoke into it sharply. "Security, what's the status on Alexis?"

A few seconds passed before someone who sounded like he was eating replied. "It's been totally quiet in there."

Xander stood up. "Go check on her."

"Alright, hang on a minute."

Xander overheard the security guard setting his communicator down while saying, "The boss wants us to check on the girl."

When there was prolonged silence, Xander knew his suspicion was about to be confirmed.

"She's gone!" the security guard finally blurted over the communicator. "I don't know how she escaped! We've been out here the whole time, and no one went in or out! Nothing in the room is out of place!"

"Initiate a lockdown."

Xander put the communicator down. He needed to find Alexis. Fast.

***

Mr. Haber reviewed the fly-over images on his magtro. "I agree, Rachel. There must be an entrance to their underground base in the northeast corner. The absence of trees there is too unusual. They have been deliberately cleared out."

"After all of these years, we've finally found the base of the Domanorith, Ben," Dr. Caul stated quietly. "It's been this close the whole time. And I'm sure those kids are in there."

Mr. Haber paused before speaking again. "Jason, move the battalion to the northeast, but stay within the cover of the forest and do not advance until ordered."

"Copy," came Jason's response.

Noah was watching Mr. Haber closely. "So what will we do?"

Mr. Haber faced him. "We will head down the mountainside to join Jason and the battalion. We will have to use the main entrance to infiltrate the base, as it is the only access point we have been able to identify."

Noah's eyebrows shot up. "You mean that—"

"I mean that our arrival will not be subtle."

TWENTY FIVE

The elevator came to an abrupt stop, tossing Alexis into the wall. The doors remained shut. As she regained her footing, Alexis heard a siren begin to go off outside. Then a haunting, robotic voice echoed through the air:

"Attention all personnel: this is a complete lockdown. Repeat: this is a complete lockdown."

Alexis clapped a hand over her mouth. *They know. They know that I'm gone. The entire operative world is searching for me, and I'm trapped in this elevator.*

Beyond the elevator doors, shouts and the sounds of people running could be heard. Someone rushed to the elevator and started trying to force the doors open.

Alexis staggered backward and squeezed her eyes shut. *Go up to the ground floor! Now! Now!*

The elevator resumed its ascent, causing the person beyond the doors to let out an angry exclamation. Alexis had only moments before the elevator panel lit up, indicating that she was about to reach the ground floor. Shaking with adrenaline, she pressed her body against the side wall to hide.

The elevator came to a stop. Alexis raised her arms, readying herself to fight, as the doors slid open. No one entered. Alexis strained to listen but could hear nothing except for the deafening siren. She inched forward. Peeking past the doors, Alexis found herself staring down a long, empty corridor. Lit only by flashing emergency lights, the hallway stretched out straight before her until finally making a left turn out of view in the distance.

That might lead to the way out . . . but it might not.

The elevator shook, as if it had been called to a different floor. In a split-second decision, Alexis leapt off the elevator and charged down the corridor, her ears pulsating from the siren and her motions disorienting in the strobe light. As she approached the left turn, Alexis slowed to a stop and checked behind her. The corridor remained empty, and the elevator doors had closed.

Alexis faced forward, lifted her arms, and guardedly crept around the corner. To her astonishment, she found herself standing at one end of a vacant foyer. There was a set of thick metal double doors on the opposite side. Alexis nearly let out a cry of joy.

That's got to be the exit!

Alexis bolted for the doors. Suddenly, she was grabbed from behind. Letting out a scream, she frantically struggled to free herself from the man with bulky, hairy arms who held her violently in his grip. She heard him laugh, and then he pushed her hard to the cold floor. As she grappled to regain her breath, the man used his heavy boot to roll her onto her back and pressed his heel into her chest, pinning her down.

"My, my, what have we here?" he asked, standing directly over her.

Alexis stared, terrified, at the overweight, middle-aged man who was hovering over her and blotting perspiration from his forehead with his tie.

"Get off of me!" Alexis grunted, squirming to get away.

The man only pressed his boot down harder, keeping Alexis trapped. "Allow me to introduce myself. My name is Gerard. I work with Doctor Gaige. We've been looking for you."

Alexis started to raise her burning arms, but Gerard swiftly kicked her in the side. She felt her ribs crack, and a terrible searing sensation spread throughout her chest and abdomen. Crying out in agony, Alexis dropped her arms to her sides. Every breath caused her excruciating pain.

The man seemed to recognize that Alexis had been rendered too weak to attack. He lifted his boot off of her and knelt at her side. To Alexis's horror, she saw his eyes flash red.

"Now that we've gone through our introductions," Gerard said loudly over the emergency siren, "you're going to come with me to pay a visit to my dear colleague, Xander."

Alexis shifted, groaned, and fell still, the pain in her chest making it impossible to move.

Almost talking to himself, Gerard went on, "You see, Xander took over as Head of Intelligence a few years ago. The committee decided that I was losing my ability to do the job, and they voted Xander in to replace me. I pretended to be cooperative, waiting for the day when I would get a chance to regain my position. That day has come. I am going to demonstrate that I still deserve to be in charge."

Alexis shuddered. Gerard's tone was so menacing that it was clear he intended to kill.

"Xander has had no clue how to run this operation," Gerard's spat. "His plans have been ridiculously cautious, leading to one delay after another. I knew that I needed to correct things. You see, little girl, I was the one who coordinated that attack on you at the bonfire party last Saturday night."

Gerard seemed pleased to see Alexis's eyes widen in disgust. He smiled. "And were it not for some minor interference, my plan would have been successful. But my chance has come again. Finding you here is fate. I am going to correct this situation, once and for all."

All Alexis could do was shake her head.

"Don't worry." Gerard's tone was mocking. "I will offer to spare Xander's life if he steps down as Head of Intelligence and surrenders to my control. If he refuses . . . no, he won't refuse. The threat of you and Drake both dying by my hand will be enough to persuade him to cooperate. Xander's emotions make him far too vulnerable."

Delirious from pain, Alexis attempted again to lift her arms. But the unbearable aching in her rib cage prevented her. Desperate, she scanned the foyer for an object that she could command as a weapon. There was nothing.

Gerard pulled something from the pocket of his suit coat and spoke into it. "I've located the girl.

Ground floor. In the foyer about twenty yards from the main entrance."

"Excellent," replied a woman with a nasally voice. "We're coming up on the elevator now."

There was a sound in the distance, which Alexis knew came from the elevator at the far end of the corridor. Then she heard footsteps approaching. Soon, Alexis was being looked down at by a man with black hair and a woman with a long nose.

"You found her, Gerard!" the woman with the nasally voice proclaimed, observing Alexis as if she were a trophy.

Gerard puffed out his chest. "Yes. I wondered if our little friend would get closer to escaping than Xander believed she could. So I slipped away from my search group and came up here. I had only been hiding in the foyer closet for a few minutes when, sure enough, she showed up and made a run for it. I caught her in the nick of time."

"Another reason why Gerard should be Head of Intelligence again, wouldn't you agree, Antonio?" the woman asked the other man.

"I will be in charge again," Gerard quickly corrected her, getting to his feet. He motioned to someone else whom Alexis could not see. "Our little friend will probably need your assistance. She slipped and took a nasty fall, the poor thing."

The person standing behind Alexis lifted her from the ground. Alexis suppressed a scream of pain as she was moved. Her head swirled and her sight dimmed. When her vision cleared, Alexis saw that it was Drake Spencer who held her in his arms.

Drake smirked when he saw her shocked expression. "Hey, Alexis, how are your plans coming along for homecoming?"

"Now, now, Drake, be nice," Gerard chided while Leslie and Antonio laughed. "Just because we got you out of the infirmary doesn't mean that you should tease those who are still injured."

A grin spread over Drake's face.

Gerard gestured again to the thing he held in his hand. "I say it's time that I contact Xander, don't you?"

***

"Xander, it's Gerard. I know where the girl is."

Xander could barely hear what Gerard was saying, due to the blaring emergency siren. Holding his communicator closer to his ear, Xander moved to his computer and swiftly began scrolling through the live feeds from the security cameras that he had hidden around the base.

"Where is she?" Xander asked, his sharp eyes scanning the monitor. "I will send a team to get her."

"No need to send anyone. I've got her with me in the basement, and she's being quite cooperative."

Xander stopped on the video feed from the ground floor foyer. His blood went cold. "I see."

"Why don't you come down to the basement and meet us?" Gerard went on cordially. "I think that when the time comes to explain this whole mess to Doctor Gaige, it will sound better if he hears that it only required a quiet little handover to return her to the infirmary rather than an emergency response. Plus, it will be much less scary for the girl, wouldn't you agree?"

Xander stood up straight. "You say that you're in the basement?"

"Yes, I was instructed by the leader of my search group to come down here."

"Who else is with you?"

Gerard spoke pleasantly. "I'm alone. No need for you to bring anyone else. I will wait for you in Pod L."

"Very well. I will be there in approximately fifteen minutes. I need to scale down the security response first."

Xander ended the conversation and put his communicator away. Then he slipped his telron into his pocket.

So it comes down to this.

TWENTY SIX

"In the basement? A quiet little handover?" Leslie repeated, sneering gleefully. "Think Xander bought it?"

The emergency siren shut off.

"Ha! It sounds like he bought it." Gerard chuckled and bent over Alexis, who was still hanging limply in Drake's arms. "Now, my little troublemaking friend, shall we go? Xander will be waiting for us."

A flash of light was the only warning they had before the doors exploded open with a tremendous boom. The floor shook. Sparks and debris filled the air. Then a huge cloud of unnaturally thick, dark smoke began filling the foyer.

"It's The Organization!" Leslie screamed.

"Come on! Come on!" Gerard motioned frantically for the others to stay with him. "Get away from the doors!"

As more of the strange smoke poured into the foyer, Alexis made a renewed effort to free herself from Drake's hold, but the horrific pain in her chest forced her to drop back in his arms. Panting in agony, Alexis could do nothing as Drake carried her away from the exit. Drake raced around the corner with the others, fleeing along the corridor toward the elevator, every step he took brutally jarring Alexis's ribs. Through the smoke and her tears of pain, she could barely make out that the doors of the elevator were closed. She shut her eyes.

The elevator is broken.

"This thing is jammed!" she heard Antonio shout.

Reopening her eyes, Alexis saw Antonio hitting the elevator call button furiously.

Leslie began trying to pry the elevator doors open with her hands. "We have to get out of here! We're going to be outnumbered!"

"Look behind us! Look at that!" Drake yelled.

Alexis raised her head to see what had caused Drake to shudder. The gigantic cloud of dark smoke had rolled around the corner and was slowly advancing toward them.

"It's a smokescreen! There are agents hiding in it!" Leslie screeched.

Antonio pulled out his weapon. "Let's take the stairs! Where are the stairs?"

"The stairs are back at the other end of the corridor!" Gerard pointed toward the smoke. "We'd have to cross through the smokescreen! We'd run right into the agents!"

"So let's cut off the agents before they reach us!" Leslie reached out and yanked off the cover of the fire alarm.

Immediately, a strobe light on the wall started to flash. From somewhere behind the smoke, Alexis heard the sound of the fire doors slamming shut.

"Those doors will hold them for a while." Seeming to relax, Antonio put his telron away and faced the elevator again. "I'll try to override the elevator program and get it to open."

Gerard still studied the dark wall of smoke, which kept creeping silently toward them. "There are agents in there. I know it."

"Don't be ridiculous, Gerard." Leslie gestured down the long corridor. "There's no way that they made it all the way from the foyer to in front of the fire doors before I pulled the alarm. Those agents are stuck behind the doors for now, at least."

Gerard's breathing grew strained. "They're in there. I'm sure of it. But I will not let them win. Not when I have the ultimate collateral." He pulled out his telron while shouting toward the smoke. "I have the girl! I will hurt her even more than I have already if you come any closer!"

Ignoring the crushing pain in her chest, Alexis did her best to yell. "There are four operatives down here, including Drake! They're armed and—"

"Shut up!" Gerard warned Alexis. He then began waving his weapon. "Show yourselves or I will hurt the girl! I swear that I will hurt her!"

Gerard's voice echoed away into silence. Alexis still saw nothing except for the massive wall of smoke moving ever closer.

"This is my last warning!" Gerard screamed, suddenly aiming his telron at Alexis's head.

"Then I suppose that leaves us with little room for negotiation," a voice behind the smoke replied.

Gerard let out a surprised cry as Leslie gasped and Antonio whirled around. There was a nerve-racking pause, and then Mr. Haber stepped out from the wall of smoke with his magtro aimed.

"You!" Gerard barked. "Put your weapon down!"

Revealing nothing in his expression, Mr. Haber set his magtro on the ground and used his foot to push it behind him into the smoke. He gave Alexis a glance before putting his eyes on Drake. "Hello, Mister Spencer."

Drake's face blanched. "Mister Haber? You work for The Organization?"

"And you, Mister Spencer, decided to aid The Domanorith?"

Drake threw his shoulders back. "Don't try to guilt me. I know all about what you do. You hide important scientific information from the world so you can have the glory all for yourselves."

"They have indoctrinated you well, I see," Mr. Haber noted sadly. "Yes, sometimes we are forced to protect truths in order to prevent them from being horribly misused."

"Enough!" Gerard interjected, beads of sweat dripping down his forehead. "If you want the girl to live, get down on your stomach! Now!"

Mr. Haber obeyed, prostrating himself on the floor.

"And if you have any cowardly friends hiding in the smoke, Mister Haber," Drake added arrogantly, "tell them to show their faces and do the same."

"You're the coward, Drake," Noah replied, emerging from the smoke with his magtro aimed directly at Drake's head.

Drake's confident expression faltered before he forced a mocking smile. "What is this, a high school reunion? Is Miss Hinshaw gonna come out next?"

"No, I am."

Wearing camouflage gear and face paint, Jason appeared out of the smoke with a magtro in each hand. He pointed his own weapon at Gerard while keeping Mr. Haber's magtro aimed at Antonio and Leslie.

"Don't make any quick movements," Jason instructed in his low voice. "Let Alexis go, and all of you get down on the floor."

Leslie and Antonio fearfully raised their arms and dropped to their knees. Drake set Alexis onto the ground. As her feet touched the floor and she bore her own weight, Alexis felt as though something tore her chest. Crying out, she began to fall.

"Alexis!" Noah reached for her.

But Gerard grabbed Alexis, yanking her against him. He pressed his telron against her head. "Drop your magtro, young man."

Growing faint, Alexis saw Noah freeze. Eyes filled with fury, he placed his magtro on the floor.

Gerard addressed Jason next. "You, too. Put those weapons down or she dies."

Jason placed both magtros at his feet, his unrelenting stare never leaving Gerard's face.

"Now get on the ground," Gerard growled.

No one moved.

"Do it, gentlemen," Mr. Haber said, watching Gerard closely.

Jason and Noah exchanged a look, and then they both lay down not far from Mr. Haber.

Leslie sprang to her feet, pulling her telron from her suit coat. "They're unarmed! Shoot them, you fools! Shoot!"

"No!" Alexis screamed.

As Leslie took aim at Noah, Mr. Haber sprang up and threw himself into her. The impact caused Leslie to lose hold of her telron, which landed on the floor.

"Stop!" Gerard bellowed.

But the fight continued as Antonio scrambled to his feet and pointed his telron at Mr. Haber. Immediately, Jason dove forward, grabbed his weapon, and shot at Antonio. Antonio was hit by the beam of orange just as he fired at Mr. Haber. The streak of red from Antonio's attack veered off course and impacted Mr. Haber in the leg. Antonio, struck squarely by Jason's shot, collapsed and did not move.

"No!" Gerard spun around with Alexis as a shield in front of him. "Stop or I will kill this girl!"

Again, Gerard's cries were ignored. Leslie broke free of wounded Mr. Haber's hold, and Noah snatched up his magtro and lunged for Leslie's telron before she could get to it. When Drake saw what was happening, he intercepted Noah, and the two young men became locked in a violent wrestling match. Drake twisted and punched Noah in the face. Noah flipped Drake over, pinning him down.

With Alexis in his suffocating hold, Gerard continued shouting. "Drop your magtros! Drop them now! I mean it! I will kill this girl!"

Mr. Haber, unarmed and limping, jerked up his head and eyed Gerard. "Do as he says, gentlemen."

Things suddenly became eerily quiet. Jason set his magtro alongside Mr. Haber's weapon. Noah put up his hands. Getting to his feet, Drake vengefully grabbed Noah by the shirt and punched him again.

"Stop it!" Alexis yelled, horrified.

His arm poised to hit Noah again, Drake stopped when he heard Alexis's cry. "Don't . . . don't tell me what to do, Alexis," he uttered, though he let Noah go.

"That's right, Drake. They're not in charge," Leslie encouraged. "Now, cover the others."

With a weak nod, Drake pulled a telron from his jeans pocket and aimed it unsteadily at Mr. Haber and Jason.

Smirking with satisfaction, Leslie strolled over near Noah and picked up his magtro. "Why don't I take care of this for you?" She next collected her own telron, which she pointed right at him. "Now, get up, young man."

Staring straight ahead, Noah stood, ignoring the blood coming from his nose. Leslie pushed Noah forward so he was in front of Alexis, who remained locked in Gerard's arms.

Almost within reach of him, Alexis searched Noah's face for a glimmer of assurance in his gray eyes. But Noah seemed to be looking past her as if she did not exist.

Leslie leaned close to Noah's ear. "You poor boy, you were almost a hero, but you failed." She grinned at Gerard. "I think we should make this a little more interesting, don't you?"

Gerard shifted with agitation. "Fine. Be quick about it, though."

Leslie eyed Drake next. He still had his telron pointed at Mr. Haber and Jason but was staring, white-faced, at Antonio's body.

"Drake," Leslie cooed, "you should have a reward for doing so well tonight. You're going to be the one to kill this boy. Kill him while the girl watches."

Drake became totally still. "What?"

"You heard me." Leslie motioned to Noah. "You're going to kill this boy. Right now."

"We . . . we aren't going to take them as prisoners?" Drake almost whispered.

Leslie narrowed her eyes. "No, we are not going to take them as prisoners."

"No, Drake. Please. Don't do it," Alexis begged. "Don't listen to—"

"Shut up!" Gerard growled, shaking Alexis roughly.

The motion caused a new surge of pain in Alexis's ribs. As she grimaced in agony, Noah winced but did not look away.

Leslie continued observing Drake. "What's the matter? You're not having second thoughts about joining us, are you?"

Drake hesitated before shaking his head.

"Very good." Leslie stepped away from Noah while aiming her weapon at Mr. Haber and Jason. "Do it, then. Now."

"No! Don't hurt him, Drake!" Alexis pleaded, barely able to breathe. "Please!"

While Alexis yelled for mercy, Noah turned his head and looked Drake in the eyes. Noah's face was devoid of emotion. Drake shook as he lifted his weapon and aimed at Noah. Seconds passed. Finally—slowly—Drake lowered his arm.

"I can't do it," Drake whimpered

"You can't?" Leslie laughed. Keeping her telron pointed at Mr. Haber and Jason, she aimed Noah's magtro at Drake. "Actually, I really think you can."

"Leslie! What are you doing?" Gerard demanded.

Leslie's reply was fierce. "The boy has to prove himself worthy of joining us."

Drake's eyes grew wide.

Mr. Haber voice was even as he spoke. "Mister Spencer, you do not have to do what she tells you."

"I don't have a choice." The desperation in Drake's voice was obvious as he eyed Leslie. Quivering, he pointed his weapon at Noah again. "I'm sorry, Noah."

"No!" Alexis cried out, her arms feeling as though they were on fire.

The next thing Alexis knew, a blinding white light had shot from her hands. The uncontrolled, massive force threw her into Gerard, who stumbled and lost hold of her. As she fell to her knees, Alexis heard Leslie scream in pain and rage. Raising her head, Alexis was met by the horrifying sight of Leslie writhing on the ground, her face burned and badly disfigured.

"You did this to me!" Leslie screeched at Alexis, getting to her feet and readying her weapon. "You did this!"

"Leslie, stop!" Gerard regained his footing. "I won't let you hurt the girl!"

But Leslie did not seem to hear as she aimed her telron at Alexis. "You did this!"

All Alexis saw was the flash of red from Leslie's weapon before she was pushed out of the way of the attack. Alexis heard someone cry out in agony and collapse in front of her. There was another burst of red from a different direction, and Leslie screamed once more. After that, there was only silence.

Alexis dared to raise her eyes. Leslie was dead on the floor, her arm still pointing a weapon in Alexis's direction. Gerard stood close, his telron aimed for Leslie. Alexis wincingly pushed herself up on one arm and looked for the others.

Then she saw him.

Noah lay in front of her, blood coming from a wound that had been caused by Leslie's strike. The strike that had been meant for her. Alexis cried out as the reality of what had happened crashed down upon her. She couldn't think. She couldn't breathe. She felt numb.

"Oh no. No. Please no. Please," Alexis whispered. She reached out her hand and brushed his hair. "Noah? Answer me. Please answer me. Noah? Noah?"

Noah did not move.

Alexis collapsed on top of him and sobbed.
Noah is dead because of me. Noah is dead. Dead.

"Get up."

Gerard gripped Alexis's arm, pulling her to her feet. Alexis did not resist. Nothing seemed real anymore. She did not even feel pain.

"Come on, Drake," Gerard snapped. "It's time for us to exit this little party."

Drake could barely hold himself up against the wall while his shell-shocked gaze stayed fixed on Noah's body.

Suddenly, a small flash of light caught Alexis's attention. The elevator panel had lit up. Someone was coming. Through her tears, Alexis scanned the smoke-filled room and spotted Mr. Haber, who briefly let his eyes meet hers. Mr. Haber had seen the light, too.

Drake moved with strained steps to join Gerard. "Where . . . where did the other guy go? The guy in all the military—"

"Get down! Get down!"

Jason came running out of the smoke, magtros in both hands, motioning for Mr. Haber to take cover. Leaping forward, Jason threw himself over Noah's body. An instant later, a huge flash of fire lit up behind him. The explosion rocked the floor. Drake fell to the ground. Gerard lost his balance and struck his head against the wall. Freed again from Gerard's grip, Alexis began crawling away from him. Her hand hit something: Noah's magtro.

"The doors are open. Send Dave in to help with evacuation of the wounded. Prepare medical response for one critical and one serious," Jason said into his magtro. He tossed Mr. Haber's weapon to him. "Ben, take Noah and get out. I'll cover you."

The smoke was becoming thicker as Mr. Haber limped across the room and hefted Noah's body over his shoulder with surprising strength. Another agent, whom Alexis could barely see through the fog, charged through the fire doors and lifted her up. Meanwhile, with magtro raised, Jason spun around, hunting for where Gerard and Drake were concealed in the smoke.

"Go, Ben. Go Dave." Jason barked. "I'll find Drake and trail you out. The battle is heavy outside, but the battalion is ready to give you cover."

The agent carrying Alexis began running down the corridor, headed for the foyer. As they reached the exit, the smoke cleared enough for Alexis to see Mr. Haber carrying Noah's motionless body over his shoulder.

Far behind her, Alexis heard the elevator chime.

TWENTY SEVEN

The elevator chimed. Inside, Xander pressed his back against the side wall and gripped his telron, waiting as the elevator finished coming to a stop on the ground floor. The doors slid open. Xander hesitated. With most operatives tied up in the battle near the main entrance, he did not know how long it would be before he could get assistance. But Xander did know that Alexis was in grave danger as Gerard's captive, and every second mattered.

He had no choice but to proceed alone.

With tense, deliberate movements, Xander stepped from the elevator into the corridor, which was filled by a massive, dark cloud—no doubt, the remnants of a smoke screen. Squinting to see through the thick, swirling haze, Xander coughed and raised his telron.

"Gerard, it's me. Where is Alexis?"

There was no response.

I'll never be able to get a clear shot, Xander determined, though he kept his weapon at the ready. *I need to buy some time.*

Xander began advancing.

"I saw you on a security camera when you called me, Gerard. I know that you weren't in the basement. You were up here with Antonio and Leslie. So make this easy. Where's Alexis?"

"I will gladly tell you," a crazed voice replied, "if you cooperate with me."

Xander spun toward the sound. Through the smoke, he saw two figures approaching. He soon identified Gerard, sweating and wide-eyed, pushing Drake forward. Ignoring an oozing wound on his scalp, Gerard had one arm clamped tightly around Drake's neck and was using his other arm to point his telron at Drake's head.

Xander kept his own telron raised but moved his finger away from the trigger. "What are you doing, Gerard?"

Gerard laughed unsteadily. "What am I doing? I'm getting my revenge! I'm regaining the respect that I lost when you took everything from me!"

Xander inched forward. His shoe struck something, causing him to glance down. Antonio's body was on the ground. Xander put his finger back on the trigger of his weapon.

"Xander, disarm and surrender to me." Gerard jerked his head toward Drake. "Otherwise, this boy dies."

Xander's gut told him it was a hoax, yet he could not take a chance—not with Drake's life. Keeping his focus on Gerard, Xander complied, crouching down and setting his telron on the floor. As he stood back up, a flash of movement in the smoke to his right caused Xander to do a double take. Someone else was with them.

"There, you see?" Xander heard Gerard remark. "That wasn't too hard, was it?"

Xander refocused on Gerard to reply, but he saw that Gerard was talking to Drake. Gerard's threat had been a hoax, after all. Released from Gerard's grip, Drake began laughing nervously while rubbing the red mark on his neck. Gerard turned, pointed his telron at Xander, and addressed him once more:

"Now let's decide what we're going to do with you, Xander." Chuckling peculiarly, Gerard kicked Xander's telron out of reach. "Yes, what shall we do with our dear friend here?"

Over Gerard's shoulder, Xander again saw the silhouette of someone passing noiselessly through the haze. Xander put his eyes on Gerard's and replied:

"I've done everything you've asked. So let Drake get out of here, and tell me where Alexis is located."

"Did I mention that I killed Leslie?" Gerard sounded freakishly amused.

Xander's voice caught. "You killed Leslie?"

"She's right over there." Gerard gestured to her body on the floor.

Xander stared. *Gerard has gone mad. Is it possible that he'd hurt Alexis, too? No, he wanted to study her powers so badly that there's no way Gerard in his right mind would . . . but Gerard isn't in his right mind anymore.*

Xander peered at Gerard anew, trying to gauge whether or not he could wrestle the telron from his hands. Seeming unaware of Xander's intentions, Gerard went on speaking to him in a tone that was pleasant:

"I want you to surrender to my control. I want you to tell Doctor Gaige that I should return to being Head of Intelligence. I want you to do everything that I order."

"Alright, I'll go along with your demands. Let's go meet with Doctor Gaige," Xander said, almost laughing at his pathetic attempt to reason with a crazy man.

"Liar!" Gerard suddenly shouted, his voice consumed with fury. He waved his telron. "You're lying! Get down! On your knees!"

"No, Gerard, don't kill him!" Drake blurted out. "He'll cooperate! He said he would!"

"Don't kill him?" Gerard repeated through clenched teeth. "Don't kill the bane of my existence? Don't kill the reason my entire world fell apart? Of course I will kill him, but I will make him suffer first."

Gerard pointed his telron directly at Drake, leaving Xander with no more time to think. Xander sprang forward, tackling Gerard to the ground. At the same time, a beam of orange light came flying through the smoke, headed directly at where Gerard had been standing. The beam of orange exploded against the wall as Xander pinned Gerard to the floor.

"Don't move, Gerard," Xander ordered, breathing hard.

"Don't either of you move," came an unfamiliar, low voice.

Xander whipped up his head. A man was emerging from the smoke who appeared only a few years younger than himself. The man had a buzz cut, was dressed in camouflage gear, and skillfully aimed a magtro at them. Xander released Gerard and carefully raised his own hands, though his eyes scanned the room to see if Gerard's telron was close. Gerard curled up and remained on the ground, whimpering and muttering incoherently.

The man in camouflage observed Gerard with disdain and then spoke to Xander. "If I take the boy, will you be alright here on your own?"

Xander did not hide his surprise. "Yes. I can take care of things here."

"Very good. I'll take Drake." The man kicked Xander and Gerard's telrons across the floor so they were within Xander's reach. He tipped his head scornfully in Gerard's direction. "You take care of that slob."

Keeping a close eye on the stranger, Xander picked up his telron, got to his feet, and aimed his weapon at Gerard.

The man in camouflage appeared satisfied. He turned to leave but stopped and looked back at Xander. "By the way, Alexis is alright."

Xander gave him a single nod. "You should get out of here. My reinforcements will be coming soon."

"You're letting them get away! You're a coward!" Gerard screamed, kicking his boot hard into Xander's knee.

As Xander grunted and collapsed to the floor, Gerard grabbed his telron and fired a frantic shot at him. Xander rolled out of the way before he was struck by the burst of red. With a frenzied cry, Gerard aimed at Xander again. Xander raised himself up on one arm, pointed his telron at Gerard, and fired.

A burst of royal blue exploded out from Xander's telron and slammed into Gerard's chest. Gerard dropped to the floor and breathed out for the last time.

Silence followed. Xander pulled himself off the floor, limping on his injured knee, and faced the man in camouflage. The man's eyes moved from Xander's face to the telron that Xander held in his hand.

"It would be preferable if you didn't tell anyone what you saw here," Xander stated, putting his telron away.

Jason raised his eyes, observing Xander. "I understand."

Jason turned and led Drake away, disappearing into the smoke.

TWENTY EIGHT

"Fifteen-year-old female. Struck by a car in a hit-and-run at approximately four o'clock this afternoon. Positive loss of consciousness. She was taken to the closest emergency room, where she was diagnosed with a right wrist fracture and non-displaced fractures of right ribs six and seven. Given her injuries, the decision was made to transfer her to this ER for a higher level of care. En route, the patient remained hemodynamically stable with a GCS of fifteen. Any questions for us?"

"Yes, several," the emergency department doctor replied, putting her pen into the shirt pocket of her scrubs. "Where are the records from the other hospital?"

"Records?" The paramedic flipped through the papers on his clipboard and checked underneath the stretcher. "I guess the folks at the other ER didn't send them with us."

The doctor sighed and turned to put orders into the computer. "First, no one notified us that they were transferring this patient, and secondly, they didn't send any records? What hospital did you say that you transported this patient from?"

When there was no response, the doctor looked up. The paramedics were gone. She walked quickly to the door of the trauma bay and checked the hallway. Finally, she turned back around, eyeing the nurse incredulously.

"The medics took off already. Can you believe that?"

The nurse shook his head. "You know how those small rural hospitals are. Never do a complete workup. Always botch the transfers."

The doctor sighed again and then smiled at Alexis. "Alexis, I'm sorry about all that. We'll get it sorted out. But first, let me start with you. My name is Doctor Teramo. How are you doing?"

"I'm fine." Alexis glanced around the trauma bay. "I'm alright."

"Your parents know that you're here, and they are on the way." Doctor Teramo took a seat by the stretcher. "In the meantime, I'd like to examine you, and then I'll get everything ordered that we need."

Alexis nodded. "Sure. Okay."

After the doctor completed her exam, she placed more orders in the computer and left the trauma bay. The nurse adjusted Alexis's IV fluid before following after Doctor Teramo. Finally alone, Alexis lay back in the stretcher, listening to the slow, steady beep that was coming from the cardiac monitor. Her chest remained sore and her head hurt, but the medications that agents had administered to her during evacuation were easing the pain. The medicines also seemed to be dulling her mind, and Alexis was glad. It was easier to be groggy than to think about Noah.

"Alexis!"

Alexis lifted her heavy eyes and saw her mother rushing into the trauma bay. Her father and Nina were close behind.

"Hi, Mom," Alexis replied, unable to hold back tears.

Liz began crying herself as she stroked Alexis's forehead. "We've been frantic. I received a call from a nurse at a hospital I'd never even heard of before. She told me that you had been hit by a car and were being transferred here."

Alexis's father, Robert, sat in a chair next to the stretcher. "Earlier today, I got your message about where you were going after school. So the accident happened while you were at that search party near Planter's Field?"

"Yes," Alexis said, her speech growing thick.

"Wow! You got a real cast?" Nina asked while poking an IV fluid bag.

"Uh-huh," Alexis mumbled exhaustedly.

Alexis wanted to stay awake—to tell her family how much she loved them—but the effects of the medications were becoming too hard to fight. She let her eyes close.

"Go to sleep, honey," her mom whispered. "We'll be here when you wake up."

***

"Enter."

Xander pushed the door open. The meeting room was dark except for one dim light directly over the far end of the table. Dr. Gaige sat with his chair turned away from the door. Xander hobbled into the room, the sound of his crutch echoing on the concrete floor. As the door shut behind him, Xander glanced around. No one else was there.

"How are you doing, Xander?"

Dr. Gaige's voice was calm and pleasant, which told Xander that he needed to be careful.

"It's only a knee sprain," Xander replied. "It will heal."

"That's good," Dr. Gaige remarked. There was a pause before he went on. "Tell me, how did the girl escape?"

"She used her powers to get out of the infirmary. In review of the security camera footage, the first sighting of Alexis is by the elevator bay on the third floor. From there, she rode up to the ground floor. You are obviously aware of what happened after that."

"I understand that you had the guards stationed outside of the girl's room. In hindsight, do you think that they should have kept watch over her more directly? That perhaps security should have taken priority over the girl's privacy?"

Xander adjusted the crutch under his arm. "Perhaps."

"Some valued operatives died tonight."

"Yes," Xander told him, relieved to hear the return of a slight edge to Dr. Gaige's voice.

"Leslie?"

"Killed by Gerard. The specifics I am not sure about. The security camera footage is useless, given the amount of smoke that filled the hallway."

"Who else?"

"Antonio. He sustained a light attack to his chest. I do not know who fired at him."

"And Gerard? How did he die?"

"I killed him."

"That must have given you pleasure." Dr. Gaige almost sounded as if he were smiling.

"No, it did not." Xander kept his voice even. "Gerard was not himself. He attempted to launch a light attack at Drake and then at me. I had no choice."

"Such a pity to lose him." Dr. Gaige sighed. "And the boy? Drake? I hear that he got away?"

"Yes, an agent took him while I was alone and injured. The smoke was too thick for me to get a clean shot."

There was another break in the conversation before Dr. Gaige went on:

"Xander, how did The Organization find us? How did they discover where this base is located?"

"I don't know."

"So let me make sure that I understand. The boy, Drake, is now with The Organization, and he knows about our operatives and our plans to obtain Number 407."

"Yes."

"Number 407 is still within the girl, who also is in the care of The Organization. She, too, has seen much of our facility and our operatives."

"That is correct."

"The Organization obviously knows where we are located, and they could return at any time."

"That also must be assumed."

"So as Head of Intelligence, Xander, I am curious to know what you would suggest we do."

"Evacuate everyone immediately and destroy this place."

"That would prevent us from pursuing the girl and doing our work."

"Some issues are more pressing at the moment."

"Perhaps so," Dr. Gaige stated. "So we shall abandon and destroy this place. And then?"

Xander hesitated.

"And then we will regroup," Dr. Gaige finished for him.

"Yes. Of course. It will take time to establish a new base, but we will regroup," Xander made himself say.

"Indeed. This is only a temporary setback," Dr. Gaige went on, almost to himself. "They have not stopped us forever. We will return stronger. We will have a new plan, and we will gain control of Number 407."

Dr. Gaige swiveled around in his chair. Xander nearly gasped aloud when he saw Dr. Gaige's eyes flash red.

"And you, Xander, will lead that operation."

TWENTY NINE

"We can now confirm that Drake Spencer, the second missing high school student, is safely home. Drake was located by a search group near his high school. Like his friend, Tanner Ricks, Drake is reportedly amnesic to the events of recent days. We are told that police and psychologists are planning to work with both Drake and Tanner in the hopes of obtaining more information."

The news broadcast cut to the anchorwoman seated behind the newsroom desk. She continued speaking into the camera:

"And in other news, we are getting more reports about that massive explosion, which occurred early this morning some miles from Planter's Field. No one was in the area when the explosion happened. We are told that the blast was caused by a buildup of volatile gases in a previously unknown, abandoned underground mine. The fire department spokeswoman states that there are no other mines in the region, and that the surrounding communities are in no danger. We will bring you more information as it comes in. For now, this is Heather Bower of Channel Five News. The better news for your lunchtime."

Dr. Caul shut the monitor off and turned to Kate. "What updates do we have from our people about that explosion?"

"Sounds like Doctor Gaige made a very clean getaway," Kate replied, reading the information on her computer screen. "Reports indicate that The Domanorith completely destroyed their base, and no evidence was left behind."

Dr. Caul looked away. "So we are left to wonder where and when The Domanorith will return."

"Return?" Albert coughed in surprise. "Do you really think that Doctor Gaige and his operatives could ever regroup and become the force they once were?"

"Yes, I do." Dr. Caul faced him. "We will enjoy peace for a while—perhaps a long while—but Doctor Gaige and his operatives will be back one day."

Albert appeared alarmed. "What are we going to do?"

"We will wait. We'll watch very carefully, and we will wait."

"And the girl?"

"Alexis will continue living her life," Dr. Caul stated simply. "When she's ready, we'll work with her to better understand her powers."

There was a sound from Dr. Caul's magtro. She put it to her ear.

"It's me, Ben. Yes, how's Noah? I . . . I see. I'll be right there."

Dr. Caul rushed for the door.

"Is there anything I can help with?" Albert called after her.

She opened the door, pausing to look at him. "You can pray. Pray to whatever god you believe in that Noah Weston will live."

***

"Alexis, honey? Molly's here. Can I send her in?"

"Sure, Mom."

Alexis peered thoughtfully out her bedroom window. The afternoon sun was bright, and the fall-colored leaves on the trees rustled gently in the wind. The serenity of the scene made it almost impossible to believe that the events of the night before had ever happened. But when Alexis moved to sit up in bed, the pain in her side was an all-too-vivid reminder of every horrible moment, culminating with the heart-wrenching sight of Noah's body being placed on a stretcher in the evacuation helicopter. He was alive, she had overheard the medical agents say, but in critical condition. Alexis had not heard anything since.

There was a soft knock on her bedroom door.

"Lex, can I come in?"

"Sure."

Molly flung the door open, ran to the bed, and threw her arms around Alexis. "I've been so worried about you!"

"Ouch," Alexis groaned.

"Sorry!" Molly jumped away. "Oh, Lex, school was absolutely crazy today. You heard about Tanner and Drake right? That they've both been found?"

"I heard."

"And they're both okay! They didn't come to school, though. I heard they're talking to the police and some doctors."

Alexis leaned gingerly on her pillow and nodded.

"And everyone's been talking about you, too!" Molly was moving her hands animatedly as she spoke. "They know you got hit by a car while you were helping in a search party. You're like a hero now."

Alexis felt her cheeks redden. "No, I'm not the hero."

"Well, I think you are. Everyone else does, too. Except Crystal. She was really grouchy and telling people that you only joined the search party because you wanted to get on television."

Even Alexis could not help laughing.

"So should I tell you the big surprise?" Molly asked, a gleam in her eye.

"Surprise? What surprise?"

"You're the freshman class homecoming princess! We voted today, and they announced the winners during sixth period. You won!"

Alexis went slack-jawed in disbelief.

"Everyone in our class was so impressed by what you had done to help Tanner and Drake that they wanted you to have the honor! It's the coolest thing ever!" Molly gushed. "And Tanner is our homecoming prince, of course. Isn't that perfect?"

"I . . . guess so," Alexis replied, still stunned.

"And you'll never believe this: Drake asked me to go to the dance with him! I'm so happy! We need to go dress shopping tomorrow, okay? What color of dress are you going to get?" Molly did a twirl, landed on the bed, and eyed Alexis intently.

"Dress?"

Molly giggled. "Don't do this to me. We need to be serious. What are you going to wear?"

"I'm not going."

It seemed to take a while for Molly to process what she had heard. "Are you insane? Are you sure that you're not still concussed?"

"Mol, I don't have a dress, I don't have a date, and I—"

Alexis jumped when a phone began to ring.

"That's your phone! You'd better answer!" Molly squealed delightedly. "I know who it is!"

"My phone?" Alexis repeated, bewildered. "I don't think I have my—"

"It's right here." Molly reached down and pulled the phone from a pocket of Alexis's dirty jacket. "Here! Answer it fast!"

Alexis stared. *I left my phone with Noah. How did I get it back?*

"Come on! Answer!" Molly jammed the phone in her hand.

Alexis fumblingly cradled the phone to her ear. "Hello?"

"Hey, Alexis. It's Tanner Ricks."

Alexis nearly dropped the phone in her lap. "Hi, Tanner. How are you doing? Are you okay?"

Eavesdropping shamelessly, Molly grinned at Alexis and flashed an enthusiastic thumbs-up sign.

"I'm actually doing pretty well," Tanner went on. He laughed slightly. "The doctors don't think I'm nuts, and I feel completely fine. So I think I'm gonna be alright."

"I'm so glad to hear it," Alexis told him.

"Thanks." Tanner's tone became serious. "But how about you? I heard what happened yesterday."

"I'm a little sore, that's all. No big deal."

"It is a big deal. You got hurt trying to help me. Thank you." Tanner paused. "Alexis, I have no recollection of what happened over the past few days, but I do remember dancing with you at the bonfire party. I also remember that there was something I wanted to ask you but never got the chance."

Alexis wondered if she was crazy to suspect what he was about to say. "Yes?"

"I know this is really late notice, but I was hoping that you'd go to homecoming with me."

To Alexis, it seemed that time stopped and a billion thoughts flew through her head in an instant.

"It's okay. You don't have to say yes," Tanner went on. "I guess it was pretty stupid of me to think someone hadn't asked you already. I—"

"No one's asked me," Alexis told him. "I just—"

"Tell him yes!" Molly commanded in a whisper. "Tell him yes! Yes! Yes!"

"Yes. I am saying yes," Alexis heard herself utter.

"Really? That's awesome." Tanner sounded like he was smiling. "Hey, I'll let you go. I'm sure you need to rest. I'll talk to you soon, though. Are you going to school tomorrow?"

"The doctor cleared me to return, if I'm feeling alright."

"Same here. If you come, I'll look for you before first period, okay?"

"That sounds good."

"Bye, Alexis."

"Bye."

Molly let out a celebratory cry. "Yes! Double date! We definitely have to go dress shopping after school tomorrow!"

There was another knock on the door.

"If Molly is hollering in there, Lex must be doing well enough for me to come in and say hi, too."

Molly rolled her eyes. "Come in, Marcus."

Marcus opened the door. "Hey, Lex, how are you feeling?"

"She's great!" Molly proclaimed for her. "She's our homecoming princess, Tanner Ricks asked her to the dance, and we're going to go dress shopping for our double date!"

Marcus raised an eyebrow. "You're feeling up to all that, Lex? It's not worth wearing yourself out over a stupid school dance."

"Mar-cus," Molly groaned.

Marcus chuckled. "I know, I know. Enough lecturing. In fact, Molly, we should both head out she can rest. Lex, give us a call if you decide to head to school tomorrow and want a ride."

"I will. Thanks," Alexis told him gratefully.

Marcus gave Molly another look. "I'll be waiting in the car. Don't talk her ear off. She's got to recover."

After Marcus slipped out, Molly turned gleefully again to Alexis. "Can you believe this is happening? It's everything you wished for. The man of your dreams is taking you to homecoming."

Alexis looked out the window and did not reply.

***

"Noah isn't breathing on his own yet?" Dr. Caul nervously eyed the ventilator.

Ralph's expression was grave. "He lost a lot of blood from that light attack, Rachel. Surgery was tenuous, to say the least."

"What does that mean exactly?"

"It means that his condition remains critical."

Dr. Caul turned to Mr. Haber, who was seated near the bed with his injured leg propped up on a footstool. As their gazes met, Mr. Haber leaned forward and dropped his head into his hands.

"I promised his parents that I would protect him, Rachel. Noah has been like a nephew—like a son—to me."

Dr. Caul stepped close to him. "You did protect him. You protected Noah, and you protected Alexis, Tanner, and Drake. You saved those kids' lives."

"And Tanner and Drake won't ever have to know what they went through," Ralph added. "The medications that Tanner received from the Domanorith made him amnesic, and what I administered to Drake during evacuation will have the same effect."

Mr. Haber sat up. "But Noah—"

"Noah will survive," Dr. Caul insisted, though her voice faltered. "He has to survive."

There was a pause before Ralph asked, "Are you going to update Alexis?"

Mr. Haber and Dr. Caul looked at each other.

"She deserves to know," Ralph told them firmly. "She would want to know."

Dr. Caul wrung her hands. "She has already been through so much, and she's still recovering herself. I was hoping to give Alexis more time."

Ralph gestured to Noah's cardiac monitor. "Rachel, we might not have time."

***

"Goodbye, Jackie."

"Goodbye?" Jackie set her suitcase down with a laugh. "Xander, why are you being so dramatic? It's not like we're never going to see each other again. In a week, we'll be working together in our old lab again, just like our PhD days. "

Xander said nothing.

Jackie peered at him closely. "You are coming to work at the old lab, right? Until the Domanorith have a new base?"

"No, I'm not." Xander did not quite meet her gaze. *Geez, Jackie, don't look at me like that. Not now. Not after everything.*

"What? Where are you going to go?" Jackie pressed, her voice shaking slightly.

"I can't tell you."

Her eyebrows rose in alarm. "But you will notify me as soon as The Domanorith have the new base ready, right?"

Xander finally faced her. "Look, it's my fault that you wound up involved with all of this. Had I known what . . . I never would have . . ." He shook his head. "Jackie, you have a chance for a normal life. You will be able to use your intelligence and education the way that—"

"What makes you think I want a normal life? You're not the one to make that decision for me. I want to continue the research that I began at the base. The science I get to explore by working for The Domanorith is far beyond anything the rest of the world is even capable of imagining."

Xander started backing away. "I have to go."

She took an anxious step after him. "Promise that you will find me."

Xander only turned and disappeared into the airport crowd.

THIRTY

"I think you'll start a new trend, Lex. Before long, casts will become the newest must-have accessory."

Alexis held up her casted arm, examining it in the reflection of Molly's bedroom mirror. "We can only hope."

Molly came up next to her and smiled warmly. "But seriously, that cast won't matter. No one is even going to notice it. As I said at the store, your dress is stunning, and you look amazing. You're like a super model! I can't wait until Tanner sees you. He is going to freak out!"

Alexis turned to one side, still trying to get used to how grown up she appeared in her floor-length, emerald green gown. Then she turned to her friend. "Well, you look totally gorgeous yourself, girl."

Molly spun around in her black dress. "Thanks! I hope Drake likes my outfit, because I sure love it!"

Alexis could not reply, suddenly struck by the haunting memory of Drake aiming his weapon at Noah. She closed her eyes, feeling sick.

"Hey, are you okay?" she heard Molly ask. "You're super pale all of the sudden."

Alexis reached unsteadily for a chair. "I need to sit down for a minute, that's all."

But Molly was already moving for the door. "No. I'm getting Marcus. You need to go home and rest right now."

Molly bolted from her bedroom. Still shaking, Alexis changed into her regular clothes and sat down. Her phone began to ring, and she pulled it out from her jacket pocket. The caller ID was unknown. Clearing her throat, Alexis answered:

"Hello?"

"Alexis, it's Rachel."

Alexis heard the strain in Dr. Caul's tone, and a lump immediately formed in her throat. "You're calling about Noah, aren't you?"

"He's not doing well, Alexis."

Alexis stood up slowly, unable to speak.

"Alexis, we were hoping to give you some time to recover, but when Ralph gave us the update, we thought that you might want to come and see Noah soon."

"I want to come right now."

"Agents tell us that you're at Molly's house. Hang tight, and we'll have transport there soon."

Alexis peeked out the window into the evening light. Behind her, she heard the bedroom door being pushed open. She turned as Molly entered with Marcus close on her heels. Alexis put her phone down and hastily wiped the tears from her eyes.

"Hey, Lex." Marcus observed her worriedly. "Let's get you home, okay?"

Alexis motioned to her phone. "Thanks, but my dad is coming. I, um, just called him."

As if on cue, there came the sound of a vehicle with a large engine pulling into the driveway.

"Geez, that was fast." Molly checked out the window.

"He, um, was already in the area." Alexis draped her dress over her arm. "Thanks, guys. See you soon."

"Did your dad get a new car?" Molly continued looking curiously through the window. "What kind of an SUV is that, anyway? It's like a—"

"I'll let myself out," Alexis interrupted. "Thanks again for taking us shopping, Marcus, and thank you for helping me find a dress, Mol."

Alexis hurried from the bedroom and out the front door. She ran as best as she could to the end of the driveway, where a massive vehicle was waiting. Jasper hopped out, opened the passenger door, and helped her climb inside. Then he quickly got back into the driver's seat and began skillfully maneuvering the vehicle down the driveway.

Alexis dropped her head, letting her tears fall. *Noah can't die. He can't.*

***

"Jasper reports that the train departed the school on schedule. Alexis will reach headquarters soon," Kate reported over the magtro.

"Copy," Dr. Caul replied. She put her device away and turned to Mr. Haber. "I hope we're doing the right thing for her."

"I do not know if we are, Rachel."

Dr. Caul watched him for a moment. "You need some rest, too, even if only for a few minutes. Why don't you go lie down? I will stay here with Noah."

"Thank you, but no. I would prefer to remain where I am."

Dr. Caul nodded understandingly. "I'll go meet Alexis and bring her in."

***

As soon as the door slid open, Alexis leapt out of the train car and began running across the Headquarters station. Far ahead, she saw Dr. Caul step out of the elevator, appearing tired and worried.

"Where is he, Doctor Caul? Can I see him right now?" Alexis panted, ignoring the ache in her ribs.

"Yes. Come with me."

Alexis hurried into the elevator behind Dr. Caul. The doors closed, and in silence they rode up to a floor where Alexis had never before been. She sprinted out of the elevator but came to an abrupt halt. She was standing in the middle of what looked like an intensive care unit. The lighting was dim, and everything was unnervingly sterile and quiet. Taking in the sight of medical workers and strange machines, Alexis felt the reason for why she had come sink in fully. Fighting new tears, she shrank back with dread.

"This way," Dr. Caul said to her.

Dr. Caul passed Alexis and began walking down a hallway. Both anxious and reluctant, Alexis went after her. They continued down the corridor until Dr. Caul stopped in front of an unmarked door and knocked.

"Come in," they heard Mr. Haber say.

Dr. Caul gestured to the room. "Go ahead."

Alexis apprehensively pushed the door open. She stepped inside, not ready for the sight that met her eyes: Noah lay motionless in a large bed on the far side of the room. His eyes were closed, and he was ghostly pale. There was a plastic tube coming out of his mouth, which was connected to a breathing machine. His bed was surrounded by wires and monitors, while hanging bags of medicine and fluid were running through the IVs in his arms. Alexis could only stare, too stunned to move or speak.

"Miss Kendall, I am so very sorry that we have to meet this way."

Alexis looked to her right and saw Mr. Haber seated in a chair. Despite everything that Alexis had witnessed him deal with, Mr. Haber had never appeared more exhausted or frightened to her than he did at that moment. The despair on his face scared Alexis more than anything.

"Alexis, you're welcome to come closer, if you want," she heard Ralph say.

Alexis peered again toward the bed. Ralph was walking toward it. He looked so different, dressed in his long white coat and with a stethoscope hanging around his neck. Ralph slid an empty chair next to Noah's bed and motioned to Alexis. She moved across the room and nervously took the seat.

"We'll step out." Ralph nodded for Dr. Caul and Mr. Haber to join him.

The three adults left, closing the door behind them. Alexis looked down at Noah in overwhelmed silence. The young man lying on the bed was not the Noah she knew. Noah had an aura of quiet, fierce strength and an enigmatic depth behind his eyes, but the patient on the bed seemed almost devoid of life.

Alexis shuddered and glanced around. The only sounds were the soft, repeating hiss of the ventilator and a beep that indicated Noah's heart rate. Alexis peeked up at the cardiac monitor. Noah's pulse was only forty-three beats per minute, as if his heart was too weak to go any faster. Alexis again looked down at Noah's ashen face. Cautiously, she reached through the wires and cradled one of Noah's cold hands in hers.

"Noah? It's Alexis. Noah, I'm here," she whispered.

With the agonizing realization that Noah probably could not even hear her, Alexis gripped his hand more tightly and let herself begin to cry.

"Noah, I'm not going to leave you, okay? I'm not going to leave your side until I know that you're going to be alright."

As she spoke, the beeping sound sped up, causing Alexis to check the monitor again. Noah's pulse had jumped up to sixty-one.

Can . . . can Noah actually hear me?

Alexis leaned closer to him. "Noah? Do you know that I'm here?" She clung even more tightly to his hand, the contact seeming to make her own grow warm. "Thank you for teaching me, and thank you for saving my life. I'm sorry that I've been so stubborn. I promise that I won't do stupid stuff anymore. I'll shoot whatever fruit you want me to. I won't go to parties when I shouldn't. I'll really be a good student, I swear. So don't leave me, okay?"

Alexis's hand became hot, causing her to look down. To her astonishment, a soft white glow was surrounding their joined hands. As the glow brightened, the beeping of the monitor increased even more. Alexis turned to the monitor and then back to the bed. She stopped. Noah was awake and gazing right at her.

The door was burst open.

"Forgive the interruption, but the monitor outside indicated that he's becoming more tachycardic." Ralph rushed over. "Alexis, please allow me to . . ."

Ralph came to a stunned halt when he saw Noah watching him alertly. Ralph peered at Alexis and then, with a smile on his face, spoke to Noah:

"It's good to see you, young man."

Dr. Caul and Mr. Haber came to the bed, their expressions of fear turning into elation when they saw Noah awake. Dr. Caul laughed. Mr. Haber dropped into a chair with relief.

Ralph kept speaking to his patient. "Noah, I am going to ask you to obey a few directions. This will help me begin to determine if I can remove that breathing tube. So please . . ."

While Ralph commenced with his examination, Alexis stepped away from the bed and made her way for the door, her hands still warm as she wiped the tears from her eyes.

"Miss Kendall?"

Alexis peeked over her shoulder. Mr. Haber was watching her inquisitively.

"I'm going to head home," Alexis explained. "Noah will be alright, but I'm sure he needs to rest."

Mr. Haber nodded.

"I'll have Kate arrange a train," Dr. Caul said to her, still smiling. "And we will have Jasper waiting at the school to take you home."

"Thanks."

Alexis moved again to leave but stopped, remembering that there was something else she needed to do. Quietly, she went back to Noah's bedside. His eyes met hers.

"You dropped this last night," she said, placing his magtro on the bed. She smiled. "Rest well, Noah. I'll see you soon."

THIRTY ONE

"One more photo, girls!" Liz enthusiastically held up her camera. "Ready? Smile!"

A flash lit up the room.

Alexis laughed. "Okay, Mom, that's enough. I think Molly and I have posed for about a million pictures by now."

"I don't mind, Mrs. Kendall. Take all the pictures you want." Molly admired her reflection in the mirror above the fireplace. "It's not every day that I look so glamorous."

The doorbell rang.

"They're here! They're here!" Nina scurried into the living room. "Lex, your boyfriend is here!"

"I'll take care of this." Robert got off the couch with feigned somberness. "I need to meet the young man who apparently thinks that he can date my daughter."

"Be nice, Robert!" Liz called as her husband strode toward the foyer. "Remember, he's not on trial!"

Nina was agape. "Is Dad going to take him to court for bringing Lex to a school dance?"

"Nope," Alexis told her with a wink. "I think everything is going to be fine."

But even Alexis got hit by nerves when she heard the front door being opened, which was followed by muffled talking. Soon, there came the sound of footsteps heading back to the living room. Her father reappeared. Then Tanner stepped in after him, appearing handsome in a dark suit and tie.

Tanner stopped the moment he saw Alexis, a smile appearing on his face. "Hi, Alexis."

"Hi." She blushed under his gaze. "It's really good to . . ."

Alexis trailed off when Drake entered behind the others. It was her first time seeing him since they had been evacuated from the base of the Domanorith.

Molly promptly struck a coy pose. "Good evening, Drake."

"Hey." Drake grinned at her. "You look great."

"Thanks!" Molly replied, casting a thrilled glance at Alexis.

Drake turned to Alexis with a casual nod. "And how are you? I heard about what happened."

Alexis managed to keep her voice steady. "Oh, um, I'm fine. And you?"

Drake shrugged. "I feel like the same guy I've always been."

Alexis did not reply.

"Alright, everyone!" Liz gestured to her camera. "Now that the gentlemen are here, I want a group photo!"

Alexis sighed. "Mom."

"Only one or two more," Liz promised, motioning for the boys to move in closer.

Tanner and Drake obediently headed over to join the girls in front of the fireplace. Molly giggled, making room for Drake to stand close to her. As

Tanner came over to Alexis, he gave her another smile. She found herself smiling back.

"Alright, here we go!" Liz took the picture, checked the image, and shook her head. "Drake has too much red eye. Let me turn up the lights."

Alexis shivered but made herself take some deep breaths. *Calm down. It's okay. It's all over now.*

Liz readied the camera once more. "Okay, everyone, let's try this again!"

Tanner gently put his hand on the small of Alexis's back. Though she sensed her stomach flutter the way that it always did when she was near Tanner, Alexis noted that she felt nothing more. And she was not surprised. In her heart, Alexis knew that she had experienced emotions far deeper for someone else, and those feelings had changed her forever.

The camera flashed again.

Liz reviewed the photo with satisfaction. "Much better."

"Hey, I'm sorry to rush things, but we should probably head out," Tanner remarked to the group. "They're doing all the royalty stuff at eight."

"And just a heads up: there still are media folks lurking around," Drake added as they began walking toward the front door. "Someone with a camera might be across the street. Pretty sure I saw him when we got here."

Molly buttoned her jacket. "The paparazzi stalked you guys? That's crazy! I hope they get a good shot of my hair, at least."

"I hope they just go away," Tanner muttered with disdain, helping Alexis into her coat.

Robert trailed them into the foyer, his expression stern. "So, Tanner, you'll be getting my daughter home by nine, right?"

Tanner hesitated. "Oh, uh, I—"

"Dad," Alexis interrupted with exasperation. "Stop kidding around."

Robert chuckled.

With a roll of her eyes, Alexis turned to Tanner. "Dad's joking, so that means you've passed inspection and we're allowed to get out of here."

Tanner laughed, seeming genuinely relieved. "Phew. Glad to hear it."

Liz opened the front door, waving as the group headed out into the chilly autumn evening.

As they made their way off the porch, Tanner gently took Alexis by her arm. "You really do look beautiful tonight."

Alexis set her eyes on his. "Thanks. I—"

"We're taking a limo?" Molly's exclamation echoed. "No way!"

Tanner chuckled and shook his head. With a giggle, Alexis pulled her attention from Tanner and looked down the driveway. Molly was marveling over a black limousine, which was waiting for them.

"Of course we're taking a limo." Drake puffed out his chest with pride. "Only the best for us."

Gabbing excitedly, Molly climbed into the backseat behind Drake. Alexis gave her family a final wave and then allowed Tanner to help her into the limo after the others.

"This is the fanciest ride I have ever been in!" Molly went on elatedly. "Too bad Marcus couldn't drive us to school in something like this every day, Lex!"

Alexis laughed lightly with amusement. "Yeah, too bad."

As the limousine pulled out of the driveway, Tanner took Alexis's hand in his, and she found herself settling into a comfortable silence beside him. Molly and Drake did most of the chatting, and Alexis was glad. Seated next to Tanner, Alexis found that she did not know what to say or think, or even the way she was supposed to feel. She had become part of two very different worlds: one simple and familiar, and the other profoundly complicated. In one world, life revolved around friends and family, Tanner, and the reality she had always understood. In the other world, Noah, incredible purpose, mystery—and even danger—were waiting. As part of both worlds, Alexis knew that she could not claim either fully as her own. But, she wondered, would the day come when she would have to choose?

Lost in her reflections, it was not until Alexis sensed the limousine slowing that she glanced through the window. They were pulling up in front of the school.

Tanner opened the door, got out, and extended his hand. "Shall we, fair maiden?"

Alexis did her best at an English accent. "Why yes, good sir. We shall."

Tanner escorted Alexis toward the school's entrance. Molly and Drake followed. When they neared the doors, there was an unexpected flash of light, which caused Alexis to cry out in alarm.

"It's another photographer," Tanner growled, guiding Alexis quickly forward. "I'm sorry about this, Alexis. I don't know why they're bothering to take pictures of me now, anyway. What I'd like are some pictures from the last few days so I knew what happened."

Alexis stayed quiet. *No, Tanner, you wouldn't want those pictures. I promise.*

There was another flash from the photographer's camera as Tanner and Alexis made it into the school with Molly and Drake on their heels. Once the doors shut behind them, Tanner breathed out with relief. His smile returning, he led Alexis down a stairwell, which was decorated with flowers and twinkling lights, toward the sounds of music and excited conversations ahead. They soon reached the entrance of the gymnasium and stopped to take in the sight.

"Wow!" Molly came up next to Alexis, clapping with excitement. "Isn't this amazing?"

Alexis nodded earnestly in reply. The gym had been transformed into an elegant ballroom. A large chandelier hung overhead. White lights draped gracefully across the ceiling, and flowers and ornate columns decorated the perimeter of the room. And at the front of the gym, students were laughing and dancing near a stage where a DJ played music.

Drake nudged Molly. "So how about we go tear up the dance floor?"

"Sounds great!" Molly giddily let Drake lead her away.

After the others disappeared into the crowd, Tanner turned to Alexis. But before he could say anything, a voice rang out over the music:

"Tanner! Alexis! There you two are!"

Alexis looked over her shoulder. Mrs. Frank, her English teacher, was waddling toward them.

"My, my, don't you look lovely tonight," Mrs. Frank told her.

"Yes, she does," Tanner agreed.

Alexis's eyes darted to Tanner, and she blushed again before responding to her teacher. "Thanks."

Mrs. Frank motioned to her watch. "We'll need you both by the stage in thirty minutes. We're going to take the royalty photos and have the official dances." She smoothed her floral print dress. "Now if only I can find our wizard," she mumbled to herself before scurrying off.

Alone again, Tanner held out his arm to Alexis. "Shall we go be royal?"

She nodded. "Sounds gr—"

"Hi, Alexis!" Julia entered the gym and bounded to Alexis's side. "You're so beautiful! How are you feeling?"

"Better, thanks." Alexis gave her a hug. "I'm glad you're here. I thought you weren't coming."

"I wasn't, until Sam asked me." Julia sheepishly tucked her short hair behind her ear.

Alexis's mouth fell open. "Sam Warren? I thought he totally annoyed . . ." Alexis saw Julia's cheeks turn pink. "Ah, Sam doesn't really annoy you, does he?"

"No," Julia admitted. "Not at all."

Sam strolled up. "Hello, Madame Princess!"

Alexis peeked at Julia and then grinned. "Hi, Sam. It's nice to see you. Tanner and I have to go, but I hope you two have a great night."

"Thanks," Julia replied, her cheeks still rosy.

With another smile, Alexis faced Tanner and placed her arm in his. The two of them started for the stage, but once they wove deep into the crowd, he unexpectedly stopped in the middle of the floor.

"May I have this dance?"

Alexis laughed. "Right now?"

"Sure. Why not? We have time."

"Then I'd love to."

Tanner stepped close and put his arm around her waist. As they began moving to the music, Alexis looked at him thoughtfully. For the first time in a very long while, she felt like a normal high school freshman. Life was safe and simple, and those she cared about were alright. Sighing contentedly, Alexis gazed around the room, trying to take in every detail of the moment. But then she did a double take, and her heart thumped in her chest.

No way. There's no way he could be here tonight.

Yet Alexis was certain that Noah Weston stood alone in a corner of the gym, his discerning gray eyes scanning the crowd. Though his hair was combed and he wore a suit, Alexis could see that he had in his earbuds. Noah was not there for the dance, she knew. He was on alert, as always, watching and protecting.

Before Noah noticed her staring at him, Alexis refocused on Tanner and stepped from his embrace.

She was trembling. "Tanner, will you excuse me for a minute?"

"Of course." Tanner's brow furrowed. "Are you okay? Do you need to sit down or something?"

"I'm okay. And I won't be gone long. I promise."

Giving Tanner a smile, Alexis darted off. Skirting around the other students, she made her way toward Noah, her pulse bounding harder with every step she took. Noah's eyebrows rose in surprise when he noticed her approaching. Then, unexpectedly, he began walking away.

"Noah," Alexis called after him, confused. "Noah, where are you going? Wait. Please wait."

Noah seemed to hesitate before he halted and turned around. His business-like expression wavered when his eyes met hers. For a few seconds, they watched one another without speaking. Finally, Alexis moved toward him.

"Noah, why—"

He interrupted her with a slight tip of his head toward the back door, and then he went outside. Alexis understood his meaning and followed, stepping through the door into the waning evening light. She glanced around. No one was there. Breathing in deeply, Alexis headed away from the gym, the music from the dance fading into nothing as she continued along the moonlit path toward the courtyard. Up ahead in the shadows, she saw Noah standing among the trees and waiting for her.

"Noah, what are you doing here?" she demanded. "You're still supposed to be at Headquarters getting medical care."

He shrugged aloofly. "I'm just doing my job."

"Your job?" Alexis shook her head. "I think you have other things to worry about right now. Do you have any idea how sick you were? How almost dead you were?"

He set his eyes on hers. "I'm sorry that I haven't been able to see you until now."

Alexis paused, struck by the way he watched her. "It's alright. You were super sick. In fact, like I said, you shouldn't be here at all, and—"

"Tanner Ricks is a good guy, Alexis."

Alexis stopped again, and it was a while before she mustered a reply. "I . . . I don't get what you're saying."

Noah inhaled slowly. "Alexis, I have to walk away tonight—walk away from you—and continue my life as an agent for The Organization. Tanner doesn't have to do that."

"I still don't understand," Alexis insisted, although an ache was rising in her heart that told her she understood more than she wanted to admit.

He looked off into the distance. "Doctor Gaige killed my dad when I was little. My mom never got over it, and my older brother was so distraught that he left home. I haven't seen my brother since—I assume he's dead, too." Noah blinked hard. "Doctor Gaige was also the reason my mother was murdered." He resolutely set his eyes back on Alexis. "Doctor Gaige and The Domanorith destroyed everyone I cared about, Alexis. Everyone. That's why I chose to help The Organization. I want to destroy Doctor Gaige and all who work for him."

"Noah, I—"

"That's also why I can't let myself care about anyone else," he continued, quietly unrelenting. "I can't worry about losing someone ever again."

"I think what you're trying to say is that you're worried about losing me."

Noah dropped his head with a resigned sigh. "I tried. I tried not to care about you."

A thrill rushed into Alexis's heart. "So you . . . you care about me?"

A faint, reminiscent smile appeared on Noah's face. "On the first day of school, when I saw you walk—or trip, actually—into Ben's classroom, I knew I was in trouble."

Alexis giggled and shook her head.

But Noah's smile disappeared. "I came here tonight because I wanted you to understand."

"Noah, caring about someone isn't something you just ignore. You can't pretend you don't feel something if you do."

"Well, I had gotten pretty good at ignoring and pretending, until you came along." Noah's face clouded over. "Seeing someone hold a weapon to your head . . . wondering if I'd be forced to watch you die . . . I knew that I could not keep going if I lost you, too."

A breeze swayed the trees, causing Alexis to shiver. Noah slid off his jacket and put it around her shoulders. There was another pause as they watched each other. Then suddenly, Noah placed his hand behind her head, drew her to him, and pressed his lips against hers. He held Alexis for one long moment before letting her go. Alexis did not move. Her pulse was racing. Her legs felt wobbly. She wondered if her chest might burst from joy. Noah Weston had kissed her. He cared about her the way that she cared about him. It seemed too wonderful to be true.

Noah searched her face, seeming to read her thoughts. For one fleeting moment, happiness shone in his eyes, but then they clouded with regret. "Alexis, I'm part of something that I can't run from— something I don't want to run from. I'm training to be a Protector for The Organization. It's my life."

"Noah, please—"

"And just like I won't be able to protect and train you properly if my emotions are involved, you won't be able to live a normal life and enjoy everything you deserve if you're mixed up with me."

"Maybe I don't want a normal life."

"Geez, don't say that. Don't take what you have for granted. You're intelligent and beautiful. You've got a family that loves you. You have friends and school and cheerleading. You have a great life." Noah gestured toward the building. "A life that you should be in there celebrating."

Alexis let her attention drift toward the gymnasium. She could hear the sounds of music and laughter coming from inside, reminding her of the secure, familiar world that awaited her there. Yet as she listened, Alexis felt something powerful stir within her. She knew that the world behind those gym doors was not what she wanted. She wanted something more. Determined to tell Noah how she felt, Alexis faced him again.

"Noah, I . . ."

But Alexis fell quiet, struck by the sadness in Noah's eyes. To tell Noah how she felt would only cause him more pain. And no matter what she wanted or how much she longed for Noah to understand, Alexis vowed never do anything to hurt him. Holding back tears, she handed him his jacket and stepped away.

"When will I see you again, Noah?"

"Monday. First period, as usual," he answered. "That is, if Ralph clears me to go."

"Ralph didn't clear you to leave? Did you sneak out of Headquarters tonight?"

"Yeah. They'll be mad," Noah admitted with a grin.

Alexis sighed. "Okay. And when do we train next?"

"Soon. I think that . . ." He broke off and motioned again to the gym. "Hey, we can talk about this later. There are a lot of people waiting to see you in there, including someone in particular who is anxious to dance with you. So get going. You deserve to enjoy this night."

Alexis nodded. "Thank you, Noah."

Noah retreated so far that he could barely be seen in the shadows. "Don't thank me. I'm just doing my job."

He took a few more steps, and then he was gone.

Alexis slowly turned and walked back toward the gym. When she reached the door, she stopped to let the wind stroke her face. Her life intersected two worlds, and there was nothing she could do to change that. If she needed to make sacrifices because of her powers, she was willing. If she had to handle experiences no one else understood, she could do it alone. And if must care about someone in silence, she would.

After a final glance at where Noah had stood, Alexis opened the door and stepped into the gym. She walked purposefully, taking in the carefree scene. Soon, she spotted Tanner waving at her from where the other members of the homecoming court were gathered. With a smile, Alexis began making her way across the dance floor to join him.

Where her life would lead, Alexis could not say. But whatever path she would have to take, she would be ready. And for Alexis, that was enough.

ACKNOWLEDGEMENTS

First, to my fans. Your support means everything.

Nick, thank you. You are an incredible support—not to mention, the best story editor a girl could hope for.

My family, always.

Cookie, you're the greatest little buddy ever.

Heather W., your unwavering enthusiasm was appreciated more than I can say. Thank you for your help, which was literally cover-to-cover.

To the rest of my 142 ladies: Madeline K., Christine K., Teresa R., and Nikki T., I am forever grateful for your ideas so selflessly given, talents, friendship—and dance parties.

Kim H., you're a sparkling gem. Your suggestions, editorial eye, and insights into the teenage mind were invaluable.

Katherine S., holy smokes, you are money. What you noticed and the feedback you gave pushed me to make this novel better.

Becky H. and Holli M., thank you for venturing into beta reader land. Your remarks were spot-on.

Brian Halley at Book Creatives, thanks for making the perfect cover.

Made in the USA
San Bernardino, CA
09 September 2017